SAVING HER

HOT HEROES SERIES BOOK ONE

AUTUMN RUBY

Blake's Angel!.
Love
Autumn Ruby ♡
xo

Saving Her
Hot Hero Series Book One
Autumn Ruby

Contents

Editor: Pam Gonzales @Love2readromance
Cover Design: Matador Designs
Formatting: Rachael Tonks @ Affordable Formatting

To our beautiful daughters, may you always follow your dreams.

Saving Her.

PROLOGUE

"It sounds tougher than I ever imagined, you're not doing bad for a little weed." I tease down the phone line as my little brother, Marshall, fills me in on his last two weeks of being on the frontline. It sounds like absolute torture. I didn't imagine it to be so tough when he'd first told me he was signing up to the army.

"Shut up, Candyfloss," he hits back.

"Probably not." I can almost picture him smiling down the phone. It'd been weeks since we'd last spoken. It'd been weeks since I'd spoken to him and although I probably wouldn't tell him, I miss him so much.

"I gotta go, sis, love ya."

"Love you, Marshy, keep safe, titch." And with that, he hangs up, and I carry on putting all the things that I really don't need back on the shelf. Two jumpers, a tight fitted t-shirt and a pair of sunglasses to be exact. I'd never be able to go travelling if I carried on like this.

I give my sister-in-law, Evelyn, a call and check in with her. She sounds a bit fed up, so I arrange a girl's day for tomorrow when she's off work. We decide on a bike ride, I really need to avoid the shops as much as possible!

Next, I head to my happy place, the local library, armed with everything I've read this week. I spend ages wandering the shelves endlessly judging books by their cover, although experience tells me I probably shouldn't. I settle on four romances, a crime thriller and a cookbook for some healthy eating inspiration.

Outside, I pile everything into the boot of Bluey, my Mini Cooper, and head home to change before I meet up with my best friend Rainy, for tea and a much needed catch up.

The rest of the day flies by, and Rainy is her usual cynical self, telling me all about her latest dating dramas. We follow up the meal with ice cream at my place and she ends up staying over, so is still with me the next day when my phone rings as I'm getting changed for my ride with Evelyn. I see that it is Evelyn and ignore the first two calls as somehow I'm running late again. I pick up the third time knowing something must be up for her to be that persistent, maybe she needs to cancel.

"Hi, babe, you okay?"

"He's gone, Candy." My heart drops to my stomach, and my whole world stops turning. She can't mean...

"What do you mean gone?" Heavy sobs come down the line, and I refuse to believe what I know she is trying to tell me.

"Marshall, they just came and told me, he was killed yesterday...in a shootout."

"No...It can't be true. I just spoke with him yesterday." "Candy, I don't know what to do." More heart-breaking sobs, and I drop the phone, collapsing to the floor in my own state of complete shock. Rainy runs over to me. "Candy, honey, are you okay? What's happened?" Her voice is a blur through my tears, and it feels like I've just become a by passer in my own life. It's like I'm standing in the middle of a bad dream and can't wake up. My minds racing, thinking up realistic explanations of how this could all be a mistake. Rainy talks to Evelyn for a minute, and I notice she's white as a ghost when she turns her attention back to me. "Come on, we gotta get you over to Evelyn's, you two need to be together. I'll call your mum on the way."

I don't remember much about being bundled into the car or the drive to Evelyn's place, but I vividly remember seeing my sister-in-law's beautiful features wracked with pain and how she looked as broken as I felt, when she answered the door to us.

That was the day everything in my life as I knew it changed. That sickening day when I learnt the true depth of grief and how hard it is to let go of someone who means the world to you. That was the day I lost my brother.

CHAPTER ONE

Candice

I watch on in horror as the whole scene unfolds before me. Over the roar of gunshots and people running and screaming I hear my phone bleep, and in a trance like state, I pick up.

"Candy, Candy, can you hear me, are you okay?" I don't respond, I'm frozen stiff in terror, too scared to stay and see more bodies die in yet another rebel shoot out, and too afraid to run in case my sudden movements attract much unwanted attention. The air is growing thicker around me and I try to focus on Rainy's voice at the other end of the phone. She sounds panicked but she really has no idea. How could she? England is a million miles away from everything that surrounds me now.

Terror.

Death.

Stale heat and musky air accompanied with a backdrop of gun shots, which Rainy can apparently hear.

"Was that a gun shot? Jesus, Candy. Run and get the fuck out of there!"

My response comes easily as if on autopilot. "If I run they'll shoot, I need to stay calm, talk to me. Tell me something normal."

"Normal, oh god. I can't think of anything. What's happening?"

I slowly turn and start walking away from the chaos replying, "There's another rebel attack."

"Fuck, where are you? Are you safe?"

"I'm right in the fucking middle of it," I hiss.

"Oh my god, oh my god, Candy, this is terrifying. I don't know what to do."

"Just keep talking to me," I plead, needing something other than raining bullets and men dropping like flies behind me.

I start walking, slowly, calmly looking straight ahead and try to focus on the voice of my best friend who is making possibly the worst attempt to calm someone down ever.

It's weird how, in the face of pure unadulterated danger, you experience a sort of peaceful serenity as suddenly there's only one thing that matters.

Getting out alive.

I pace forward quickly, but not at a speed that would catch the attention of the rebels and put me directly in the firing line. Time feels like it's moving in slow motion around me, and the sounds become distant, almost as though I'm swimming under water, everything is muffled and unclear. I focus on Rainy's trembling voice.

"Stephan called again today," I hear her gulp, forcing the information out while holding back tears.

"And?" I bark out, my voice not sounding like me own.

"I didn't pick up. I mean I wanted to, but you know how I felt when he didn't come to my party and then there was that stupid bitch. I can't even remember her name now but you know the one I mean."

"Mmm," I mumble back, unable to focus on whatever she's talking about, but needing to hear her voice all the same. A thick sob escapes her lips and hits my ears making me feel so guilty for putting her through this.

"Don't," I demand.

"I can't help it, Candy. What if this is the last time..."

"It won't be. Fuck Rainy, a little positivity wouldn't go a miss." My only response is further sobs and words I can't decode over the sounds of her crying into the phone.

"Jesus Christ, I'm not dead yet!"

I can't pretend the threat is not terrifying. I'm stood right in the middle of an attempted food donation from the international aid response team and shaking from head to foot. I should have known this would be a target.

They've been intercepting with foreign aid attempts more and more in the past few weeks, and I wonder whether the desperate humanitarian crisis the families and children here are facing is being portrayed any better in the news at home than it was a few months ago when I flew out.

"What's happening now?" She asks, her voice growing quieter and weaker, like she's fading away from me.

"I'm not sure, I can't see much...just a lot of smoke."

"What was that?" She screams upon hearing another loud bang as a gunshot fires behind me.

I speed up, my heart is racing, and each step I make brings a little more hope I might survive yet another horror scene. Rainy calls me 'kitty cat' sometimes, she's always saying I must have nine lives to survive everything I have.

"Hang on...I've seen some kind of centre. I think I might be able to make it."

I strain my eyes to the left, too afraid to turn my head, I can feel the pulse of adrenaline pumping through my veins and become aware that my entire body is shaking.

"You can do this," Rainy shouts back, I could always rely on her for encouragement but this was a far cry from her trying to convince me I suited my bangs when I had them cut in. "Please tell me you're coming home after this? The place sounds like a fucking hellhole, Candy."

Her voice becomes glitchy and I can barely make out her sentence. She disappears from the end of the line as my phone signal cuts out but I keep the handset glued to my head. I feel like the tin man from Wizard of Oz, each of my joints are frozen solid, not from rust, but from sheer terror. Although, I haven't dared to look back, my previous experiences of open shoot outs are emblazoned in my mind's eye, so I know exactly what the scene behind me will look like.

Horrific.

Feeling like I'm about to step onto hot coals, I tentatively put one foot left slightly. I know any slight movement could catch their attention, so I keep walking slowly and wait for the next round of shots to be fired.

As soon as I hear them I'm away, sprinting for my life towards the alleyway, and even when I reach it I don't stop. I can barely breathe, and the heat of the day feels like it's burning through to my soul. I keep going until I can't hear the sound of shots anymore and make my way round to the back of what turns out to be a health centre, raising alarm that an attack is highly likely.

I don't hang around for the evacuation; I can't afford to die out here, not after losing my brother just over a year ago. I collapse in a heap on the floor about three blocks away from the attack and kiss my locket holding a picture of me and my brother, Marshall.

Rainy puts my extra lives down to luck, but I know, just like when he was alive, he's got my back, and I genuinely believe he's my guardian angel now. How else did I always manage to walk away from death's door unscathed, almost unaffected, well apart from the odd nightmare?

I take a few minutes to catch my breath before making my way back to base. I'm caught by surprise when tears prick my eyes, and suddenly I'm a sobbing, shaking mess on the ground. My back's against the wall, and I hold my head in my hands feeling completely overwhelmed. When will any of this end? Despite having been here for nearly six months and doing my homework before signing up to volunteer, I still feel I know nothing about the war here. However, I do know that seeing more innocent kids and families lose their lives in attacks like today is heart breaking and becoming increasingly common.

The peace deal signed a few months ago may sound like a success story back home in England, but here in South Sudan, things couldn't be more hopeless.

By the time I pull myself together, dusk is falling, and I know from the deafening silence around me that the rebels have moved on, for now at least. I wipe my tears on my white linen shirt and gather myself to begin the walk back to base where things felt safer, and I could think more clearly amongst friends.

Although it's evening, the air is still warm, and thankfully the casualties had been able to make their way to the health centre as the rebels had decided they'd done enough damage for one day. My denim cut offs expose my skin, and I swat away the mosquitos that are hovering now that my repellent is wearing off. It's a false sense of security walking back along the winding dust track to base. The calm after the storm, you could say. It was always like that after an attack, the mood of the whole country seemed to quieten and become sombre. There was no one around, and usually I'd feel a little intimidated. Yet, after what's just happened, I feel numb to the world around me, and I'm lost in my own thoughts.

By the time I make it back, most of the volunteers have gone to bed, and there's only Sally and Julie left at the open fire pit.

"Oh my god, I was so worried." Sal hurtles towards me.

"I'm okay, it was a nasty one though, they must have had a heads up we were coming. Who's giving them their intel?" I ask, thinking out loud.

"I dunno, babe, but I wish someone would shoot the informant instead of kids and innocent families," she says with a heavy sigh.

"Me too," I murmur.

"Let's get you checked over, lovely," Jules cuts in and her mothering tone has my eyes brimming with tears, again. They don't fall, my body is too emotionally drained to cry or do anything other than let Julie fuss over me.

CHAPTER TWO

Blake

I check in with Greyson on my way for my morning coffee. "Don't you ever take a day off, bud?" I smile upon hearing his usual banter on the other end of the phone. He already knows the answer, I hadn't had a day off in almost twelve months. A full year since my girl had left me, and it felt like fucking hours. Minutes sometimes. Aimee had been my best friend for as long as I can remember. Okay, we weren't lovers, but to me, we were more than that. We were friends, and in my world genuine friendship is about the only thing that's hard to come by. Everything else can be bought.

Watching her health deteriorate as the leukaemia had taken hold had been harrowing and is something that will plague me for the rest of my life.

"Did ya get a call from serge, about helping to build a Peace Centre and keep the rebels at bay?" G asks.

"Yeah, I got the call alright. Reckons it'll only take a few of us on the job if we enlist the locals to help," I reply, sceptically.

"Sounds about right, assigning two of his best snipers to some shitty project and giving us zero fucking resources to come up with the goods." His fury at our sergeant is audible in his tone, and brings a smile to my face.

"I'm sure he thinks we're still in training, everything's always some kind of test or challenge with him. Why can't he just let us get on with what we do best?"

"I hear ya, G. He tell you where we're headed?"

"South Sudan. The ass end of fucking nowhere."

"I dunno about that, G, but I've said I'm in. I need the distraction and the basic exercises just aren't cutting it for me lately. At least we can get hands on and stuck into this for a few months."

"A year, Blake. He said a year."

"Same thing," I shrug. Time had stood still since losing Aimee. Day's bled into nights, nights into weeks and weeks into months. I wasn't living, I was merely existing.

"Well, let's hope there's plenty of decent Sudanese women to get our... What did you just say? Hands on and stuck in?"

"Hell yeah, to that," I reply laughing down the phone, and I'm still smiling as I hang up. Greyson is a good bloke, one of the best I know and one of the few if not the only person I trust. Since losing Aimee, the guy's been my rock. I've never done anything with the UN before, so I'm a little apprehensive, but feel better about it knowing that he will be out there with me.

"An espresso with an extra coffee shot to go, please," I order.

The waitress doesn't move, she just stands there gawking at me, so I clear my throat and order again. She must be at least ten years younger than me, late teens I'm guessing.

Her cheeks flush crimson in embarrassment from being caught staring at me, and she fumbles around preparing my coffee. I glance down admiring the diamond encrusted Rolex on my wrist and clear my throat again loudly enough to hurry my little fan along.

This is me. Surviving the rush of London city life one coffee break at a time. I'll last all day making deal after deal for my dad's company, and finally eat a steak around seven. Then I'll hit the bottle and find some faceless brunette to fuck.

The waitress passes me my drink over the counter and looks up at me all fidgety and nervous. Jesus, if daytime Blake makes her nervous, she'd run a fucking mile away from my after dark alter ego. And she'd be right to; I chew girls like her up and spit them out for breakfast. I inwardly groan as my mind flickers to the leggy brunette I left in tears last night after she'd started up with some shit about me using her. I'm still not sure what she was expecting from me, I couldn't have made it any clearer that I'm not a second date kinda guy.

I make my way down Regent Street and towards Laine Corporations, picking up to the second call of the day.

"Hi, Mum."

"Blake, honey, are you on your way to the office? The meeting is set for nine sharp."

"Have I ever been late for a meeting?"

"Okay, I know. I get it. Just wanted to remind you, that's all," she croons.

"Mum?" I cut her off, knowing she doesn't give a flying fuck about the meeting, she is just using it as an excuse to check in on me. "How are you?"

"Good Blake, you should stop by soon. I'd love to see more of you."

Sigh. "I will, I'll come over in a few days. You should probably know I've been drafted as part of a UN Peacekeeping troop to help build a Peace Centre for the next year."

"A Peace Centre?"

"Yeah, I think it's serge's not so subtle hint that we need some time out after Afghan."

"That's probably the first thing I'd agree with him on in six years!"

We both laugh, her and serge were definitely not on the same page when it comes to my career plan. Then her tone turns serious.

"Where?" Fuck, did she always have to be so direct. So casual then bang, straight in for the kill. She'd give the snipers in my squad a run for their money any day. I keep my tone casual so as not to freak her out.

"Bor."

"Bor, where the heck is that?"

"South Sudan, so I'll see ya soon, Mum, love ya." I hang up promptly avoiding the million questions that she would have followed by the quit-the-army-and-move-back-home speech.

Checking the time, 8:50, and straightening my tie, I stride into Laine Corporations and make a mental note to have the security guard fired. He didn't even look up as I passed him, and if he hasn't seen me, anyone could be in here. I catch Amelia with her usual pout in my direction full of lust; she'd clearly had her lips done again. It must be the fourth or fifth time this year, so we're obviously paying her too much. I reach Dad's office at precisely 8:55, and I'm handed an agenda with a bunch of papers as I take a seat in the glass walled boardroom. I can see from the look on my dad's face, it's gonna be a long one.

Taking my seat, I glance around the room and even in my custom suit and designer shoes, I could never belong here. The business was part of my life but for everyone else around the table, Laine Corporations was it. Thoughts of Afghan flooded my mind, distracting me momentarily from the circus before me.

"Welcome everyone; we're here to discuss the takeover of Jennings Hold Limited and the small matter of Mrs. Jennings putting a last minute claim to her stake in." Dad looks serious, but from what I heard the Jennings are small fry, so he probably doesn't give a shit either way.

I chip in, "The way I see it is, we've got two options. We either do the decent thing and offer to buy her out, or we make the deal behind her back and risk her going after us down the line."

"Or I could...you know. Persuade her."

"There won't be any need for that, thank you, Jason."

Dad throws a shut-the-fuck-up glare at my brother which matches my own, and this time I don't even feel bad for him. He makes things worse for himself, and why the hell Dad even invites him to meetings like this one anymore is beyond me. He's usually either half cut or half asleep and only ever makes things more difficult than they need to be.

"Mrs. Jennings knows the game, I spent one of our Christmas parties with her way back."

"Get in there, bro, I bet you did," Jason chips in slyly. I ignore him for the sake of my father, hoping he'll disappear.

"There's no way you'll get a deal this big past her, but she won't miss the chance to screw Mr. Jennings over, either. Since the divorce, she's been hell bent on revenge. Get her in, I'll explain things to her and buy her out. She'll expect a decent amount, but it'll be worth it in the long run."

"Thank you, Blake, that sounds like a good move forward." Jason pushes his chair back with a huge sigh glaring at Dad and storms out. He's such a jealous bastard.

"Be quick though, I've only got four days. I've just signed up for another year." Dad recoils at the news like an injured puppy, nods quietly and continues working his way through the agenda. I'm only half listening but am surprised to hear the rumblings of a deal that would finish my dad's best mate and his Barbie girl daughter, Tiffany, off for good. I switch off, mentally preparing for South Sudan, and for the first time since agreeing to go, I'm wondering what I've let myself in for.

Candice

I wake up feeling as though I've slept off a world of problems and still feeling slightly shaky from yesterday. I'm the first one up at camp as usual, and the cool air is a welcome change as the sun is still making its appearance. I can see it rising over the woodland area, and it reminds me how lucky

I am to be alive. I take a slow deep breath in, filling my lungs with morning oxygen, and slowly let it out exhaling all the negative vibes. I feel rejuvenated and ready for a fresh day. Except, even once I'm dressed and making my way to base, a niggling feeling of danger still plagues me.

Our camp in Bor is the only one of its kind within the region, set up to support the families affected by the civilian war that's tearing South Sudan apart. When I'd first arrived, I had felt like a lost soul with no real sense of direction. There had only been a handful of volunteers willing to enrol as the situation remained dangerous.

Julie and I had signed up for the advanced first aid training, and the adventure it bought with it had been a whole lot more than either of us bargained for. Mum and Dad had watched the news in horror from the safety of their sofas back home in the Cotswolds and begged me to call it quits, go home and get a regular job. Maybe even go back to school. Of course, I refused every time. I *need* to be here. Losing my brother had been the final straw in my year of all round shitness, and if it hadn't been for my best friend, Rainy, encouraging me to travel again in an attempt to 'pull myself together', I really don't know where I'd be. I had never envisaged being here all these months later.

Things had been more settled back then, especially when the UN stepped in and a peace deal had been announced, but after I arrived things had quickly escalated. The situation was nothing like it had been portrayed on the news I'd watched back home in preparation. When the rebels had turned against the president all hell had broken loose, and the general consensus was every man for himself. We were in uncertain times, and the environment reflects my feelings perfectly. Chaotic and unsure. Slowly trying to find my way and piece my broken heart back together the same way you would approach a complicated thousand piece jigsaw.

We've all spent the first few months setting up a makeshift health centre and school for the local children, which has been more difficult than I'd expected. Barely any of them are traditionally local. They've fled from all over to escape the horrors of war, which makes the language barrier almost impossible as there are so many different languages in the mix. I set up a small shack and began spending time in the community, talking to parents about the importance of keeping things as normal as possible for the little ones, that means attending school.

In the first few weeks we had barely a handful of children, but free craft materials and a hearty snack soon had them pouring in and the class is now full of an enthusiastic bunch of steady attenders. They love coming, and I absolutely love teaching them. It takes up all my spare time, and every minute I can get away from the hospital I spend with the kids. They add much needed hope and happiness to an otherwise dismal situation.

Pulling on my medical gloves, I start my shift by taking the temperature of each of the patients and ensuring they all have fresh, cool water to drink.

Blake

*S*ince we landed in Bor, it's been nonstop work every day. I'm just glad to have my best friend...well more like my only friend, Greyson, here with me. The whole reason the UN got involved, was to teach the Sudanese army how to defeat the rebels. Or at least protect themselves from them, but it wasn't going to plan today and another civilian crossfire has kicked off. The heat is stifling, reaching at least 90 degrees on most days. The smell of death and blood lingers in the air, and the sound of bombs, bullets and fear has become the norm to me, and yet it doesn't show any sign of easing up.

"Come on you bastards," Greyson screams. There are more rebels approaching now, the last lot are dead. We're lucky that we have not lost anyone from our squad, this week at least. "They're coming, Blake." I take out my binoculars, and yes, he is right, the bastards are nearly within reach.

"I count ten at least, G," I tell him, using the nickname I gave him on our very first day of our army training. "We got this, bro." We aim our weapons west in the direction they are coming from, and wait for a clear shot. It seems to take forever, when in all seriousness; it's probably only a few minutes. Signalling down to G, in 3..2..1... Fire. We start firing in complete sync and take them out one at a time. They soon source our location, and bullets fly in all directions.

"We need to move, G."

"Let's go then, Blake, what are we waiting for?" His passion for this is something else.

"We can make it to the outbuilding before they approach," I

say, signalling to the right. We run, just reaching the inside of the building, as they fly around the corner.

"Five left, Blake."

"Yeah, I see, man."

"I will take the left if you take the right?"

He nods in agreement and without hesitation, we are firing again.

"I see four down, man. Where's the fifth?" I question him, our eyes trained for any movement. We cautiously move out of the outbuilding going over to each body and checking to make sure these fuckers are dead. Suddenly a sharp pain slices through my knee, well I think it's my knee, the burning sensation seems to have taken over my entire leg. "I'm hit, man. I'm hit." Greyson's reactions are too quick for the last man standing, and it seems to play out in slow motion right in front of my eyes. I watch guns being aimed. Bullets start to fly, but Greyson is just too quick and takes him out with a bullet straight to the head. He is over to me in seconds as I lay on the floor clutching my leg. The blood's pouring from it as I try to add some pressure to relieve the burning sensation. "Thanks, G," I say through gritted teeth.

"Shut the fuck up, bro, Let's get you to the medical centre." He shrugs it off as if he didn't just save my life, he is trying to act cool, but I can tell he is anything but. He scoops me up and carries me the half a mile to the truck with a tortured look on his face, and we haul ass to the nearest makeshift hospital. It's around twenty minutes away, but in my semi-conscious state it feels like we are travelling a hell of a lot longer. "Hang in there," he repeats over and over again, and I'm trying to, but his voice is fading out like a distant echo.

"We're here man," he says as we pull over and another wrack of pain slams through my leg. I try to get out of the truck, but my body just won't move. Without hesitation, he throws me over his shoulder before bursting through the doors. I feel breathless and tired at the same time as my vision starts to blur. I faintly hear muffled voices then the darkness takes me, and it all goes black.

CHAPTER THREE

Candice

*A*ny distraction from the doom and gloom of the rising number of patients in the last few months is a welcome one. So, when the hottest guy I have ever laid eyes on is taking up one of the beds on my morning shift, he's got my full attention. He's sleeping for the most part, and I read up on his notes. A gunshot to the knee, nasty, he's not going to like the recovery time on that.

I glance at the small pile of army uniform, folded on top of a pair of well-worn soldier's boots, and then back to him. His strong tanned arms and shoulders are visible over the white cotton sheets he's tucked up in. His dark, barely there stubble, outlines his chiselled jawline, and I watch his gorgeous face for a minute as he sleeps. The surgery went as well as it could by the look of things, but he's still going to be in here for a while, which makes me smile to myself.

I'm daydreaming, still holding his notes when his eyes flicker open, and he catches me off guard.

"Hi." His voice is raspy from the anaesthetic, "Could you get me a drink, please?" I pour a drink of water and find myself speechless staring into his deep green eyes. He's looks like an advert for Calvin Klein, rugged and strong with the eyes that command all of your attention as soon as you so much as glance his way.

"Thanks." He smiles as his fingers touch mine when he takes the glass, and a surge of excitement ripples through me. I pull my hand away awkwardly, reminding myself that he's a patient.

"Hi, Blake, nice to meet you. I'm Candice, I'll be looking after you today."

"The pleasures all mine," he growls in a low, husky tone that sparks feelings of desire in me, that I haven't felt for a long time.

"Let's get you freshened up then," I offer, fighting to keep my cool and professionalism.

"No arguments from me with that one. How are you coping in here with no air con, it's horrendous?"

"I guess, it does get hot in here at times," I throw him a smile, trying to be my confident self. I can tell he sees straight through me, which pisses me off. Why should I be different with him? He's just like any other patient, another warrior hurt in the fight for good. There had been so many after the last bomb dropped, we are barely coping. Every bed in the makeshift ward is full. I begin swirling some warm water from the kettle in with a bowl full of cold and help him sit up. My hands fall around his neck as

I help him shuffle himself into an upright position so his tightly toned torso is fully exposed, and I breathe in sharply on sight of it. His body is solid but not too muscly, and the touch of his skin makes me so much hotter than I already am in this stifling heat. Who am I kidding? Blake Laine is definitely *not* like any other.

I begin to sponge him down. "You know, you could probably do this yourself, if you're up to it?" He places a hand over mine and speaks in a hushed tone.

"And miss out on a little cutie like you putting her hands all over me, not a chance."

I pull my hand away as a flurry of embarrassment mixed with excitement overcomes me. I can sense his eyes burning into the side of my face as I work, and a magnetic force pulls my eyes to meet with his. His face is perfection. Huge green eyes stare back at me, before I peek down and take in his full, kissable lips. My cool facade crumbles, and I look away quickly to avoid letting him know just how much I fancy him. I've never been affected by a man like this before.

"Little cutie. I bet you say that to all the girls."

"No," replies Blake. "I don't usually talk to girls, I just fuck them." I feel my cheeks burn flame red as an amused smirk spreads across his beautiful mouth. Flawed by his crude remark, I carry on taping up the bandage and fussing over his knee. He's flirting and it's unnerving. His eyes search for mine and when he locks our gaze, I feel like they're burning deep into my soul.

There have been so many men come through our volunteer centre in the last few months, but none have commanded my attention the way Blake Laine does. Despite his injuries, his body is physically strong and his presence powerful. Both of us felt the searing desire to tear each other's clothes off just from our hands touching.

"You'll be out of here and breaking hearts in no time," I think aloud.

"I'm no heartbreaker, Candice," his murmur dripping in sincerity. "I told you, I fuck women. I worship them. I fulfil their wildest fantasies, but I never let them in close enough to break any hearts."

I'm not giving him the satisfaction of embarrassing me, so I quickly swipe back. "You're quite the gentleman aren't you, Blake."

"I can be gentle, Candy, if that's what you prefer?"

"Only my friends call me Candy, and I haven't made my mind up about you yet."

"Then I beg your pardon, Candice," he mocks in a voice that's dripping with amusement before adding, "as I don't have friends who are girls." He seems deadly serious about that last part. Not knowing quite what to say, I maintain my best indifferent face and hurriedly finish up washing him as the intensity of being with Blake is getting to be too much.

"Maybe I'll be the first," I add, dismissively.

"Is that what you want, Candice, to be my friend?" He looks at me with a sincerity that demands an answer, but he's not going to get one. I'll bet he's totally used to getting what he wants with women, but I won't be his latest conquest. No thank you.

"What I want is for you to follow orders and get better, and get your filthy mind back to thinking about something useful again."

"Woah, following orders, hey," he feigns shock. "I didn't have you down as the dominant type."

I can't help but giggle, he's ruthless, and I kind of love it.

Just as I'm finishing up, the door bursts open, and Sally pushes another trolley through at high speed. Great, just as my night shift is coming to an end another emergency is on our hands. I immediately spring into action running over to them, but it quickly becomes obvious this one isn't going to make it. I grab the bundle of blankets from under his trolley and pass them to Sal who quickly piles them over the gaping wound in the man's chest. He's moaning in pain, too proud for words or tears.

Sally shakes her head signalling there's no point in taking up the doctor's precious time with this one, his suffering is beyond repair. I lower my head close to his face and hold his hand tightly in mine looking straight into his eyes. He knows. Shit, he's fading fast, I reckon he literally has seconds to go. "You have made your loved ones very proud, and you are a true hero. I will get the message to them, don't worry. Rest now." His eyes glaze over. He's gone.

A tear rolls down my cheek. It doesn't matter how many times you see death, it's always devastatingly painful. With every soldier taken, I feel a piece of me crumble inside. I know I will never be fully whole after this. Each time I take a break and visit home, it's like I leave a piece of me here in these four walls surrounded by these true heroes. I know it's where I belong. Sally squeezes my arm motioning for me to release his hand, so she can cover him with the blanket she is holding.

When I look up, Blake is watching me with an intent stare and an expression that I can't decode. Not lust but not concern either. Something that closely resembles admiration.

CHAPTER FOUR

Blake

Two weeks later

*S*he's watching me again from across the room, like she has been for the last two weeks. I know this because I haven't been able to take my goddamn eyes off her. She is on my mind more and more every passing second. It's like she's a hot wire straight to my untamed cock and every time her blush spreads across her pretty face, I wanna see just how far it spreads across her beautiful body. Just the thought has me adjusting my crotch again! "Hey Candy," I call from the other side of the room.

Hey eyes dart over to meet mine and making her way over she asks, "Can I get you something, Mr. Laine?"

"How about your phone number?" I reply. Right on cue and just as I anticipated her cheeks turn a deep shade of pink. Happily knowing I have embarrassed her, I ask her my original question. "Do you think it would possible for me to go back outside for a little while again today? These walls are driving me crazy, and if big Baz over there doesn't stop his snoring, I won't be responsible for my actions." I smile smugly, there is no way she will be able to resist coming with me, just like she hasn't for the past two weeks. Her playing it cool game is waning fast.

"Actually, you're in luck. I'm just about to take my break, I guess you can tag along, if you like."

"Well gee, thanks, Candy. You're gonna have me thinking I'm getting special treatment, the way you're carrying on."

"You wish."

"I never have to wish, I always get what I want in the end. Now, will you please call me Blake, for god sake."

She giggles and rolls her eyes at me. "Okay, Blake."

We make our way outside at a steady pace as I'm trying to get this knee better to get the fuck outta here. I've been stuck indoors too long, and this place is driving me mad. With the exception of getting to see Candice every day, of course.

"It sure is a nice day," she chirps as we reach the door.

"Yeah, it is," I say sulkily.

"Someone's feeling grumpy," she continues in the same shitty tone I just gave her because I'm feeling pissed off.

"Can I ask you something, Candice?"

In her best flippant tone she replies, "You can ask, Blake, but it doesn't mean I will answer." Which makes me smile, she is just so goddamn cute, even when she is trying to be all stand-offish.

"Do you want this?" I ask watching the sweet smile fall from her soft lips replaced with a more serious expression.

"Want what, Blake?" she answers nervously, her eyes widen into two innocent pools of blue. She's not fooling anyone.

"Come on, Candice, enough with the small talk, it's bullshit. You know as well as I do that there is something between us," I say gesturing my fingers between the two of us. "I know you can feel it. I've watched the way you are around me for the last two weeks, and I have had enough of this pussying around. Why are we avoiding the inevitable?"

She lets out a sigh and takes a deep breath like she's preparing to give me a piece of her mind. Her nostrils flare slightly and her forehead creases up, and I'm instantly regretting being so forward with her.

"Okay, so firstly, I wouldn't say inevitable, it's kind of a turn off, but I'm not going to insult you by denying that yes, of course, I feel something too, but..."

That was all I needed to hear. I pull her towards me so that her body is flush against mine, and her perky breasts push up against me. Her girly scent of flowery shit invades my nostrils. Something shifts in my chest, and my mind tells me to hold onto her forever and never let go. I lower my face so I can feel her breath on me, she looks up at me through fluttery lashes and her eyes burn with lust. I lean down a little more leaving my lips just barely touching hers, waiting for her consent, just hoping I haven't overstepped the mark. I soon realise I haven't when she presses her lips gently onto mine and kisses me. I kiss her right back, my tongue finds its way into her mouth, and what a gorgeous mouth it is, she tastes of strawberry and mint. After what feels like forever, we both pull away breathless. She starts looking around straight away.

"Oh no, Blake, what if somebody saw us! I can't be seen kissing one of the patients!"

I can't help but laugh at her flustered state, and I pull her into my arms as she slides her arm around my waist placing her head on my chest. It strikes me how happy I feel in this moment. I only met her a few weeks ago, and for some reason, I feel like I have my whole world in my arms. To be honest, that scares the shit out of me.

Candice

I shift along the bench needing to put some space between us, I can't think straight when he's so close beside me. Ever since I came to work that day and saw the very handsome Mr. Laine, I'd imagined what his gorgeous mouth would feel like pressed against mine, and it was beyond any of my wildest expectations. His lips burn like fire, and his kiss is so demanding and passionate. It sounds cheesy, but I felt like we really connected, and I mean, more than just wanting each other's bodies. I want all of him, every last inch, and I know he can see it on my face as his eyes are bursting with the same pure desire every time he looks my way. I'm relieved when he breaks the silence.

"Well, that was unexpected. I ask to stretch my legs, and you lose all control and attempt to seduce me...and to think, I had you down as the shy type."

I throw him a scowl. "In your dreams, Blake." He gives a small chuckle.

"They do say, it's always the quiet ones." He winks, and I've had enough of him for one break time. I don't mind the banter, in fact I quite enjoy it, but I don't like the tension between us now. His kiss had demanded more than I think I'm ready for. After the last dating disaster I'd sworn off men for the foreseeable future, that was part of my decision to sign up for the volunteer programme in the first place. I needed some thinking time, especially after losing Marshall. I touch my locket at the thought of him and wonder what he'd make of Blake. I looked up to meet his eyes, so green and inquisitive. "As I was saying..."

"Don't," he says cutting me off by pressing a finger to his lips. "I'm not asking for anything, so you don't need to talk. In fact, I prefer it when you mouth is right here." And he kisses me with a peck that lingers long enough to send a rush of excitement directly to my core. The sensation of his course stubble against my cheek is like a rough diamond, rugged and beautiful all at the same time. His smell of sweet, spice and citrus is invading my thoughts. God, I want more. I need to get away from him, I'm becoming obsessed! He must sense my awkwardness, and I'm relieved when he stands up easing the tension between us.

"We don't have to talk about any of this. The way you're lookin' at me says enough."

"You are seriously annoying."

"And you are seriously fucking sexy when you're mad at me. Remind me to piss you off more often. The way you bite your inner cheek while you think up a comeback makes me wanna take a chunk out of your ass."

I suppress the urge to laugh and shake my head in despair. "You are way too cocky for this to be anything anyway."

"So you've considered it then? Us being something?" A sly smirk spreads across his gorgeous mouth, and I don't know whether to smack him or kiss him again.

"You can see yourself inside, Mr. Laine." I don't give him the opportunity to complicate me any further, and I don't hang around to watch him hobble back inside. That'll teach him a lesson. When I glance back, his face is an absolute picture. I don't think he can believe that I've left him to get up and about on his own. It wasn't planned, but the push is probably just what he needs to get back some of his independence.

With Blake back in bed and the rest of the men on the ward as settled as they could be with their pain relief administered, I drift into the kitchen area and slip off my ballerina style pumps; enjoying the feel of the cold hard floor against my hot and sweaty feet.

It's been such a hectic few days, and working full time in this heat is exhausting. I can't wait to meet up with Sally after work, she's not going to believe he kissed me just like that, out of the blue. I tidy the worktop, and make sure all the medications are locked away before making my way round to the school area.

I see Julie's working again, even though she's post night shift and meant to be sleeping before she's back on duty tonight. The woman's a machine, she never stops.

The kids are enjoying a game of football, although no one looks particularly like they know what they're doing. Julie's whistle gives the impression it's all serious business, and there's an uproar when the tiny referee, who I know is just six years old, holds a red card up in the air following a nasty tackle. The group charges at her, and I watch on at what looks like it is going to be chaos but soon hear the sound of laughter fill the air. I love this bunch of kids, they have so very little but are so full of joy and laughter that spreads like wildfire. I challenge anyone to spend five minutes with them without a smile, it's impossible.

I join in, snatching the ball while they're all in a huddle trying to grab it, and as soon as they realise what's happened they're chasing my tail trying to get it back. Aliya's confidence is growing, and I'm taken aback when the usually shy little girl runs straight up to tackle me. The little minx! I seize her up blowing a huge raspberry kiss onto her stomach, and they're all laughing again and wanting one of their own. I don't disappoint, and whoever doesn't pull their top up slightly indicating they want a belly razza gets a tickle instead. All except for little Yasin, who is the smallest of the boys and is still finding himself within the group. I ruffle his hair and shoot him a friendly wink before passing him the ball in the hope it'll get him joining in, which it does.

By the time I'm at the canteen, Sal's waiting, and I collapse next to her and eat our daily ration with a polo mint each. We're on our last six now, so I am hoping Mum sends some more soon.

"Good day oogling lover boy again?"

"I do NOT oogle. Is that even a word, anyway?"

"It is now." And we both laugh, the girl's nuts, she has a new word for everything. It's like our own little language that no one else understands, a secret girl code between friends. I was lucky to have found her as I didn't make friends that easily, girls can be so bitchy at times. But not Sal, she's as down to earth as they come, and I love her for it. It was good to have an ally out here, being surrounded by men did drive me mad at times.

"I really like him, you know," I confess between mouthfuls.

"I can tell, he's not my type, but I can see why he's definitely got something about him...A real charmer. Just be careful Candy, he's got heartbreaker written all over him."

"What makes you say that?" As if I need to ask.

"I'm not blind, Candy. That's all I'm saying. You gotta do what makes you happy girl."

"He kissed me!" I blurt out not being able to keep it from her any longer and needing to tell someone.

"Shut up! When?"

"Today, when we were outside," I shrug

"Seriously, girl, you were out there for what? Five minutes?"

I let out a light chuckle before replying, "I guess when you know, you know."

"Oh, it's like that is it?" Her face screams sass as she purses her lips and blinks her eyes at me.

"I really like him," I say, simply.

"As in *like*, like him?"

"His kiss took my breath away," I admit.

"Girl, you are in deep doo-doo," she blows out the air as though she's eaten something too hot for her mouth causing us both to giggle.

I can't help thinking she might be right.

CHAPTER FIVE

Blake

*I*t's only been a few hours since the most amazing kiss I have ever had in my twenty eight years on this planet, but I can't get her hot mouth out of my head. After tossing and turning all night, thinking about Candy and how, in so many ways, our relationship reminds me of my relationship with Aimee.

Easy.

Relaxed.

But the desire to fuck Candice's brains out outweighed anything I'd experienced before. A girl I want to fuck *and* have a conversation with has knocked me for six, and that's why I've decided I am going to ask her on a date when she comes in today. It'll have to be a shitty coffee from the canteen as I'm still not up to leaving the centre. At least that's what the doctor keeps telling me, I need to rest more. I'd have been out weeks ago, if it was up to me.

Just on cue, she breezes in the door like some sort of goddamn angel, her long blonde hair is in her usual bun on the top of her head. She's small, with perfectly defined curves in all the right places. Her blue eyes are so bright they could light up a whole room, and she has the most genuine smile I have ever seen. I let out a sigh, damn, she is so beautiful. I can't take my eyes off her, and I see she is talking to a poncy looking doctor who is smiling right back at her. He's nothing like my doctor at home, with grey hair and is about sixty, this guy is much younger. My good mood dampens, and I feel a sudden surge of rage shoot through me. What's this? Jealousy? I have never cared enough about anyone to feel jealous, but this is what it must feel like, and I don't fucking like it. I feel the need to go over to her, sweep her up in my arms and claim her mouth right in front of that poncy doctor just so he knows who the fuck she belongs to.

She must feel my glare as she stares back at me instinctively. My hard expression instantly falls off my face and is replaced by one of my reserved killer smiles. I know she can't resist, she starts to blush, and a shy smile spreads over her beautiful face. Doctor Pussy looks in my direction to see what Candice is looking at. Yes, it's me, motherfucker!

I continue listening to Ed Sheeran's new album through my phone, my blood reaching boiling point as I watch Doctor Pussy and Candice being overly friendly doing the daily rounds of the ward. They soon make it over to me.

"Hello, Mr. Laine, shall we see how your knee is doing?" Ugh, he's all sugar and smiles, and Candice appears to be lapping it up. Two can play that game. I nod politely. "Of course, doctor," I say cooperatively in response as he lifts my leg up. I look at Candy with a killer smile and give her a wink, watching her pretty eyes light up again.

"Well, Mr. Laine, another few days, and you will be good to go." Something in his voice says he will be glad to see the back of me.

"Glad to hear it, doc." He glances between me and Candice as we can't seem to tear our eyes off each other.

"Continue walking around as much as you can, and be sure to do your physio, Mr. Laine," he says as he stalks off, his voice tight and moody.

Candy comes back to me as soon as she sees Doctor Pussy off. "Blake, what the hell, you're gonna get me fired."

I laugh, "What for, having a bit of fun?"

"Shut up, you know exactly what I mean." She slaps my shoulder, and I grab it feigning injury.

"Besides, it's not like they have a queue of willing candidates waiting outside. In case you forgot, we're in South Sudan. No one in their right mind would wanna work out here."

"Well that explains a lot." She grins at me, her blue eyes dancing cheekily.

"So, what time's your break? You wanna grab a coffee?"

"Ooh, is big bad Mr. Laine asking me on a date?" she says playfully.

"Maybe I am, Miss Embers."

"Actually, you are in luck, Mr. Laine. I'm just about to take a break, and yeah, I would love to go for coffee with you. How could any girl refuse?" *They couldn't,* I think to myself wryly.

We make our way to the canteen, and I resist the urge to throw my arm over her shoulder. Something tells me she's the kind of girl that will pull back if I move too quickly, and I'm enjoying her company way too much to send her running scared just yet. "What would you like, Candy?" Her cheeks instantly blush pink, obviously feeling the sexual tension just as much as I do. "I mean, off the menu," I say quietly as she narrows her eyes playfully at me.

"I will have a coffee, extra milk, please." I order adding a black coffee for myself as Candice makes her way over to the table grabbing a couple of sugars on her way over. I watch her smile and say hello to nearly everyone she passes. She is just so beautiful, with her hair swept up high on her head and a few strands falling loosely around her face. The lady from behind the counter coughs snapping me from my thoughts as I look at her, she eyes the two coffees that she has already set down. "Thanks," I say with a wink and she smiles.

I settle down opposite of Candice, and suddenly things feel a little awkward. The only dates I have ever been on are with women who want one thing only, and it isn't a conversation. Suddenly my usual routine of a few killer smiles, a few compliments and an invitation to the nearest hotel for the night seems lame. So, I start from scratch and step into the unknown. "So, tell me about you, Candy"

"Erm, what do you want to know?"

"Everything." She blushes before replying, "Well, to start with, I usually hate being called Candy, except for a select few people, who quite frankly could call me anything, and I'd answer. I just turned twenty-four. I'm from Bourton-on-the-Water, have you heard of it?"

I shake my head, listening intently.

"They call it the Venice of England. It really is one of the most beautiful places on earth, well in my opinion."

"Where is it?"

"It's a tiny village in the Cotswolds, but we're not that far from London. I still live with my parents, Joan and Stu; they're both pretty awesome, I'm really lucky. Up until recently my brother, Marshall, lived with us, too. He died just over a year ago serving in Afghan." She reels off the information all matter of fact, but raw pain is palpable in her deep, sapphire eyes.

"Wait, what? I'm sorry to hear that, Candice. I'm also amazed that you're out here yourself after that's happened?"

"He was my reason for volunteering," she replies without hesitation.

"It might sound crazy to you, but I feel close to him out here, he was my best friend," she says on a smile.

"Anyway," she visibly shrugs her shoulders in an attempt to shake her sadness. God, she seems brave for her age and has had a seemingly sheltered life so far. She continues with a smile, "Oh, I have a best friend, Rayray, well Rainy, who I have known literally forever. She is amazing, way cooler than me, and is actually hoping to come visit soon."

"What about you, Blake, I've not stopped talking! Tell me about you." Ugghh, should have seen that one coming.

"Okay, my dad's, Jonathan, my mum's name's Elaine, and I have a younger brother, Jason. My best friend who persistently tries but will never be cooler than me is Greyson, but I call him G. I met him through the early stages of my army training, he's followed me around ever since...That's about it, I like to keep my circle small." Her facial expression changes straight away,

"Hold on a minute, Blake, your dad is Jonathan Laine, as in Jonathan Laine from Laine Corporations?"

"The very one," I say.

"I didn't realise," She says shrugging her tiny shoulders. I sit back taking in her blank expression awaiting the penny to drop and am surprised when she doesn't say anything else. Instead, she's staring off into the space in her own little world. Usually when someone discovers that minor detail about me being heir to a multimillion pound corporation, their eyes flash wide with greed, and their interest in getting to know me ramps up like a fucking Jet Ski engine starting up. Especially women. The ones I have dated have all been gold diggers. Pristinely groomed in their designer dresses and high heels and the polar opposite of my Candice. 'My Candice.' Jesus, now I sound like a complete pussy.

"So, what's your type then?"

"My what?"

"You know, on paper, what type of guy do you usually go for?" She rolls her eyes and shakes her head, taking the last sip of her coffee.

"Breaks up," she states, and I stumble up to follow her back to the ward.

"So, I'm not your type?" I push her, never doubting for one second that I might not be, I'm everyone's type for chrissake." She giggles.

"I guess you're not, no. I don't exactly have a type. I've never really thought about it before."

"Well, seeming as it's not a definite no." I throw my arm around her shoulder casually. "Are you going to let me take you on a proper date when I get out of here in a few days?"

"Mmmm, I will have to get back to you on that one, Blake. I may just be washing my hair that night," she teases.

I quickly look around to see no one is about and pin her to the wall so I am towering over her. She looks up at me through long fluttery lashes, and I look straight into her beautiful eyes which run deep as the ocean. I gently place my lips on hers and start kissing her as she matches me perfectly; I wrap my arm around her lower back and pull her into me on a growl as she throws her hands into my hair. Her body is flush against mine, and my cock is rock hard pushing into her stomach.

We pull away after a few minutes completely breathless and panting, and I rest my forehead on hers as we both take a few calming breaths. Looking straight into my eyes, she looks flushed and so gorgeous, she presses a swift kiss onto my lips. Just as we turn to start walking, Sally bursts through the door. "There you are, Candy, I have been looking everywhere for you." She eyes us suspiciously.

"Good to see you up and about, Mr. Laine."

"Why thanks, Sally, I will leave you two to it." I pull Candice in and give her a squeeze and plant a complete over the top kiss to her head just so Sally knows exactly what's going on. Candy looks a little embarrassed, but I notice she doesn't pull away.

Candice

Sally's shoulders shake with laughter as she walks off briskly down the corridor, and I chase after her, almost running to catch up. She is always like that, rushing about without two minutes to spare.

"The look on your face, Candy. You're smitten with him!" She's pegging the bedding and towels out to dry as we chat.

"Not smitten, but I'll admit I do have a little soft spot for Blake. He's actually kind of sweet, and you have to admit he's gorgeous."

"I'll give you that, babe. He's a total hottie, but the man drives me mad and not in a good way!" I laughed, he has been pretty rough on Sal these last couple of weeks, constantly finding ways to break the rules and get up and about when he's supposed to be resting. "Talking of gorgeous guys, there was one looking for you earlier, I didn't catch his name, but he was really tall and bulky, built like a tank."

"You're sure he was looking for me?"

"Yeah, you're obviously miss flavour of the month at the moment, what's your secret? I need a new approach, haven't had a decent man look my way in months, it's depressing." She rolled her eyes dramatically making me giggle.

"You're such a drama llama, Sal, maybe if you weren't so picky you'd stand a chance of getting to know someone."

"I am not picky," she sulks. "I just know what I'm looking for in a man."

"I dread to imagine what that is." We both laugh, grabbing what we need to prepare the trolley.

I turn to see a soldier striding towards me from across the ward; I can tell he's English as he's in an UN Peacekeeping uniform. I don't recognise him as one of the volunteers here, and he looks full of purpose and importance.

"Are you Miss Embers?" Last time an official approached me like this, it was bad news, and the thought filled me with dread.

"I am." He put out a hand to shake.

"Lieutenant Cameron of the Queen's Royal Briano." He steps back formally adding, "Miss," with a nod of his head. I shuffle awkwardly; glad when he appears to relax now that introductions are over with.

"I hope you don't mind me searching you out, but I couldn't quite believe it when I heard you were out here. I served with your brother, Marshall, right up until he passed. I am sorry for your loss." Just the mention of his name has my eyes brimming with tears.

"I didn't mean to upset you, Miss."

"Candy," I smile. "You can call me Candy." I instinctively reach up and hug him. He wraps his massive camouflaged arms around me, and I instantly feel closer to Marshy. He steps back slightly embarrassed.

"I wanted to give you this." He reaches into his padded jacket and pulls out a tiny photo of me and Marshall arm in arm, grinning at Nan, who I remember was taking the photo. It's torn at the edges and a little faded, but it's the best thing I've seen in forever.

"He said that if anything ever happened to him, I was to get this to you, and make sure you know that in the darkest of times he looked at you and smiled, until the very end." Tears stream down my face. "I was only gonna post it once I traced an address, but when I found out you were here, I couldn't not give it to you in person." I'm shaking and holding the photo when I notice Blake approaching us. "Blake, this is Cameron." Blake offers a firm handshake, but slides his other arm around my waist possessively. Cameron reciprocates, looking slightly uncomfortable.

"I better be going, good day to you, Miss."

"Thanks so much, this is so very precious and means the world to me. How can I repay you?"

"I served with Marshall for nearly four years, Candice, he was a great guy. He had my back through a heap of shit and getting this to you is not nearly enough to pay him back. He was one of the best...again, I am sorry for your loss, take care, Miss."

"I'll make sure of that," Blake chips in, spinning me around so I'm nestled into his chest. His closeness catches me off guard, and a feeling of home fills me.

He holds me for a few minutes while my tears dry and I regain my composure.

"Blake, you need to finish up resting your knee if you want to be out of here in a few days." He's annoyed, his jaws tightly clenched, and I can tell he really hates being a patient.

"If you're good, I'll show you what Cameron gave to me." Curiosity getting the better of him, he makes his way back over to the bed which looked like it was half the size of him. He perches on the edge sulkily as if doing what he's told and getting back into bed would kill him. I glance around, the wards quiet with most of the other patients asleep or reading, so I sit beside him on the bed and show him the photo.

"Your brother, Marshall?" I nod in response. "Woah, you guys look really alike," he smiles, "and close, too. Did you always get on?"

"He was the best," I murmur, I'm struggling to talk about him. At home it's like it's forbidden to mention his name. There is still so much anger surrounding his death. My Dad blames him for joining the army in the first place, and my Mum is simply angry at the world for stealing her son too soon.

He senses my sombre mood and places an arm round my shoulder cheekily.

"Come on, this time it's you who needs the fresh air!"

I run my eyes around each bed making sure the other patients are comfy and can manage without me for five minutes.

"I will go, you need to rest up." He pulls me to my feet.

"I don't, I'm seriously fine, and I am coming with you." He still has his arm around me as we walk outside. The heat hits us instantly, it's stifling and intense.

"So, what's the deal with you, Candy. You could not have got to twenty four with those eyes and that ass without breaking some hearts." We take shade under one of the few trees.

"I have had boyfriends, but I'm not really a couple's kind of girl. Although, my parents don't agree and have been trying to marry me off for at least the last five years." My mind wandering to my neighbour, Stephan, he must have been just as embarrassed as me by our parents' unashamed attempts at matchmaking.

"You don't strike me as the type to rush into a relationship, but everyone has to belong to somebody, Candice."

"Not me," I reply. I belong here, with Marshy and Sally and the team. They're really great, and as soon as I go home I'm always desperate to get back here. These people are like family to me now, especially Sal.

"When did you first come," he asks.

"To South Sudan? About a year ago after my brother...but before that I always travelled. Europe mostly, after college I had this dream of being an artist, and I spent a summer in Italy trying to break through."

"It's a tough business?" I'm surprised at how interested he is in me and my past, it's the first time I've spoken about my art since coming here.

"Yeah, the competition's stiff, and the level of training people get now is really high."

"Do you paint?"

"Yes, mostly, but I love experimenting with pastels too, adding texture with sequins and beads."

"I would love to see some of your stuff."

"Not likely, I haven't painted since Marshall passed, I've been too busy, and he was the one who always encouraged me. He really believed I had a gift in my work." Blake sidled up closer, and as always, I can't resist the urge to lean into him. His scent is heavenly, and he feels like some kind of sex god surrounding me with his manliness. It's overwhelming, but I love it. He places his flat palm across my cheek, turning my face to meet with his, my lips part and he catches my bottom lip between his teeth, pulling gently before kissing me with an intensity that pales every other kiss I've ever had to insignificance.

I think I'm falling for him.

We make our way back around the dirt path to the entrance, his arm over my shoulder and mine wrapped around his waist, everything is quiet, quieter than usual.

CHAPTER SIX

Candice

*F*uck! He leapt over me as time stood still around us, knocking me straight to the ground. For a split second it felt calm, like nothing had happened and he lay covering my body with his.

"Move now," his voice low and controlled, pointing two curled fingers towards a nearby bush. I froze. Great, all that training of what to do in every eventuality with snipers, landmines and bomb threats. Hours of training just gone in a flash. Nothing could have prepared me for this. She had stepped out right in front of me, just five kilometres away. She was a new face, but I could have never anticipated this. Blake had, he'd leaned in to kiss me again and froze on sight of her. His voice automatic, eyes blank, "Suicide Bomber."

Two words that would change my life forever.

The ground shook with massive force, and the sound was so loud I thought I was dead on instant. Dust, screaming, running, panic. Before I could even register that I was still alive at this point in time, he had swept me up and was running. I buried my face in his chest and prayed. He ran until the screams grew quiet, and the toxic air clouding us grew thinner. "Blake, your leg," I snapped to my senses and struggled to get free of him, "put me down I can run myself." He ignores me, I fight harder until I'm on my feet running with him, hand in hand, his grasp squeezing my fingers so tight they feel numb.

"Don't stop. Don't look back." I ran.

"Keep running, Candy!"

Heavy tears spill out as I keep running. "Blake?"

His fingers had left mine, the ground is shaking. More screams, more chaos. A second bomb? "BLAKE!" I scream his name over and over still running like he had told me to, hating my feet for carrying me further away from him. My legs keep going, putting distance between me and the chaos behind, but my heart is back there holding his hand. I am so, so scared and screaming, "BLAAAKE." Nothing. My screams fell silent over the sounds of the carnage that I am running from.

I charge into a small outhouse collapsing in a heap of exhaustion, needing a few minutes to pull my shit together. I'm panting, gasping for air from running faster than I ever have before. The smoke darkens the space dark, but I can just about make out a pair of eyes on me. I jump up ready to run but make out an older man in front of me carrying a small child. He holds her body out towards me. Shit. Is she dead? He says nothing, and it's eerily silent. I check her pulse; it's faint but still there. I place a hand over her mouth, she's not breathing. Instincts taking over, I take her from the older man, I'm assuming it's her grandfather and position her flat on the ground. He begins to sob at the relief of someone stepping in to help. I'm guessing he can't speak English, but I talk anyway, my voice sounding unfamiliar and shaking from pure fear, "I'm a nurse, please don't worry, I'm a nurse."

I tilt her head back slightly, she's so tiny, I reckon about six years old. I've done the training, but I've never done CPR for real on a child. I press down firm and sharp, counting and praying....29....30. I cover her face with my own, trying to breathe life into her and feeling like I'm watching myself in slow motion. I'm not one for drugs, but I imagine this is what a bad trip feels like. I pause but nothing happens. "Come on, princess." I'm on her chest again. Counting. Desperately praying and hoping Marshall can do something to help me out. I'm giving up hope... 27...28. Her pulse is barely there. 29.

She breathes a shallow breath, and her eyes flicker. Her grandfather sobs loudly and throws his arms around me as I sit her up a bit further, and she takes another breath. He's kissing me then the little girl, over and over, frantic with joy. This is what I trained for; I'd just saved a life with nothing but my bare hands. I felt suddenly responsible for her and know I need to get them both to safety. I looked around for the best way out of here, that's when I realise how bad the fires had gotten. "Fuck!" I shout aloud realising we're trapped. I watch as a huge piece of ceiling crumbles towards us. Before the whole fucking roof caves in, I throw the girl forward out of the door and scream for the man to run. I quickly follow leaping towards the door. "Ow," *my head*, I yelp as I fall and everything turns black.

The next thing I know, I'm lying flat on my back and struggling to open my eyes. I can hear voices talking about how well the services did in flying everyone home straight after it happened, and how relieved Mum must be to have me back with her in England. "Mum, what happened," my voice croaked. "Where…"

"Shhh, you're in North Cotswold Hospital, baby, we almost lost you, but you're home now." Oh god, she's crying. Mum never cries. Dad's here too, shaking his head in his hands. Wait, is he pissed off at me? Surely, he's not going to give me the whole 'you should never have gone out there' lecture, not now, I don't think I could take it. My head is pounding, it's like I can hear my ears throbbing, instinctively I reach up to hold my hands over my ears but they hit bandage first. Then the pain kicks in and I'm crying again. I want to know what happened, but I don't have the strength to ask. Everywhere hurts so much, and the lights are so bright. "Take a sip." Mum tips a cup slightly to my lips drenching them, it feels good. She must know as she does it again.

I mentally examine myself squeezing my leg muscles tight then releasing them, wriggling my fingers, then my toes. Everything seems to be working and have sensation, although all I feel is pain in most movements, at least I know I'm not paralysed. My eyes met dad's across the room, yep, I guessed right, he was more than a little pissed.

"Oh, Candy." He stood up, but Mum waved a hand gesturing for him to back off, and he sat down placing his head back in his hands.

The doctor entered the room with a wide grin and a handful of notes.

"Welcome back, Miss Embers, it's great to have you with us." I searched eyes for answers.

"You have been in a catatonic state for almost two weeks, my love."

"Cat-a-what?"

"A coma, Candy," Mum chipped in.

"Now that you're awake we need to run some tests to check the damage on the brain as we suspect a bleed, and we will need to obviously monitor you for a while yet. I don't want you to panic or worry too much at this point, Candice, because the fact that you're alive is a miracle with the impact of your head injury and the extent of your burns."

Burns? What had happened to me out there? I remember running and the sounds of screaming and his strong arms running with me in them even with his bad knee. "Blake?" A break in my voice as Mum wets my lips again looking confused.

"Shhh, settle down, honey, you're gonna be okay." I close my eyes and allow my thoughts to drift back to South Sudan, back to the sun and back to his arms. I can hear voices coming and going, mostly Mum's but others too. I try to process what they were saying, try to open my eyes, but they feel so heavy. It's like I'm having an out of body experience. One minute I was there, the next I'm here with my parents, it's like the past few weeks have been a dream, but the pain in my sides let me know it's all real. A sense of panic flows through my body like a blood transfusion forcing itself through every vein. I have to get back to him. Mum's voice interrupts my thoughts.

"How long...recovery...bomb...trauma..."

I slip back under letting the darkness soothe my headache, and the voices still as I find some calm. As soon as I'm asleep everything rushes back to me, memories good and bad flashing up one after the other, out of order and jumbled up. I feel like I'm crying, although I can't feel any tears in my eyes. Just numbness, followed by pain, then more nothingness. I force myself to keep fighting to stay awake. I know losing me would kill my parents, and Rainy and Sal need me too. Shit, am I dying? Is this what death feels like? I thought they said you see a light? I don't, all I see is empty nothingness, I have to fight this. My inside voice is crying out, "I'm here everyone don't give up on me." In the darkness it's like my senses are working overtime. My legs feel heavy, my side feels numb, like it's not even there in parts but my lips, my lips feel Blake's powerful kiss. I don't give a damn if we just met, the urge to have his mouth pressed against mine once more is stirring enough fight inside me to wake the fuck up.

Blake

I pace the corridor at North Cotswold Hospital like I have for the past few days after spending over a week trying to find out where they'd sent her. Once they'd confirmed the bomb had been linked to a small town terrorist movement, they'd flown most of us who were directly involved home, pronto, while they assess the situation. It was crazy how fast they could get us all the hell outta there when they wanted to, but when you put in for a day off, it can take weeks to be confirmed. I'm just thankful that Candice lives near me, and I was able to track her down. Although, it was the least they could tell me considering they refused to give me her home address, throwing all that shit about confidentiality at me. If they hadn't of given me something to go on, I'd have broken in and took it anyway.

I see her Mum and Dad are with her again today. I have not yet plucked up the courage to introduce myself. I mean, what would I say? I have only known her about a month. Granted, the best month of my life, but still... Right then the oldish looking guy, who I could tell was Candy's dad from the first time I saw him, comes out of her room. I looked straight at him, and something seems to shift in his expression.

"Blake, by any chance?" His questions brings a realisation.

"She's awake?" I let out a relieved breath I didn't even know I was holding in. "How is she doing," I ask eager to know if she is okay.

"She has not long come around, she is okay, upset and a little confused, but thankfully still alive."

I can tell there is something more he wants to say which irritates me, but being polite, I put out my hand. "Blake, Blake Laine." He takes my hand.

"Stu Embers, shall we get a drink, Mr. Laine?" An odd request I think given the circumstances, but I accept out of courtesy.

"Please, call me Blake," I state, and he nods his head in acceptance as we make our way in the canteen. I grab a bottled water.

"What you having, Mr. Embers?"

"I think I need a strong coffee."

I order his coffee, and we take a seat, an awkward silence

filling the air. "I am so relieved Candy has finally come around, Mr. Embers." He looks distracted.

"So are we, it has been a living nightmare. Listen son, I am going to get straight to the point I want to make, so I can get back to Candice. I don't know what's gone on or is going on with you and my daughter, but I need you to know we will be taking her home with us, and she won't be going back out there. I will not risk losing another child to this war, so whatever has gone on with the pair of you, it's now in the past. Do you understand?" He shocks the shit out of me being so blunt like that.

"Mr. Embers, with all due respect, I don't think that's your decision to make. Candy is a grown woman and can surely make up her own mind."

He cuts me off saying, "See boy, this is why she doesn't need someone like you in her life, you army lads are all the same, it runs in your blood, you need to serve and protect. That's how we lost Marshall, he felt the need to be out there too, but Candice isn't cut out for this. She should be at home where me and my wife can keep an eye on her and keep her safe. You may mean well, but what happens in 6 months or 12 months when you get sent on a mission, and where does that leave Candice? Just think about it, Blake, please. Is that the life you want for her? Waiting for that phone call or a knock at the door, never knowing that when she waves you off if it will be the last time she ever sees you. Because, Blake, in all honesty, that is not the life I want for my daughter after watching my wife doing the very same over our son." His words hit me like a bullet straight through my chest, he must see it written all over my face as he stands, and as he walks off he taps me on the shoulder. "It's nothing against you, son. I just can't watch the army destroy our girl. I really hope you understand that," and with those final words, he walks off.

I sit and ponder on his words for what seems like forever before I realise he is right, I don't want this for Candy. It would be selfish of me to put her through it, and with that I make the hardest decision of my life and walk out of the hospital, without her.

Jerry, my driver is waiting right outside the entrance completely oblivious to the no parking warning all around him. I nod and he knows without words where I'm going, and we make off towards Greyson's place at high speed. It takes a good hour and thirty minutes before I am at his door with some cold beers and a sorry ass look on my face.

"Alright, dickhead," he greets me. I grunt, make my way past and throw myself on his too small couch. "Why are you being all dramatic and acting like a chick," he laughs. The bastard actually laughs.

"I walked away," I say, not needing to emphasise. "Well, what did you do that for, dumbass? I thought she was the real deal." I lean up, grab a beer, open it and gulp it down.

"Her dad warned me off, said he doesn't want her with someone in the army after what happened with her brother. I get where he is coming from, G. What the fuck can I offer her, the occasional visit when we ain't on a mission?" He comes over and grabs a beer as he seats himself in the chair opposite me.

"Come on, man, you're over thinking this shit. Candice sounds like a cool girl, I'm sure she can make up her own mind," he throws back at me.

"That's exactly what I am afraid of, G. What if she realises that it's all true, and it's not what she wants. Where does that leave me?" I put my empty bottle on the table and grab another one taking yet another huge gulp as G eyes me knowing I am about to drown my sorrows. He shrugs and gulps down his own beer.

"If you can't beat um, you join them." He shrugs again while reaching for another one for himself, and this is why he is my best friend.

G and I are still sat in the same place a fair few hours later having drank a lot more beers and talking even more shit. "I get it, Blake. I mean, from what you say she's hot. I am pretty sure if I had a sexy nurse, I wouldn't wanna let her go either," he says laughing.

"It's not just that, G. I mean, yeah, obviously she is hot as hell, but she isn't like any other woman I know. She's, I don't know." Feeling frustrated I stand and pace up and down.

"She's just more, G. Do you know what I mean?" I ask him.

"Not a clue, bro, this is me you're talking to. I don't think I have ever been with the same woman more than once," he answers smiling proudly.

"Well you will, G, and when you do it knocks you on your ass." He stands and walks towards his bedroom.

"Whatever dude, this is too deep for me after this many beers, I'm off to bed. Sleep in the spare room, if ya want," And with that, the door shuts leaving me on my own with my own thoughts. I lean my head onto the back of the sofa, and no sooner than my eyes start to shut, I think of all things Candice.

In my drunken state I pull out my phone and can only half make out the contact list I am scrolling through. Then bang, I stop at 'Tiffany'. I go to press call but stop myself and mentally compare Tiffany to Candice. Tiff has short dark hair, nothing like Candice's long blonde waves, and her dark brown eyes are opposite to Candice's ocean blue. I'm feeling pissed off. Candy is everything I want, but her Dad is right, I gotta leave her alone. I'm not what she needs, I probably never will be. I made that choice when I signed my life away to the army.

I make a stupid ass decision and ring Tiff, she answers almost immediately as though she was waiting for the call.

"Well well well, Blake, this is a pleasant surprise," she practically purrs down the line.

"Okay to come over, Tiff?"

"You know it is, Blakey baby." I get a cab, not wanting Jerry to know anything about this and twenty minutes later pull up at Mount Street Gardens, right outside the apartments that house Tiffany Parker. I take a deep breath and buzz her number. She lets me in straight away, her voice low and inviting, "Come up, babe." Making my way to the elevator I contemplate my decision in coming here again, she is only going to get false hopes and, as usual, think I want more. I know I'm being selfish, but I need to fuck Candice out of my head and I know Tiff can do the job. She's familiar, I don't even need to bother with conversation, she knows exactly what I'm here for, and I know she'll be willing to oblige. I'm being unreasonable, but Tiff already knows that I am an asshole. It's all she deserves, I think to myself harshly.

Tiffany, daughter of Martin Parker and heiress to Parker Enterprises, has changed as we've grown up. She's had her fair share of shit over the years and has been sucked into a world of fast cars and the rich kid's drugs scene. Everything I avoided by signing up to the army as soon as I could. Our dads have been secret business rivals for many years, always trying to outdo each other. Little does Tiff know my dad has two huge deals in the pipeline, that will sink Parker Enterprises.

The elevator door dings, I shake my thoughts off and step in pressing floor twenty-two. Watching each floor light up as I pass, I know I'm making a huge mistake. I arrive and step out round to the lift approaching Tiff's door, which she has left ajar for me. Walking in I notice she has put some sloppy music on, and as I enter the living area she stands holding two wine glasses and wearing nothing but a black thong and bra with a black silk robe.

"Hello Blake," she says in her best seductive voice, which I find annoying.

"Tiffany," I reply with a nod over to the liquor, "okay to get some Jack?"

"Go ahead and help yourself," she says while putting one of the wine glasses down and taking a sip from the other. Grabbing a whiskey tumbler from the side, I pour a Jack Daniels straight and knock it back before pouring another knocking that back, too. I tense when I feel her hand slide over my shoulder. "What's wrong, Blakey, you seem stressed?" I turn to face her.

"I haven't come here for small talk, Tiff." I don't miss the flash of disappointment in her eyes. "Well, what have you come for then?" I trace my finger down from her throat to the swell of her breasts.

"I'm here to fuck you, nothing more." I watch as her body reacts to my touch and goose bumps spread over her whole body when I reach around and grab her ass and pull her into me so she can feel my erection. "Nothing less." She lets out a moan as she shamelessly grinds herself against me. She tries to kiss me, so instead, I turn my head and kiss down her throat.

She throws her arms around my neck, I hoist her up and she wraps her legs around my waist. While kissing and sucking her breasts, I make my way to the bedroom and throw her on the bed. I take my clothes off in record time, tossing a condom from my pocket onto the bed next to Tiff as she takes off her robe. I reach around and unclasp her bra and cup her breasts pinching her nipples hard. She cries out reaching for my cock, and I let her pump me up and down. She slides towards me and sits on the edge of the bed so her legs are wide apart, and I am standing between them as she licks the end of my cock. I place my hands on the back of her head and thrust into her mouth until I can feel the back of her throat. She takes all of it while looking up at me, eyes full of lust as I carry on thrusting into her mouth, and I still can't help but think of Candice. I pull out of her needing to fuck her properly. She stands and slides her thong down her slender legs, and I cup her pussy sliding my fingers through her, she is soaked. "So fucking wet aren't you, Tiff?" She moans as I flick her clit. "Want me to fuck you hard, don't you?"

"Yes, Blake," she is panting, breathless from gagging on me.

"Turn around," I whisper in her ear, and she does immediately. I grab the condom tearing it open and roll it onto my cock. I push Tiff down so she is bending right over the bed and with no warning I push my cock straight into her. She screams out. "Shhh, Tiff." I grab her hips and thrust into her harder and harder each time. I can feel her getting close as she squeezes my cock as hard as she can with her pussy. "Getting close aren't you, Tiff, don't come until I say you can."

I pull out of her turning her around placing her pussy right in front of me at the end of the bed and throwing her legs up so her feet are touching my shoulder. I slam straight in between her legs and thrust back and forth pounding her hard as I circle her clit with my fingers. She is screaming, and I can feel how close she is. "Come now," I command and on cue she does. I focus on the creamy juices flowing out of her and continue thrusting into her letting her fingers wrap the base of my cock until I find my own release and gradually slow down.

"That was amazing, Blakey." I slide out of her sitting on the edge of the bed and take the condom off and knot it, tossing it into the trash. Saying nothing I pad across to the bathroom and shut the door. I look in the mirror and feel like shit knowing I just used Tiff again, and it hasn't changed my feelings for Candice.

CHAPTER SEVEN

Candice

For three days I'd been back at my parents' house. Three whole days, and I'd heard nothing. Not that he had my number, but I felt like if he was really bothered he would have tracked me down. Almost two weeks have passed since the bomb that changed everything and I'm convinced he will have forgotten all about me by now. Clearly, whatever I thought we had, hadn't meant as such to him as it had to me. It's not like he would want me now anyway, I'm ruined from head to foot. I look down at my bare arms and take in the scuffs and scrapes, that the doctor says will heal over time. I can't help feeling as though I'll never be normal again.

I pull the duvet up over my head and hear my Mum's footsteps padding up the stairs.

"Come on, lovely, you need to be getting up and about by now.

Life's too short to be moping around." And to drive the point home, she glanced towards the framed photo of my big brother hugging me and grinning in our Christmas day jumpers.

"Mum, just leave me be. I need to sleep, the doctor did say I need to rest."

"He said rest, honey, not mope around and waste your life away."

"Three days, Mum, you're giving me three days?"

She makes the point of looking at her watch. "It's been nearly four now, and you'll get bed sores just lying there. C'mon, up you get," she said as she pulled on the duvet. Bed sores? Was she for real? Pouting like a petulant child, I pulled the duvet back over myself but attempted to satisfy her by sitting up.

"I'll come down for dinner if you're cooking?"

"That's my good girl, see you at 5:00. Your dad's home tonight, so he can join us, too." My spirits lifted a little. The mood had been sombre these last few days, but now I was back at home and under his close surveillance. I could tell Dad was beginning to relax a little, and hopefully his sense of humour I loved so much would be back in time for tea. When she was gone I slowly got up from the bed, pain radiating through my entire body and my side feels like it's still burning.

I was so relieved the physiotherapist had agreed to see me as an outpatient, rather than keep me in. I might not be qualified, but once she had heard of all the physio sessions I had delivered at the clinic with Sal, I think she realised I was capable of enough self-care to nurse myself back to full fitness. Besides, once they cleared me from any serious injuries it wasn't going to take long for my aching arm and shoulder to regain strength. It wasn't the pain that bothered me, it was the ugliness.

I'd peeled back the bandage covering my side last night. The red, melted skin was raw and shining. As soon as I sneaked a peek, I wished I hadn't. The burns on my arms and legs were superficial, as were the ones on my face, but the one that ran from my shoulder blade and covered my left side, stretching slightly over my stomach and round to my left bum cheek...

It was revolting.

I hated it.

I had never been vain or particularly interested in my looks, but then I had never had to be. I had always been naturally pretty and right through school I was self-confident. My parents had always praised the way I looked. I remember the way my dad had made me look in the mirror every day before school and repeat after him, "I am beautiful, I am loved and I believe in myself."

I hadn't really known what I was saying back then, I just liked the way he kissed his finger and pressed it to my nose afterwards. Now I was older, I understand the importance of those few words added to our daily routine and how they helped me–through exams, coping with bitchy girl comments and dealing with the heavy criticism thrown at me when the boys in class noticed I had developed boobs at an earlier age than most. I tried to recite them now staring into the bathroom mirror, but the words were replaced with tears which stung my burnt and blistered cheeks.

I don't know why I'm annoyed at myself. I understood the risks when I went out there, but I had hoped to avoid any serious danger as I knew the stress it would cause both my parents. They were still grieving the loss of my brother and any extra pressure would push them over the edge. Now I knew they would never let go of me again, the very thought of it was stifling.

Twisting the taps off I look at the luke warm bath deciphering the best approach, lowering myself in slowly or just going for it. I decided on the latter, I countdown out loud, "3,2,1 Ahhhh." The water feels like 100 degrees, and I've only dipped my foot in. I add a load more cold and try again. I need to feel clean. There's something about burnt skin that makes you feel dirty, and despite the pain, all I wanted to do was feel clean and fresh. Okay, I'm in. Breathe. This is possibly the most pain I've ever experienced. The doctor warned me about this, and she was right. It did seem to be subsiding as I sat upright with my body tensed to a stone and barely daring to breathe. I can feel my shoulders start to relax, and the soak actually feels good. The water gave me a different sensation to the dry, itchy, tight feeling my skin has had for the last few days. I winced as I forced myself to look down at my charred skin, it was unsightly.

"Tea's almost ready, lovie," Mum shouts up, interrupting my thoughts of self-hate.

After smearing myself in cream, I towel dry, barely touching the sore bits and give up with the thought of clothes. Opting for a loose khaki green nightie that could pass for a t-shirt dress, well almost, and a pair of fluffy flip flop slippers, I make my way downstairs following the smell of spicy chicken, Mum's favourite recipe. It wasn't like her to have the tv on when we we're about to eat. Wait, was that voices I could hear. Oh no, I should have anticipated this. Mum has always been the hostess with the mostess, and believes there is nothing a family dinner can't fix.

Yep, I should have known.

"Surprise!"

My eyes scan the room, there's: Rainy, my childhood friend; Stephan, the boy next door they've been trying to set me up with for years; Aunty Julie; cousin Brett; and a couple of girls from the W.I. "Mum, can I have a word, please. *In the kitchen,*" I hiss under my breath.

"Sit down, Candy. People just want to wish you well, everyone's been so worried," my dad's was tone soft but his eyes demanding. I turn to Mum, she's ushering me into the nearest chair piled high with cushions. This was going to hurt, which she had pre-empted, probably so I couldn't use the pain of the burns as a reason for not joining the little dinner party she had put together.

My side is so sore that I'd forgotten the extent of the bruising and burns to my face. My hair is still damp and with my usual bun, the injures to my face are clearly visible. I must be a sight for sore eyes as their voices grow quiet when I walk into the room. Everyone seems to draw a breath, before all talking over each other to wish me well. I pushed myself for a fake smile, it was more of a grimace but the best I could do. Wincing as I lower myself into the chair, I can feel every part of my burnt side stretching until I am resting on the pile of cushions. Mum was dishing out her chicken concoction, but I couldn't stomach a full meal. I'd barely eaten since I'd been home. Dad reached over and placed a reassuring hand over mine.

"It'll do ya good, Candy, it's just what you need."

He was probably right. I lifted a forkful up, and the pain in my shoulder peaked to a sharp spasm that made me drop my fork. My cheeks flamed red, but I could feel dad's eyes on me, urging me to carry on for Mum's sake. Everyone wanted to know exactly what had happened, 'all the juicy details', as Aunty Julie had put it.

"Give her a minute to think straight. Bloody hell, you're like a pack of hyenas." This time I cracked a real smile, my first in days. You could always count on Rainy to stick up for me; she was a true friend for life.

"Let's talk about something else, I'm sure Candice is desperate for some fresh conversation," Dad said as he squeezes my hand gently letting me know he's on my side.

Stephan's chest puffed up speaking boldly, "Well business is booming at the Garage, and I'm thinking of branching out...in fact, I've been to check out another plot today."

"Wow, Stephan, that's great, good for you." I cringed as Mum patted him on the back. He didn't stop there...

"Don't worry, Candy, I had a feeling things might not work out, so I kept your job open for you as receptionist. Although, with the new garage opening, I may be able to offer you the position of personal assistant." His eyes grew wide with anticipation awaiting my response. I shovel a fork full of food in to buy some time, looking to Rainy to rescue me.

"Go on then, girly, tell me how you're holding up?" Her voice was full of genuine concern, and it overwhelms me. Tears prick my eyes as I try to hold them back knowing how much they will sting if they fall to my scuffed cheeks. Aunty Julie reaches out and squeezes my shoulder without thinking.

"You let it out if you need to, lovely."

"Argh," I yelp out as the pain radiates through my shoulder and down my arm. I drop my fork again, food splattering off my plate. Julie is fussing over me and apologizing. I jump up forgetting my injuries for a minute, pain radiating through me. "Stop! I yelled." "Everyone, just please go," I broke down and dad helps me back upstairs. I can hear Mum apologizing to her WI friends for my little 'outburst.' She could be so thoughtless at times. Dad tucks me back in while I continue to sob before wearing myself out and falling to sleep.

I can see Blake's face as if its right there with me, feel his eyes meeting mine across the room. I feel giddy and girly and enjoy this flirty side I didn't know I had until now. We're back on the ward, me nursing his leg and him watching my every move. I reach down to adjust his pillows, and he brushes a stray hair away from my face. My lips burn with the desire to kiss him. Then a bang, and we are running. My head hurts. His face is moving further away from mine. "Blake," I call to him. "Blaaaake."

"You're okay, you're okay. I've got you." I wake with my sheets drenched with sweat and my body shaking uncontrollably as Mum holds me looking tired and really worried. It takes a few minutes to realise what's happening. "It was all a dream, Candy, your home. You're safe now, sweetheart." I lay back down, not closing my eyes in case it all comes back again. Mum stays with me for a while until I settle a bit. "You okay?" I nod weakly.

"I'm okay, Mum. Go back to bed." This time it's Sal I dream of. We're laughing at the state of each other after delivering a kids PE lesson at the volunteer centre. The heat makes playing rounder's completely unbearable. Sal, and I were not the sportiest of people at the best of times, but this was ridiculous. The kids run rings around us, and we're both bright red from running mixed with a touch of sun burn.

"You look a bit funny, Miss Sally. Are you going to be sick?" laughs one of the kids.

"Miss Candice looks even funnier," a little girl points out, and she is right, my bun has half fallen out and is hanging to one side. My mind wanders back to the ward and there I am with Blake again. He is smiling at me and complaining to Sal about the food again just to wind her up.

"It's not the bloody Ritz, Mr. Laine," she pretended to swat him like a fly. Then everything catches fire, the kids, my hair, the buildings around us, I'm screaming to Blake but no sounds coming out. I'm trapped and can't see a way out. I'm shivering in terror, and the heat of the fire is all I can feel getting hotter until I can hardly stand it. I jolt awake and can't settle for the rest of the night, there's a restless feeling in my bones. I toss and turn until finally around 4am and almost getting light. I make my decision, I'm going back. My body may be ruined, but it still works. I have to live. Not just for me, but for Marshall, too. He'd been robbed of his life too soon, and I owe it to him to live enough for the both of us.

Now, I just have to figure out how to tell Mum and Dad in the morning.

CHAPTER EIGHT

Blake

*B*ack at my Mayfair apartment, I sink into my massive black leather corner sofa that's far too big for just me and enjoy the calm of the spacious monochrome surroundings. The space couldn't be described as homely, but its simplicity was enviable in the heart of chaos that is central London. A huge plasma tv hangs on the wall and everything about the room screams bachelor pad, which is ironic considering a lady has never crossed the threshold. It's a two storey penthouse suite in central London with the most amazing views over Hyde Park, and the whole of the city for that matter. That's the reason I bought this place. It feels a million miles away from the world below, just how I like it.

My phone sounds telling me I have a text. I know it will be Tiff before I look at the screen, but I still look anyway. Twenty-six missed calls and six texts; the latest text is one worded *'asshole.'* I knew I was making a monumental screw up going there the other night, but I honestly thought I could fuck Candice out of my mind. I couldn't have been more wrong as she is all I have thought about since.

Trying my hardest to think about anything other than the woman I've been obsessing over since being back in London, I turn my thoughts to what lies ahead for me tomorrow. I couldn't turn down the twelve month contract offered to me to help build a rehabilitation place for all the children and adults affected by the war. Plus it gets me the hell away from here, from Dad, the business, endless hangovers and from missing Candice. I mindlessly flick through the channels on the tv not interested in actually watching it. My flight leaves for Juba at five in the morning, and I know all too well what waits ahead there. The constant noise, stifling heat, distinctive smell and sound of bullets flying around. Anyone else would be dreading it but not me, I can't wait to go.

I stand and make my way over to the glass windows, place my head onto the cold glass and let out a sigh. Don't get me wrong, the army is where I love to be. Feels like home, but going back there is also going to remind me of the one thing in my life I have had to walk away from. My heart starts beating faster at just the thought of her despite my attempts to put her to the back of my mind. I have never felt so attached to anyone in my life, not that I'm not close to my folks, but this was different. Thoughts of my family remind me that I haven't even bothered seeing them since I've been back in London. No doubt they'd be too busy to meet up anyhow; it was at least a three week notice period before I'd get an appointment with either of them anyway. I didn't mind, I'd gotten used to it over the years. We had that kind of relationship, I wouldn't want them up in my business all the time, pardon the pun.

Despite our issues, I still know I'm lucky to have had a more than privileged upbringing. I've pretty much never wanted for anything, but that hasn't made me the spoilt brat that Jason is now. I appreciate that he had a rough start up until my parents adopted him at age nine. Apparently, his mum, who is dead now, was a first-class junkie, and he doesn't even know who his dad is. He has played on that his whole life to get everything and anything he wanted without realising our parents would have gave him it all without the pity party. He has always been weirdly jealous of me, I know it and so does my dad. Like through high school, when I had finished with one of my 'girlfriends', he always wanted to pick up the slack, which was fine by me because I was never interested in a relationship anyway. Well, up until I met Candice that is.

I recall going to a college party that our parents didn't want me to go to, and he was always there to rat me out and generally be a dick like that. Spoilt little fucker. I hate the way he has a knack of making Mum feel guilty after everything she's done for him. I don't know how he still carries a chip on his shoulder when our folks have treated him exactly the same, if not slightly better than me, and he wasn't the easiest of kids to love. I think he's got worse these past few years, his expensive lifestyle has made him greedy and ungrateful.

I do feel a bit selfish leaving dad with just Jason for support, and I've already had endless phone calls with him this week pleading with me not to go back. I have tried to explain that this time is different and that I'm not there to fight, instead I'll be helping repair a small town that is apparently completely broken by the civil war. Truth is, he doesn't give a shit where I am or what I'm doing, as long as I keep a hand in with the family company. My dad, myself and Jason each own a third of Laine Corporations. To my dad it's like a giant ass game of monopoly. We buy out companies in financial hardship and break them up for parts, which makes us a shit ton of money and even more enemies. It's now a multi-million pound company, so my dad can't understand why I want to risk my life. But I have to do something for myself. Yep, I reap all the benefits of Laine Corporations with practically zero input. Except for when a big deal needs closing, just like the one we are currently working on, and then I get called in to seal the deal. Even then I have to deal with the constant moaning from Jason as to why he wasn't good enough to negotiate and oversee contracts. It wasn't a trust thing, our folks had always trusted him implicitly when it came to big decisions, but this was one of the biggest deals we would ever do and I know my dad's torn.

It had finally come to the day when he needed to decide where his loyalties were. Friendship or business. Despite his best attempts and massive opportunity, Jase had never bothered to learn enough about the business world to earn the respect of our partners and never posed enough of a threat to our rivals. Dad always joked when we were on our own that business is in the blood, and I always felt a bit uneasy with the joke, but now I've seen how quickly Jason's shitty choices have cost us hundreds of thousands. So, I can see why dad's losing confidence in him.

I give up with the tv wondering why anyone pays all that money to the network when they never put anything decent on. I climb into bed and starfish, revelling in the comfort. You really can't beat your own bed. I try and force sleep which never comes easy for me. Especially since leaving her in the hospital that day, all I can picture are those bright blue eyes that resemble the ocean, that perfect scent of girly flowery shit and them little scattered freckles on Candice Embers beautiful face.

I had left her behind without so much as a goodbye. The only woman in my life that causes my heart to beat so fast it feels like it is going to explode straight out of my chest. I know if I went to say goodbye, I would never have been able to leave her and drag my sorry ass back to London. I know I need some time to heal, to see if leaving her was the right thing to do. I also know she is living back at her folks in the Cotswolds just a few hours drive from me, and I have thought so many times about jumping in my car to go get her and bring her home with me. But her dad's words replay in my head, and I stop myself from doing just that.

I must eventually find sleep as I wake to the sound of my alarm ringing, but it feels like minutes since I first closed my eyes. I grab a quick shower get dressed, and I am out the door in record time and on my way to the airport. Greyson was meant to be flying over with me, but instead he wanted to take one of the few scheduled flights as he likes to hook up with the air hostesses or anyone with a pulse on the way. He's pretty famous in the mile high club stakes.

All the way to the airport I get a shitty sinking feeling that I'm running out on her. I share a beer with a few of the lads I recognise from training, but am feeling like I can't be bothered with anyone and just wanna be on my own. So, I keep to myself for most of the journey. There's only a few of us coming back out here as part of the UN peacekeeping commitment. We're under strict orders not to tackle the rebels, only dampen the damage as much as we can. It pisses me off that my leg still isn't classed as healed, and I'm signed off from frontline duties, but at least the centre gives me an escape from the business and something to focus on for the next few months.

I arrive at Juba airport, and as soon as I step off the plane the dry heat hits me straight away and the smell I haven't missed at all since leaving, lingers in the air. I make my way to the car rental, pick up a jeep and haul ass to the Peace Centre. After a fifty minute journey through the middle of nowhere, I reach Bor. I pull up outside, and it strikes me that even though the team looks busy, and there's definitely enough hands on the ground with all the local volunteers, they're lacking in leadership. They've had a two week head start, and the centre is literally a pile of bricks. They've come up with nothing. Well, that's about to change now that I am here, it's the main thing that I like to do, take control of a situation. It's what I'm renowned for, both at home and in my squad.

Candice

*M*um and Dad, I don't expect you to understand, but I had to go back. I promise I will ring when I land and stay in touch more. I won't put myself in any danger, but it's become my life. The centre, or whatever's left, is my home for now. It's where I

feel close to Marshall. Please forgive me, I love you both loads.
Candice x

I scribble 'Mum' on the envelope and prop itup on the hallway sideboard. I'm chickening out, and it feels really shitty. On the other hand, so did staying here and living a half-life with a job as Stephan's assistant and under my parent's constant surveillance. I need to finish what I started and if I waited, it would have only been harder on them. My phone flashes up with a text.

Am outside babe, hurry up, RayRay.

I bet Rainy was loving this. She's rarely gotten any action lately, and it feels like it's been me getting swept in drama and chaos for a change. We're soon on the road. Rainy keeps the lights off like she's kidnapping me, she's clearly watched one too many episodes of Prison Break.

"You sure about this, girly?"

"Never been more sure of anything."

"I can't be here right now, it's too full on...and they both seem to have upped their quest to marry me off to Stephan since I came back." I roll my eyes.

Rainy's laughing, "Oh god, there's your reason alone to get the hell outta here!"

"You know he's not all that bad, he's just a bit of a closed book, I reckon he's gonna burst out of his shell one day and give some woman the time of her life!"

Well, it won't be me." I've known that boy since he moved in, and he is like an annoying cousin to me. Always teasing and telling me some weird facts about the world, well mostly about cars and engines. There's quiet for a moment as we approach the airport.

"I sure as hell will miss you, girly," she says looking genuinely sad.

"Told you, as soon as you get that teaching qualification, you're on the first plane out there...you'll love it, Rayray."

"I can imagine sun, sea, sand..." she trails off dreamily.

"And a shed load of dying men, yup it's the dream," I add sarcastically.

"You shouldn't joke about that stuff, Candy. What you do out there is serious shit." I frown, and adjust my bun a little tighter.

"I know, I was only messing." We pull over and she gives me the biggest hug. It kills my side but I don't care, I need it. "You're the best friend a girl could wish for, Rainy. Make sure you make time for fun while I'm gone and write me billions."

"I'll write you as soon as I get in." And I know she will. I'd fallen lucky the day we started preschool together in our matching pigtails that we'd both pulled out. She would never know how much she meant to me, and I know she loved me exactly the same.

"Stop it, you're making this into a goodbye, and you know I hate them. You promised..."

"Sorry, babe, I'll text when I can, love you," I say as I jumped out of the car before she got upset. She revved off quickly like I knew she would. Waving would have definitely resulted in tears. I watched as she sped off flashing her lights at me and beeping as she turned the corner. It was me who was in tears at the reality that it really might be goodbye. Stop it. I chastise myself, I couldn't think that way, or I'd never do anything remotely exciting and might as well turn around right now and marry Stephan. The very thought dried my tears, and I was soon boarding the plane and settling down in the window seat I had booked online. I'm exhausted, not just from the lack of sleep but from the exhaustion of the effort in every move.

With my side so badly burnt, it's like the rest of my body has to work overtime to compensate. Every twist and turn carefully measured and worked around, so I'm barely moving the broken skin. I feel like a robot, the old me but trapped in someone else's shitty body. I hope that I am going to the one place where I know I'll be useful and will give me the sense of purpose I need to keep going. At the centre, every pair of hands, however able, is needed and appreciated like no other place I've ever known.

I drift in and out of sleep for the next seven and a bit hours trying to get comfortable in the tiny space as I'm sat next to two larger women both snoring loudly. Thoughts of Sally are playing on my mind, it's weird how she hadn't been in touch. I guess she has been too busy dealing with the chaos after the bomb. I force the image of Blake's irresistible face out of my head once more, disappointment flooding over me. I really thought what we had was real. I scrunched my eyes tightly closed trying to block him out, but like always, I could still see his dark eyes locked on mine. At least the next few months at the centre would take my mind off him.

A tall blonde guy with a killer smile flashes me a wink as he stands up to reach the overhead cabin. It lifts my spirits. Who knows, I might even meet someone on this trip who is actual boyfriend material. My heart sinks as if it is in tune with the plane's descent, what am I thinking, a boyfriend is the last thing I need. Hot bod over there wouldn't be winking if he had seen my destroyed body, he'd be flinching in disgust. Instinctively I trace a finger up my side and hug myself, turning to face the window. The sight of the vast desert brings me some inner peace, and I let out a sigh. "I'm back, bro," I whisper. "I'm right here with you."

I throw my rucksack over one shoulder groaning as the weight pulls down on my sore shoulder even though I'm trying to balance it on my good side. I attempt to pull down my case from the hand luggage bit, impatient to get off the crowded plane and into the fresh air. I struggle for a few minutes on my tiptoes before an arm reaches over mine and lifts it down for me. A strong firm hand is wrestling my rucksack from my arm.

"Allow me, Miss."

Hot guy flashes me another cheeky grin, his bright pearly whites dazzling against his deep tan. The pain in my shoulder has me saying, "Thanks a lot, you sure you don't mind?"

"Course not, honey; want me to carry you too?"

I cringe, he really is too much. I feel my cheeks blush red. "Just the bag would be great, thanks."

He's reading my luggage tag-the snoop!

"With pleasure, Miss Embers."

We head out to wait for a taxi, and once he's placed my bags down I sit on one, lifting my face to the sun. It's amazing, just past midday so it's at its hottest, too.

"What's a pretty little thing like you doing out here, then?"

He stood next to me, so tall that even when I look up all I see is leg. "Visiting the army camp, are ya? Got a fella out here?"

Not wanting to give anything away I carefully reply, "I'm working at the Peace Centre.

"Woah, no way, that's where I'm headed! We can share a cab."

Awkward...I eye him suspiciously. "Well my boyfriend's meeting me when I get there," I lie, trying to gauge his reaction.

"Cool, I'll get to shake hands with the luckiest guy in South Sudan."

I giggle shyly, sweeping my side fringe up from my face for a few seconds of cool air. He notices my burns straight away, and I quickly smooth my side fringe down again uncomfortably and put my head down. Would it always be like this? I agree to the taxi ride, and am seriously weirded out by his bolshiness jumping into the backseat next to me; I was hoping he would of rode upfront with the driver.

"So, what's the plan when we arrive?"

"We?" I giggle. "I don't even know your name."

"It's Grey." He throws me his best smouldering look.

"As in fifty shades?"

"Woah, baby, if that's what you're into, I'm down for it."

Surely he's not being serious, but he smoulders on suggestively, and I can't help grinning. We fall back into our own thoughts staring out of the window, and I wince as the taxi driver throws me into him every time we take a corner.

"I usually have to put in a bit more effort than this. Sheesh, for someone with a boyfriend you sure do keep throwing yourself at me."

"You really are too much, Grey." He shoots me another smoulder.

"Thank you, Miss Embers, I consider myself a professional when it comes to women."

I burst out laughing not caring if I bruise his ego, which incidentally I don't as he smiles, too.

CHAPTER NINE

Blake

I make an early start, trying to avoid the blazing heat of the African sun that I know will reach crippling heights by lunch time making volunteers for labour work thin on the ground. I stop and reach for a drink of water enjoying the feeling of the cool liquid sliding down my throat. I whip off my top using it to wipe the sweat off my forehead and carry on in just my pants. The centre is starting to take shape and the foundations are set, so we are moving onto building the frame this afternoon. More and more volunteers have been showing up the past few days to help get this place up and running. There is so much going on around us between the soldiers, volunteers, nurses and so many local kids who are all eager to help. It's pretty amazing how everyone is coming together.

Unexpectedly out of nowhere, my heart starts beating so fast I think it's going to explode. I get a shiver right down my spine, and my whole body feels like it has a current of electricity flowing through its veins. I turn my head looking both ways in confusion before my eyes land on the blonde getting out of the cab, it then all makes sense because my body has always reacted like this around her, Candice Embers.

"What the fuck?" I say to myself, she must sense my stare as she looks straight back at me; a blush spreading over her beautiful face does nothing to hide her shocked expression. Obviously, not expecting to see me here, she bites on her bottom lip as she tries to hide her smile.

Just then, I notice a tall male get out the cab and sling his arm straight over her delicate shoulders. Rage flows through me, and I start to make my way over while my blood is reaching a boiling point. My fists are clenched at either side of my frame, but everything starts to cool as they both turn in my direction and I recognise Greyson, but I still want his arm off her.

"Blake," they both say in unison while looking at each other in confusion.

"Do you wanna get your arm off my woman, G?" I say smiling as Greyson immediately removes his arm and clasps hold of me.

"Good to see you, man. I didn't know this was Candice. No way! Punching above your weight there, bro. She's a stunner," he says winking at her, and she smiles down coyly.

Shit, she looks even more beautiful than the last time I saw her.

"I will give you two some time," G says as he makes his way over to some of the others helping out and who are equally as pleased to see him as I am.

84

"I don't know what to say, Candy. What the hell are you doing here?" She looks up at me through those long ass eyelashes.

"Hi, Blake, I don't know really. I just couldn't keep away, I needed to come back. I couldn't just sit at home and let my mum and dad suffocate me."

"But you're burns? Are you well enough to be here?"

The darkness that clouds her wide blue eyes kills me.

"Please don't mention them, I just want to forget it all, Blake. It's all too much."

Her name on my lips awakens feelings that I have spent the last few weeks trying to forget. I don't know what to say to make it better.

"Candy, I'm so sorry."

"You have nothing to be sorry for."

I don't know whether to tell her about my conversation with her dad, or if it will make things worse. Why am I second guessing myself so much?

"I know you came to find me, Blake, and I don't blame you for running. I don't expect anyone to want me like this. I get that what happened has ruined everything, but if we can just get along, as friends maybe, then I'd really like it."

Friends. The word hits me like a cold slice of ice through my chest. I do the only thing I can think of that will change her mind and lean in to kiss her.

As before, she can't resist and she's kissing me back with a burning passion and her taste of strawberries and mint is mingled with wet salty tears. I pull her in closer, and she cries out in pain.

"Fuck," I throw my arms away from her and into my hair in frustration.

"I'm sorry, Blake," she sobs. "I'm just not ready, and I'm not sure I ever will be. My body's in bits and so am I."

I can see the honesty in her eyes, I shouldn't say what I am about to as I know I'm making promises I can't keep. "I'll wait. As long as it takes, I'm not going anywhere, Candy. We're not done here, not by a long shot, and for the record, I didn't run."

She looks up at me all wide eyed and inquisitive, but I can't tell her about the hospital. She might blame her Dad, and she needs her family now probably more than ever. "I'm mad as fuck that you're even out here as I know your doc would have said it's too soo..." She cuts me off.

"They did, but I know how to look after my own body. It's everything else that needs to heal. That's why I'm back, there's nowhere else I feel more like myself than out here with this crazy team surrounded by chaos. I need to find myself all over again."

"I get it, I do and not that I've ever done 'friends' before, but for you I'll make an exception." The heavy crinkle between her eyebrows lifts, and her pretty blue eyes are sparkling again. She throws her arms around me. I panic, she feels so good. I'm guessing she knows I'm about to kiss her again as she pulls away faster than my lips can reach her.

"Catch you later."

"Sure, see you around," I reply. Like I can completely take it or leave it when we both know she's all I'll see round here.

Nothing else exists for me when she's in the picture, just that tight ass and huge blue eyes that light up whenever I'm around. I watch her walk away and can't help wolf whistling after her. She sashays her ass side to side purposefully teasing me before shaking her head playfully. "Fucking friend zoned," I mutter out loud frowning.

I make my way back to Greyson I want every fucking detail of how he came to be in a taxi with my girl. As I'm walking her dad's words play over and over in my head, *'never knowing if it will be the last time she sees you.'* Knowing he's right, what can I offer a girl like Candice?

Other woman were just happy taking my body or my money or both, they never wanted anything in return. I made it clear from the get go that there was nothing more up for grabs. I was London's most unobtainable bachelor. Most lads in my circle were jealous of me, and most of the woman wanted to fuck me, if they hadn't already. I'd made quite the reputation for myself in the local press, even hitting the national papers at times. But none of that mattered to her.

She was not like any other woman I had ever met; you could see the truth in her eyes every time she spoke to me, and for the first time, I want to give her the same. She deserves the real me, not some watered down shittier version whose full of banter and flashy cars. Although, she deserves all that too, I think to myself.

Candice

I walk inside the centre asking, "Hi Julie, where's my girl?"

"Oh no, has no one told you? She's missing, Candice."

"What do you mean missing?"

"Missing since when?"

"Sit down, lovely." I wince as she virtually pushes me into the nearest chair, the bend forcing my broken skin to fold. "No one's seen her since the bomb went off. She might have been back that first week as there was no one about, but I came back last Tuesday and haven't seen or heard anything from her."

"Oh my god, Sally."

Familiar arms wrapped around me from behind.

"Blake, we have to find her...what if she's been taken?"

"Shhh...Don't worry, baby. We will get her back to you in no time, me and Grey thrive on this shit."

"I'll help. I know her better than anyone, that's gotta count for something."

Blake passes a sly shake of his head to Julie. Does he think I wouldn't see that, I'm not stupid!

"We're low on the ground," Julie chips in. "With Sally gone there's hardly anyone on nursing duties, and beds are already full."

I'll give her that, she's not messing around. The centre looked like organised chaos, even more so than usual, and a pang of guilt strikes me as I realise I would probably be more use here than out there searching for Sally. Blake disappears from behind me, and I feel a little relief knowing that he's gone to find her.

"Don't say 'gone'," I lash out, she's missing not gone. You make it sound like she's not coming back, and she is. She wouldn't leave me, she just wouldn't."

"Blake's been amazing while you've been gone, he's barely slept trying to find her. Now Greyson's with him, I'm sure they will be able to find her together. Like he said, it's what they're trained to do."

I manage a small nod, wiping my wet cheeks on the edge of my t-shirt and join Julie stacking the medicine cabinet ready for the trolley rounds. My dark mood lingers over my face, and we don't speak. I have nothing to say.

An hour or so later my eye catches the open doorway still awaiting a door to be hung, and in the distance I see Blake and Greyson making their way towards the sand trail that I know leads to mountains of nothingness. Their side by side, backpacks on and in their old camouflage gear as if prepared for a war. The sight sends a sickly feeling to my stomach. The fear of the unknown was so great, but if anyone was going to bring Sally back I trusted it would be the two of them.

I am still trying to make sense of Blake's feelings for me, but what I know so far is that he cares about me a lot. He knows how much my Sal means to me, and now he even knows my brother was taken from me too soon in this cruel place. I'm one hundred percent certain he will do everything in his power to make sure she is returned to me in one piece.

The confidence in their own ability is evident in their proud walk, heads held high, shoulders back each marching in time with the other. The sun is setting, and I keep watching because I can't tear myself away from the image of them both.

I know I could never bring myself to be with a man like him, well probably any man at all, but I'd give everything to go back. Tears stung at my eyes again. That kiss, the way his fingers felt when they ran through my hair, the way he looked at me like he wanted to devour every inch of me...Stop it, I chastise myself breaking my gaze to fasten the lids back onto the tablet jars...As magical as it was, it was just a memory now.

Blake had wanted that version of me and I'd give anything to have the old me back. It's surreal that just a few weeks ago we were together, and I was on top of the world. I tuck a strand of hair behind my ear, my finger tracing over one of the burns and shudder at the reminder that he deserves so much better.

"You really like him, don't ya, girly."

I don't reply.

"C'mon, let's see to our men." She winks and we take off towards the ward with the filled up trolley.

Jules was right, the ward is full to the brim, and we would be rationing the paracetamol at this rate. It was strange not seeing any familiar faces. Everything had moved round to cram more people in. The new centre was clean and bright, but it wasn't even properly built yet and was nowhere near ready for this many bodies. The heat was stifling, even in the early evening, and it was eerily quiet with everyone lost in their own thoughts, including me. "You're going to have to do better than that, if you want to get that blood pressure up." I refill the first patients jug and hold a glass of water to his lips. The hours shoot past as I make my way around a total of thirty four men and five women.

My side is aching, and it's beginning to sting when I'm twisting. Even though I'm wearing the loosest possible t-shirt dress, the fabric is constantly catching on my side and bothering me. I take off my hygiene gloves and allow the wave of tiredness I've been resisting all evening to wash over me. I never used to get tired, really. I'd just always be on the go. Now, it's like my body's using all my energy to heal my skin, and there's barely anything left by the end of the day. That said, I'm restless and know I won't be able to settle while Sally's still out there.

"You knocking off, girly?" "Yeah, night, Julie. I'll see you at six for morning rounds."

"That you will, sweet. Now, be off with ya, an' get some rest."

It wasn't far to my place, a short walk through the grounds of the centre and the tents come into view. Mines pink which seemed pretty cool coming out here, but now it looks kind of awkward and out of place. I feel like I should have gone for a boring khaki green or navy blue to be sensible. I have to admit, though, in the sea of sludge canvases mine and Sally's pink and orange pop up numbers do lift my spirits. As soon as I unzip and step inside, I find a note from Blake on the end of my sleeping bag.

Get some rest. We will find her. Blake X

I hug the scrap of paper to my chest. He knew me so well and understands how worried I'll be and knows I won't be able to sleep.

He's amazing.

I carefully pull my top off over my head and start the hefty process of cleaning and changing my dressings. Every inch of the deep burn stretching down my side aches. I know I'm overdoing it, but it feels like I'm living, I feel alive out here like no other place. Especially, now that Blake's here, too. Okay so, we can't be together, but I still love being around him.

Our silent agreement to stick together as friends makes me so happy, and I can't quite believe we're back out here together after everything that happened. It's kind of surreal. He's exactly the same, flirty and gorgeous; the thought of him being with someone else fills me with dread. I've accepted things will never be the way I had hoped they would before the bomb, but I still want him. It's selfish, I know. He could have his pick of any woman he wants. Luckily there are hardly any girls here, so at least I won't have to see it, I think that might just kill me.

I settle down with my chick lit romance novel from home, I'm skimming rather than reading, my mind flitting. I leave my door zipper open knowing there's no one around but leave the mosquito net closed, allowing the fresh air to drift over my body. My nipples harden as I read about the alpha male going down on the main character. Images of Blake kissing me immediately overtake the words on the page, and I turn on to my stomach letting my bare chest press into the sleeping bag causing my nipples to stiffen even more. I slip a hand over my breast cupping it as I imagine Blake's soothing touch in place of my own. I read on about how he pleasures her further and I imagine Blake's tongue licking between my thighs, instantly becoming hot and wet underneath.

I peek out of the tent making sure nobody's around and daringly circle over my nipple the way the alpha male is doing in my book...the way Blake would if I let him. I trace my finger along my burn and flinch away, it's so gross and the uneven crusty texture sickens me. Scrunching my hand up into a fist then shaking it out, I try again, I need to do this. The conversation with my nurse back home comes back to me once again. "How will I ever be with anyone, you know, like that..."

"Oh, sweetie, look at you. You'll have men falling at their feet, you're a knockout. You just gotta learn to love yourself."

"How? I'm disgusting. Look at me." "I'm looking straight at you, you're a beautiful girl with your whole life ahead of you. Don't let this define your future, Candice."

"I feel like it's already ruined me. What would you do?"

Her caring tone ringing in my ears, "I would learn to like myself before thinking about anyone else."

"How?"

"Touch your scars, as often as you can, get used to the feel of them, get to know them. The more familiar they are, the more they will begin to feel part of you. When you can touch them without flinching, that's when you're ready."

She must have sensed my distrust because she lifted her own shirt and showed me her very own scar that went across her lower spine before winking at me, tapping the side of my nose. That was the first time I'd stopped crying since it happened, I don't know if it was simply the shock of her showing me her scar or her kind words, but I must remember to thank her when I am home next. I slowly, steadily, try again and quickly withdraw. It's no use, I simply can't do it. I let out a sigh and hear Julie heading for her tent two up from mine.

"Night, Candy," she sounds dead beat.

"Night, Jules, sweet dreams, girly." I close my full zip now and decide to sleep naked again, I know the fresh air will be good for my wound. The temperature's dropped now, and I lay a white cotton sheet over myself and allow my mind to wander. As usual, I can't get comfy and moodily roll onto my side knowing I'm in for a long night. I place a hand under my pillow to give me some extra height and feel a crumpled piece of paper. I pull it out.

Sleep tight dreaming of my hot body sex bomb.

He's such an idiot, but I follow his instructions!

As soon as the dark of night takes me under, memories of the fire come back to me. The small girl who almost died, the panic on her grandfather's face. The feeling of sheer terror chokes me, and it's like the smoke is stealing my breath. I can't see Blake, but I sense him trying to reach me. So, I silently scream his name before my eyes snap open, and I find myself in a sweaty, quivering mess. It takes a few minutes to place myself, and I do what the doctor suggested focusing on objects around me to establish reality from my nightmares. But it takes a few hours before I can bring myself to close my eyes and attempt to get back to sleep.

When I do, it all starts again.

CHAPTER TEN

Blake

*W*e have been walking a good few hours through the afternoon heat, which seems even hotter with all our army kit on.

"Which way now, Blake?"

I look around and everything looks the same as last time. We walk along the sand trail for a good ten miles before reaching the foot of the small mountain. There could be anyone lingering up there, so we have our weapons in hand and ready. With a nod of the head and a hand gesture to my left, we make our way onto the pathway around the side of the mountain. Our eyes stay focused and trained on the trees for movement or any sign of life. Dusk is approaching, and the last glares of the sun are blinding. Greyson pipes up again, "Do you think we will find her, Blake? I mean, she's been gone how long, two weeks? She must have been taken, she wouldn't survive this long on her own." He has a point.

"I don't know, G, but I couldn't stand by and do nothing if she is alive. The poor girl will be frightened to death."

"Poor girl?" he questions with a frown. "How old are we talking here, Blake. I presumed she was in her late fifties or something? I mean, the name Sally isn't exactly, ya know, current."

"No, she's around the same age as Candice. She said something about Sally being named after her late grandmother."

His eyes light up.

"How can you even think about your dick right now, G? In fact, don't even be thinking of it at all. I'm not risking you near any of Candy's friends."

He laughs taking no notice of me, so I flip him off. We continue making our way up the mountain, and just as dusk sets in I hear a faint noise. "Do you hear that, G?" I ask, lifting my arm signalling for us to both stop.

"Yeah, man, sounds like an engine."

We both looked in either direction, it appears to be getting closer. We jump into the shrubs at the side of the dirt road and get down as low as possible. Thankfully we're in our camo gear, or we would have stuck out like a sore thumb. We stay completely still and silent as the loud engine gets closer before rounding the corner we just passed. I mentally note a count of three men, all armed with what appears to be ak-47 machine guns.

We let them pass before jumping out of the shrubs and cautiously follow in their direction. Around ten minutes later we come to a stop at a small bunch of shacks in the middle of nowhere. Staying hid behind the trees and shrubs we do a count of two vehicles and six men all armed. I notice one of the shacks is guarded by two of the men, and I bet my life that's where Sally is.

Looking at Greyson and nodding my head in the direction of the shack, he nods back knowing what I am saying without any words spoken. I pull out my silencer and G does the same as we turn back around watching their every move for what feels like hours, waiting for a gap so we can take these bastards out. As two men go inside one of the shacks, we seize our chance. Both aiming at once, we take the first two out instantly, seconds later the next two are also a heap on the floor. We make our way down the slight hill, keeping our eyes trained on the shack waiting for the last two to rear their ugly heads. Just as we make it to the bottom, they do.

Bullets start flying, and a woman's scream comes from inside the shack. Staying low on the ground, as soon as they stop firing and in complete unison as if it's been a planned mission for months, we take the last two out. We run over and check to make sure that they are all dead as quickly as possible before entering the guarded shack with weapons still drawn. The sight before us is horrifying. Sally is screaming behind the gag around her mouth, and she is tied to a makeshift fucking bed, I dread to think what these bastards have done to her. She recognises me, and as I make my way over slowly she calms slightly. I need to get her away from here as quickly as possible. I start to untie the knots in the rope around her wrists, which I notice are all cut and bruised, and I quickly move to the rope around her ankles.

"Hey Sally, we are going to get you out of here. I need you to do everything I ask you to, okay?" She nods her head cautiously eyeing Greyson.

"Ignore the teddy bear behind me, he likes to tag along wherever I go."

I wink at her trying to lighten the mood, and I hear G grunt from behind me but ignore him. I help Sal sit upright. "Can you stand, Sal?" She tries so hard to get up, but her leg gives in every time, and she starts to breakdown,

"I just can't, Blake, it's my ankle. It's so sore I think it may be broken."

Greyson sweeps in out of nowhere and picks her up.

"Cover me, Blake, just in case anymore shows up."

And with a nod we are out of there. Deciding not to take the dirt road, we stay in the trees and shrubs to stay hidden as we make our way back down the mountain.

A few hours later we have relaxed slightly as no one else showed up. Sally has been flat out in Greyson's arms the majority of the way. I have offered to carry her too, but he refused just holding her closer. If I didn't know him any better I would say he had a soft spot for the brunette, tattooed girl in his arms.

We finally make it to the last bit of dirt path around five miles from camp. "We did it, G." He looks in my direction and replies,

"Course we did, brother." As we smile at each other, I know he really is my brother from another mother.

Candice

I wake to the sound of the rest of the team chattering and sounding excited. Their voices are muffled by the birds singing and broken up by the sea of tent canvases. It's another bright day, it's crazy to think of the chaos that was here just a few weeks earlier. I still couldn't understand the motivation for the suicide bomb in an area where a ceasefire supposedly has been declared. The failure of the peacekeeping deal seemed to have broken the trust of Sudanese people, and it was taking all of our efforts to regain it.

I throw on one of my usual loose t-shirt dresses, this one a little different as the shoulders are cut out and it's a shell pink, rather than my standard earthy colours. The chatter changes to a commotion, and I can hear Jules shouting, "Someone wake Candy," from the other side of the site.

Oh my god, Sally! They couldn't have found her already. I practically fall out of my tent bursting out of the zipped entrance and dash towards the crowd that's gathered. I don't see any sight of them, not Blake or Sal. "What's happening?" My eyes searching wildly in hope. Before I get a response I see them right on the horizon, Sally's dainty body limp in Greyson's arms with Blake carrying both backpacks beside them. Oh god, I'm shaking all over, please let her be okay. I sprint towards them not even bothering with shoes, the sand burning my feet as I run.

I'm completely out of breath when I reach them, and Blake shouts forward, "She's okay." As soon as he's close enough, I hurl myself at him.

He catches me effortlessly, and I wrap my legs around his waist and arms around his neck without thinking twice. He spins me round before carrying on walking, a rucksack hanging from each arm and me clinging to his front like a koala bear. God, he smells good.

"Told you we'd find her," he whispers in my ear. I want to kiss every inch of him. Then the pain hits my side, a reminder that running and jumping was more than a little overdoing it, and I remember what's happening around me. He gently lets me slip to my feet, and I'm hopping around Sally as Greyson marches forward steadily. "Jesus, Sally, what happened?" I stroke her hair and grab the bottle of water from Greyson pouring it over her blistered lips. She's alive, but it looks like she's barely hanging on. Tears are streaming down my face at the relief of finding her and the shock of how poorly she looks. "If anyone's touched her, I swear to god, I'll hunt them fucking down," I seethed with anger and look to Blake.

"Woah there, little firecracker, easy does it. No one's going anywhere, let's just get her back to the centre."

"Sally, babe, can you hear me? Come on, Sal, stay with me. I'm right here. You're going to be okay." The others have formed two lines and left a gap in the middle for us to walk through as they all clap to welcome Sally back. I cry all over again, these guys are just the best.

Greyson sets her down on the bed, and I start assessing her with my first aid training kicking in. My eyes check her inner thighs for blood, there's none, no bruising either, thank god. Just a nasty gash down her lower leg and swelling to her ankle.

"Stand back, Candy, you're too involved," demands Jules.

"Like hell I will, this girl is my best friend. Don't ask me to, Julie, cos' you know I'm not going anywhere." She looks annoyed but rolls her eyes acceptingly. Good. She takes her vitals, and I begin cleaning up the injury, which isn't as deep as I first thought. Thank goodness for that, Sally's legs are one of her favourite features, so long and shapely. Her pulse is racing almost double what it should be, and she's dripping with sweat. "Heatstroke," me and Jules say at the same time.

"Jinx," we both shout as I set to work fitting the glucose drip to get some fluids into her as quickly as possible.

I'm stroking her matted hair away from her face as I wait for her to respond to the liquid being pumped inside her, she's severely dehydrated. I'm guessing by the looks of things, she had fallen and not been able to walk back to camp, but why had she been wandering off alone like that? I would be having serious words with her when she woke up.

"You better wake up soon, Missy, I was so worried. I thought you might have been taken...Wake up, Sal, I need you."

I'm fighting back my tears as I need to stay strong for her. She had no family, and I knew she considered me her most important person. I was her world and her mine. It was not like with Rainy, we hadn't grown up together, but I didn't love her any less. Now and again people come into your life and afterwards it's never the same. You change somehow because of them, they complete you when you didn't know you were missing a piece. That was me and my Sal.

"You're my world, Sal, my absolute best friend. I knew you would be okay, wake up and prove you're the tough cookie you always say you are."

Her eyes flicker. I rest cold, damp flannels across her forehead and chest, and I feel Blake wrap his shirt around my shoulders. I notice how cold I am as all five fans are blowing towards us, and I'm immediately overwhelmed by the smell of sweat and spice. Julie's ushering him back to the chair next to Greyson.

Their bodies are exhausted, they must have been walking all night to find her. I feel part of him wearing his shirt, like I belong, and I'm suddenly stronger than before, more like myself than I ever had been. I slip my arms into the sleeves and wrap it round myself. It drowns my dainty frame, and I glance over to him fleetingly not wanting to miss a thing with Sally. The look in his eyes is so loaded, it's more than want or lust. It probably matched the look in my own, I am hungry for him, I need to be with him. If only things had been different. Sadness pangs in the pit of my stomach.

"Sal, its Candy...Squeeze my hand if you hear me, sweetie." It's been almost ten minutes, and I am getting more and more worried by her lack of response. Then a small weak squeeze grips my fingers, and I know she's back in the game.

"She's awake! She can hear us! Sally, my girl, you're going to be okay. I love you so much. Thanks god, you're okay."

A raspy croak escapes her lips, and I press my ear close to her face. "Say it again, babe?" Her voice is shaky and she sounds so confused.

"Where am I?"

"Your back at the centre, Sal. It's me, Candice." Her eyes close again, but I notice a single tear fall down her cheek. My heart breaks for her, she never cries, she is literally the toughest girl I know. She's been through so much, and I've never seen her so vulnerable. Thank goodness I'm here with her, and the boys got to her in time.

My eyes lift to find Blake's eyes fixed on me. He's watching my every move, and I can tell he's loving the sight of me wrapped in his shirt as much as I'm enjoying wearing it. I carefully roll Sally into the recovery position and apply some petroleum jelly to her chapped blistered lips. I hooked her up to an IV and let the water do its magic, she's dehydrated and needs to rest.

I cross the room to Greyson who also looks completely exhausted. "What happened?"

"She must have fallen. She was miles out, though. We only just got to her in time, and we were walking most of the night, it's a good job she's so tiny!"

"He carried her the whole way, so now he thinks he deserves a medal. Seriously, G, the bags weighed more that she did."

Grey gives Blake a death stare. "Well, I'm just glad you got her back in one piece. Thanks so much."

I throw my arms around Greyson and hug him. Blake clears his throat loudly and looks furious. I go to kiss him on the cheek, but he whips his head round quickly so my lips land on his. I blush but let him have his moment, he did bring me my bestie back, after all. The feeling of electricity flashes as soon as our lips touch. It's only a quick peck, but we both breathe in deeply after it. I'm caught off guard and reminded of how amazing his tongue feels wrapped around mine. I shut the thought out of my head and make my way back over to Sally. Greyson's shaking his head as I walk away.

"You two are a fucking nightmare; if my arms had any strength left I'd be using it to bang your heads together."

"Fucking try it," I hear Blake growl, and I can't help but smile, now that Sally's back and Blake's here. I am feeling settled and much calmer than when I first arrived.

"You scared me so much, Sally." I take a hold of her hand and squeeze it gently.

"Sorry."

"Don't say sorry, silly. I'm just so glad your back."

"So am I," she says, relief evident in her voice.

She looks broken, and I silently promise to do whatever it takes to get her back to her usual sparkly self as quickly as possible. I know she would do the exact same for me. "You wanna talk about it?" I whisper.

She shakes her head in response, "I don't think I can." She's on the verge of tears, and I've never seen her so upset before.

"That's okay, you don't have to," I reassure her. "Is there anyone you want me to call?" She shakes her head.

"She's safe now, you can relax," Blake's voice is soft and reassuring. "Come on, you look wiped out, let's get you to bed for a bit of sleep at least." For once I don't argue with him. I'm exhausted with all the adrenaline of worrying about Sally gone now. I feel sapped, and I know I need to be up early for my morning class.

"What about Sal," I whisper under my breath. Greyson chips in, "I'll keep my eye on her."

"What, you mean you'll stay here with her?" "Sure, I never sleep much anyway it's no big deal."

"Well make sure you get some rest too, Grey. Thank you again, for everything." I kiss him on the cheek before we head back to Blake's tent for the few hours that are left of the night. No sooner than my head touches his chest, I crash out and for once my nightmares leave me alone, and I sleep right through until morning.

He looks so peaceful when he's sleeping, I try my best not to wake him. I carefully slide out from underneath his heavy arm and shuffle into my flip flops. A few minutes later, I'm in class and just in time before the children start to arrive. There's no bell or queuing up like at school back home, they just seem to appear in a bustle of laughter and noise with a few of the quieter ones wandering in a while later. They've come to mean the world to me during my time here and as I settle them for our morning story, I wonder what each of their future holds. It's hard to imagine a life for them outside of South Sudan. Many of them will never leave, and they shouldn't have to. All I can hope is that one day their country finds peace so that every single one of them can have the future they deserve.

The story of the little red hen goes down a treat, and the rest of the day flies by as we sing songs about farm animals and use branches the kids have collected to do simple maths and even some times tables. They all lap it up, and it fills me with pride to see how much they have achieved in a short space of time.

I wonder how Blake's day is going and what he is up to. I can't wait to see him again later and there's not much else to occupy my thoughts. Life in general is simple in the desert. It's one of the things I love most about it. You don't have all the petty things to think about, like what to eat for tea. The rations aren't particularly tasty but they're good enough, and in the heat there's never much room for wardrobe malfunctions as it's too hot to wear very much anyway. The lack of internet makes it difficult to keep in touch with everyone, so I find myself writing letters, which I know I would never do in other circumstances. Plus, it means Mum and Dad are not constantly checking in on me, which I know they would be if I was at home. As much as I love and miss them they can be unbearable at times, and I can see why Marshy was keen to get some space and freedom, we were always similar like that.

I wince as I stretch up to peg up one of the children's paintings and take a second to breathe before trying again. I've been feeling so much better these past few days that I sometimes forget about my burns, and that's when they bother me the most. I'll move too quickly, like just then when I reached up, and it leaves me in agony for hours at a time. I know I'm probably overdoing it, but I'm not going to spend weeks at a time lying in bed waiting to get better. For me it's all about a positive mind set and keeping busy. I've never been good at resting; if I'm not fully immersed in some new project or scheme then I'm bored. Working at the school is just the distraction I need right now to keep my mind off thinking about what happened. The other distraction comes in the form of beautiful green eyes and lips that I could kiss endlessly.

CHAPTER ELEVEN

Blake

Working all day in this heat is exhausting even if I'm still riding on the buzz from yesterday. I'm glad Sally is doing okay, and I can't deny how much I have missed the missions. The pure adrenaline racing through me when I'm out there is something else. It's knowing that I'm doing it for a good cause that's more rewarding than anything. I feel like I have a purpose when I am on a mission.

"It's really taking shape now, man."

Greyson interrupts my thoughts, looking around and feeling slightly proud.

"Yeah, deffo ahead of schedule by a fair few weeks."

"I'll cheers to that, B, cos' for a beer at the canteen then?"

"Yeah, G, let's get these tools packed up and get down there."

My phone rings pulling it from my pocket my brow furrows, 'Dad work'.

"Hey Dad. What's up?"

"Blake son, am glad you answered. Listen I know you are busy out there, but the Dawson's deal is in the bag, and I could do with you there to finalise," he sounds agitated.

"When you thinking, Dad?" The line goes quiet. "This weekend or the next at the latest, son. I don't like to ask you when I know you have commitments there, but you know I can't trust Jason with this. If he blabs it will all go to shit."

"It's fine, Dad, I will sort something and let you know soon as. How's Mum, anyway?"

"Oh, she's good, son. She started doing spiritual classes or something and keeps going on that the Feng Shui is all wrong in the house," he laughs. "You know me well enough to leave her to get on with it." I suddenly feel like shit for not ringing her sooner.

"Glad to hear she is good, Dad. Listen we are just finishing up here for the day, I will sort a date to get back to you when I know."

"Thanks, son, you know I appreciate your help on this. It's the biggest deal I have ever done."

"I know, Dad, you don't have to thank me."

"Talk soon, son."

With that I hang up and dial the gaffe to see what date I can get off. Luckily enough, as we are ahead of schedule, he agrees to give me the whole of next week off. I shoot my dad a text to let him know.

'Arrange for next week sometime. Will be home Friday.'

He replies immediately, which only tells me how eager he is for this to go through.

'Will do son.'

As I tuck my phone away I notice Greyson has put most of the tools back, so we finish up and make our way to the canteen for a well-earned beer. I tell him my plans to go back to London for the week and my uneasiness of leaving Candice. I feel like, yet again, I'm walking away from her.

"Simple, bro, ask if she wants to go with you. I'm sure she'd be glad of the break." He makes it sound so straightforward.

"It's not that easy, G. This is the big business dinner with my folks, and what about Tiffany? I don't really wanna risk her around Candy."

Just the thought of Tiff opening her mouth to Candice has a feeling of dread in my stomach.

"Listen, dude, if you really wanna make a go of it with her, maybe you should just tell her about what happened with you and Tiff when you went back home?"

He looks at me with as much sympathy as Greyson can manage.

"Yeah? I dunno, I mean, I know I should tell her, but I very much doubt she would understand."

"Blake, stop being such a chick. You weren't even together, yano, properly the last time around."

"Yeah, but there was something there, man. I knew it then, and I know it now."

"Ah, look at you, B; you're a pussy whipped one woman guy already."

"Shut up, dickhead, you're only jealous."

We head back to the tents and collapse for the night, and I know G is right. I probably don't need to tell her what happened when she was in the hospital, but it wouldn't be fair to introduce them to each other if she didn't know Tiff and I had some kind of history. I know how much Dad needs this, if he can lock down the Dawson's deal he'll instantly trample the Watsons, and that's all we need to take down the Parkers. That'll make sure Laine Corporations stays at the top of the game for years ahead.

Even though, I don't give a shit about the money, I feel proud of my dad and his shrewd business mind. This would be the only deal he's done that'll compromise a friendship. Martin Parker has been mates with my dad for years, he's one of the only people in business Dad trusts, so I'm unclear why he's gonna rip his company to pieces just for profit. It's not like he needs the money. I think about Tiff's face when she finds out I helped rip her VIP lifestyle out from underneath her pathetic Jimmy Choo's. She deserves everything she fucking gets, all she's done is use and abuse people trying to get some attention for herself and failing miserably. I flip thoughts of her off and focus on a much prettier face. Candice.

The idea of having her in London with me is kind of surreal, and I wanted to make it happen so bad. Weirdly, I wasn't just considering how good it would be to fuck her on every surface in my apartment. I was thinking of doing normal stuff with her. We could have dinner, see a movie; we could do just about anything and I'd lap it up. Each little tid bit she throws me has me desperate for more. I know she's nowhere near ready for anything after what happened, but I feel an urge to prove to her that life goes on. I want to make her feel normal again. Better than that, I want to make her feel special or some shit. Heal her the way she healed me when I had thought I might lose my leg. Except, I know only too well that people don't mend so easily on the inside as they do on the outside. Instinctively, and for the first time, I feel like I'm in it for the long haul. My very own little mission, and I fall asleep knowing I'm up to the challenge.

I wake to find G rummaging through my shit. "What the fuck, bro? Don't you knock?"

"Dude, we're in a tent, what the hell do you want me to knock on?"

"Shit myself then, you idiot. What are ya even doing in here? You got a crush on me or somethin'?"

He launches a trainer at my head. If I was more awake I'd annihilate him, but I'm still half asleep, so I roll over instead stuffing my face under the pillow.

"Got it, cheers."

He pulls out some shaving foam and makes off for a shave.

"You're welcome," I grumble after him, and I'm forced to get up as he leaves the tent zipper wide open. I begrudgingly get up and follow him, grab a cold shower, and I'm ready for another days work in the unforgiving heat of the desert.

"So, what's the plan with Candice tonight?" he asks as we dry off.

"I am taking her up to the peak," I say proudly.

The peak is exactly that, the highest point of a nearby mountain, and the only place I can think straight when I need to. It's not high enough for the altitude to hit and nowhere near as high as some of the others I've climbed, but the air's clearer there than most places, and I know she'll feel on top of the world.

Women love all that romantic stuff, and to be honest, I'm looking forward to spending some time with her on our own.

"Very smooth," he says.

"Anyway, what's going down with you and Sally, G?"

"Nothing, bro. Just been checking up on her, that's it really. Just seeing if she's okay after the shit she went through."

"Ahh, I see. So, it's nothing to do with the fact that she's a sweet girl with a smart mouth and basically a smaller version of you...no?"

He throws his hand up to his chest all dramatically, "Blake, I'm insulted you would think so little of me, swooping in on her when she's just gone through hell."

He is grinning like a bloody Cheshire cat now.

"Come on, man, you can't blame me. Tell me she isn't hot as fuck," he challenges me, not giving a shit what my response is. He knows she's not my type. All those tattoos and piercings have always been his thing, not mine. Not like I've had a 'thing' before. In the past it's been more like *any* thing!

"Just don't mess her around, G, cos' that will piss Candice off then I will get an ear bashing." "I hear ya, man, and between you and me, I think she is kinda cool." He shocks me with that little admission.

"You mean to tell me the lovely Sally has stolen your heart," I tease him knowing he will never admit it.

"Never said that," he huffs.

"I said she is kinda cool." And with that he heads off to make a start on building the frame for the extension to the rear of the building.

I can't really question his issue with commitment, given my own history or near relationship misses, but for G's sake I hope he can sort his shit out. He deserves a decent chick more than most. We work in silence for the next few hours thankful that the locals appear to be giving it their all now that they're more on board with the concept. Relaxing and maybe even beginning to trust us a bit, there's not many of them, most are too scared to get involved. But the few that did, work like dogs and always seek to have a ready smile despite the grim conditions and lack of decent equipment. It's only when I stop for a break, I see the texts from Tiff on my phone.

'Phone me later'

I ignore it, stuffing the phone back into my pocket and feeling my jaw tense in anger. I have to end this. I don't want anything more to do with her, but it has to be done the right way, Laine's next deal may depend on it. Given Greyson's lack of any real relationships I have no idea why I turn to him for advice, but he's the only other bloke here who knows me, and he's my best mate. So, I do.

"Tiffany's still texting, how do I fuck her off but nicely?"

"You don't, B, just be straight with her. Tell her she's a spoilt bitch and you wouldn't shag her again if your bank balance fucking depended on it."

I laugh inside at the irony of his words.

"That's just it, Grey, it actually might do."

"You really gonna let some jumped up princess have you by the balls, what's wrong with you, man? You've never been about the money before."

"And I'm not now, but my dad's worked hard for this for the

last couple of years. It's his biggest deal to date and she's not worth screwing it up for."

"Then just ignore her, with any luck she'll disappear. You want me to arrange that for you?"

His serious deadpan expression has me laughing and feeling a little better about things than before. "I think that's a bit overkill, G, but thanks." He winks at me before replacing his ear defenders and slamming the drill into the wooden post.

"Anytime," he shouts over the noise, and we are back to work and to our own thoughts for the rest of the day.

Candice

I lay out the scatter cushions on the floor ready for the next day and know he will be here to walk me to the canteen any minute. I love the way he insists on starting early just so he can finish sooner and meet me for tea.

"Hey Miss Embers," his voice soft and low.

"You all finished here and ready for our dinner date?"

"Ready."

I smile and slip my arm through his. This is what we do. This is us, he doesn't push me, and every day I feel more at home in his presence. His hand slips down my back, resting on my ass and taps it gently.

"Damn you're on fire tonight, Miss Embers." I giggle and without thinking slip my hand in his.

"Whit woooo, here come the star crossed lovers," announces Sally as we approach the group. She's recovering so well and has bounced right back to her old self. Greyson cracks a rare smile like he always does when Sal is around.

"So, what's the gossip kids?" She laughs, "What's been happenin' in the world of tiny people, Candy?"

"Well, Aliya has really come along with her English, but she's been skipping class, which isn't like her. I think she's looking after siblings, so her parents can work.

"You can't win 'em all." Blake sighs looking disappointed for me.

"Well...I can try! I'm going to put on some extra morning classes for the kids who have caring responsibilities. That way they can finish up early, and make it home in time for their parents to start work."

"You give way too much of yourself, Candy."

Sally shakes her head saying, "I really don't know how you can even consider getting up at that time every day."

I shrug and reply, "It's worth it when you see how far the kids have come in such a short space of time and how much they all love it. It's not like back home, Sal. These kids really care, they want to learn as much as they can about the world."

"You do an amazing job with them."

I melt at his words and think it's sweet that Greyson's nodding in agreement. "What about you boys, how's the centre coming along?"

"It's looking really good so far, and with Blake's early starts and my late finishes we're around two-three weeks ahead of schedule, which means we..." He throws an arm around Blake in excitement.

"Which means we have almost a whole week off!"

"We do, and there's a lot you can cram into five whole days, but firstly, I need a date," Blake announces. "What are your plans?"

I know what I hope they are, but then, if it was five entire days in bed together, would I even agree? Much as I wanted to feel his skin against mine, I'm panicking. When I'm with him I feel so ready, and the need to be closer to him is all I can think about. But when I'm on my own, thoughts of my disgusting scorched skin taunt me. There was no way I can be alone with him all that time. I can tell by the look in his eyes he wants me, and the prospect has me feeling anxious and slightly nauseas. My hand instinctively wraps around my waist and lightly claps my side as if trying to protect myself. He's noticed and reached out to squeeze my hand and holds it under the table. It's like he can see straight through my dress, in his eyes I'm naked and I blush as the heat of his hand sends a tingle straight through my underneath.

"I have a proposition for you, Candy."

Sally's staring wide eyed at us, waiting for my reaction.

"Maybe we should talk in private," I suggest, sensing his unease with everyone around.

He pulls me up, and we head to the back of the unfinished building and sit on a semi- built wall.

"So, I have a really important business deal I'm clinching this week. My dad likes me to be there with him when we finalise our bigger deals."

"There's a dinner on Saturday, and I'll need a date to come with me. Are you in?"

"So, it's not just me specific that you want to accompany you then, any date will do?" I'm being awkward and can tell it pisses him off.

"Are you asking if I want you, Candy?" He places an arm around my waist letting his hand gently stroke my hip.

"I think we both know that, already." His touch makes my stomach muscles tense in anticipation creating a hard wall that hides the butterflies suddenly swirling round underneath.

"I can't be your date. Sorry, I...I'm just not really dating at the moment." Oh god, he looks rejected. His gorgeous green eyes are filled with hurt, but he brushes it off pretending to be cool with it. "I don't mean a sit on my face kind of date, Candy. This is a business trip, you can enjoy the five-star treatment courtesy of Laine Corporations, and I get the satisfaction of bringing an absolute stunner to my business dinner. Which I have never, may I add, done before."

"They think we're serious, everyone's off my case about not settling down and boom I survive another boring week with the family. Well, definitely not boring if you come, obviously." I look away needing to think this through.

"Did I mention my balcony overlooks one of the prettiest parks in London, is a footstep away from shopping heaven and there is zero chance in a billion years that I'll force you to get naked around me?"

Jesus, it's like he reads my mind.

"Although, I should point out at this point, you are always more than welcome to take your clothes off around me. Jeez, I'd go to fucking dinner naked if it meant I could cop an eyeful of what's underneath this." He tugs at my pink chiffon kaftan playfully.

I burst out laughing, leaning my head into his. "A pretty view, you say?"

"Candice, it's the best..."

"Will you do something for me then, Blake?"

"Stupid question."

"My parents have been so worried about me since we lost Marshall. Their desperate for me to settle down and would have me marry basically any male on our street if they could. "Maybe," I'm hatching my plan as I say this. "Maybe if you meet them, as my boyfriend, they'd relax about me being out here and ease off the reins a little with the whole marrying me off saga."

"You asking me to be your boyfriend, Candy? Fucking hell, I only wanted a date."

"Very funny, you douche." "Woah, you ask me out then you're calling me a douche. What is with you?" He pushes me away playfully, before pulling me back in and catching my lips in his, kissing me in a completely over the top French snog complete with noisy moans of satisfaction before pulling away dramatically.

"Sealed with a kiss," he announces to the non-existing audience. "Right, now that's sorted, let's talk terms."

"Terms?" Wow, he really takes this whole business thing seriously.

"Yup, I have never had a friendship with a girl before, well at least not in a long time. You think I'd jeopardise that for a business deal?" He doesn't give me chance to answer. "No chance."

"Okay, first term no being naked, no undressing whatsoe..."

He cuts me off saying with a grin. "I sleep naked."

"Me, silly!" I smile. "You can I guess, if you have to."

"Wow, no girl has ever said that to me before. Now, stop flirting, you're making me blush."

My cheeks burn hot pink, and we both laugh. The sound of his is light, and I love this carefree side of him. I wonder if he's the same guy when we spend the weekend with his family. I suddenly feel a little anxious, am I out of my depth here? And meeting my family, is that really a good idea? "Any other terms before I add mine?" He looks serious, and I feel like I should add more just so we're on an even playing field. I scrunch my eyebrows up in my most serious business face.

"Yes, one more. I want the full five-star treatment you mention, no holding back, Mr. Laine. I haven't had a warm shower in months, and my last term is free time. I want Sunday morning to myself to spend however I see fit, Sunday lunch with my parents, the rest of the time I'm all yours." He kisses me again.

"Sounds perfect. Now my turn. You can't say no to anything, if I give you something you can't refuse it or my five-star treatment won't work, and secondly no getting attached and wanting to make this a permanent thing. I don't do long term, Candy. I'm a no strings attached kind of guy, got it?" I nod.

"What makes you think I'll fall for you, Mr. Laine?"

"Sheesh, are you joking, baby. Who wouldn't?"

"Last term, you let me take you on a date tomorrow, to get in the spirit of things before we go. Think of it as a trial run."

"And you're sure you're okay with me keeping my clothes on, I mean, I'm sure there's hundreds of girls that'd love to accompany you and could give you all the extras, too."

"There is...boringville. I'm asking you, and we sealed it on a kiss, so the deals done, lady." He leans back and lets out a deep over the top sigh of satisfaction. Now, let me walk you home my lovely girlfriend.

"Okay, boyfriend." I smile, slipping my arms through his before he clasps my hand instead.

CHAPTER TWELVE

Candice

The next day I can't stop thinking of our arrangement and whether Mum and Dad will believe that I have really fallen for a man like Blake. They won't like it, they'll think he's all about the money and too materialistic to care about the things that matter. I would have thought the same if I had known who he was before I met him. Being out here has given me a chance to get to know the real Blake, and I wonder how different he will be when we are back in the city and he's surrounded by all his usual luxury. I wonder what five-star treatment means in his world. In mine, it's some down time, a few tea lights and some Cadburys dairy milk chocolate.

I pull myself from my thoughts to focus on the paint by numbers we are creating in class. I've tasked each child with drawing a picture and writing the numbers in, then tomorrow we will swap pictures and everyone will have to follow someone else's numbers to create their picture. I used to love paint by numbers as a child, and I'm hoping the kids enjoy these ones. It's amazing how much I'm relying on art to teach a whole range of subjects, including languages and numbers. It makes me wonder how much more scope there is for creativity to be included in the national curriculum back home in England.

The dry heat is intense even in the early evening, so I'm glad when home time finally arrives and the class all scarpers in different directions. I wrap the white cotton of my shirt between my fingers, knotting it at the waist and rolling up the sleeves in an attempt to get some air to my body and cool off. A little flutter in my stomach appears as his words echo in my head, our first date! "Wow, don't you be going all mushy on me, Miss Embers; I'll drop by at six. Wear your hair down, you don't do that enough."

I turn to leave and see Aliya sitting just outside of the makeshift classroom, head in hands. I shuffle up beside her quietly and give her the time she needs. Which isn't much, a second later she's sobbing into my lap, and I'm wiping her tears with the tie of my shirt.

"What's making you feel sad, little one?"

"Can't come to school no more, Miss. Have to stop."

"Oh no, sweetie, that can't be right. You're doing so well with your English." I knew what was coming next, it was the same with most girls her age, and it broke my heart.

"I is big girl now, Miss. I go to work with my Mama and Grammy."

"Great sentence, Aliya, well done." I cuddled her closer. "When do you start work?"

"At tomorrow."

"What time?"

"As soon as my Da gets back from the village, I look after Chaya at the morning."

"Well then, you are in luck my little star because I have a special class that runs very early in the morning before all the other children arrive. Only three other people come, and they are very friendly."

Her tears had stopped, but her wide eyes still looked full of defeat. I wink and add, "Best thing is, the girls who come are allowed to bring any brothers or sisters along." She squeezes me with the fiercest hug, and I know she's understood every word. "So will you come, Aliya?"

"Yes," she cries again, but this time tears of joy as a smile breaks through.

"Now, if you're free I could really do with some help tidying up and getting ready for tomorrow." Her gappy, toothy grin melts me, and I give her a playful tickle on the cheek before we set about spreading out forty-two flat square cushions in a neat semi-circle ready for the next day. I begin singing, "twinkle twinkle little star," and she's soon jumping in with all the actions, she truly was the class star. There was no way she was quitting, she needed this even more than some of the other kids in class. She's a bright girl with big dreams, and her confidence is growing every day.

The time flew as we gathered up pencils and juice cartons an American NGO had donated. I glance at my watch and realise it's six already, the hours have flown by! I sensed him behind me as he ducks under the canopy, he can just about stand upright in the middle and Aliya's eyes widen. He's by far the biggest man she has ever seen! His face softens when he sees her expression.

"Pleased to meet you, little Miss." He holds out his hand and faking boldness she shook his, with a firm handshake.

"Good day, sir," Aliya said before looking to me for appraisal.

"Great job, Aliya. Now run along, I will see you in the morning, nice and early, remember." She ran off at high speed, shaking a thumb up in the air.

"Yes you will, Miss Embers, I be here."

I turned back stepping straight into his solid chest. He steadied me with a hand on my lower back sending a pulse straight down to my cotton Victoria Secret nicks. His other hand pulls my chin up to meet his stormy glare, which falters when our eyes meet.

"You stood me up." It dawns on me how much taller than me he is. His shoulders surrounding me, his presence has got me feeling like I'm in some kind of Blake bubble, and it makes my head spin. Not knowing what to say I lower my head, but he catches my chin tilting it back up. This time his eyes are smiling. "Great singing though, Candy. You can serenade me anytime." *Grrr he'd been there the whole time!* Before I can respond his soft lips kiss my forehead.

"Don't do it again." Now, let's go eat, then I can show you your surprise.

"Don't be telling me what to do, Mr. Laine. You know you won't get away with that, and just so you know, I hate surprises.

I'm a planner," I reply with a shrug. He rolls his eyes and grabs my hand pulling me out of the canopy.

"Food, my little firecracker, you need to eat." As if to answer, my tummy rumbles, and we both giggle. His hand over mine has me thinking about that soft kiss he just planted on me. Why didn't he kiss my lips? It was obvious I wanted him to. In fact, it's all I want!

Damn it! My shirt's still tied up revealing some of my scars, I can't believe I didn't realise this sooner. I quickly unknot it and smooth it down with my free hand hoping Blake hasn't seen anything, if he had, he hadn't let on. We join the others in the makeshift canteen, and sit like two teenagers giggling at the back of the school hall. Sally's constantly making jokes about Blake's obsession with me, comparing him to a secret agent following me round on an undercover mission. "No, actually, look at those doughy eyes, you're more lovesick pup than MI5."

"Lovesick pup," he repeats, raising one eyebrow and staring straight at me making me smile.

"There's nothing puppy about this one," I laugh.

"Yeah, I see myself as more of a predator; I eat girls like you for breakfast, Candy." He jumps up, reaches across and starts biting my ear making dramatic roaring sounds.

"Somebody save her," shouts Sally, whacking him on the back.

"Time to go before I ravish you in front of everyone."

"Hell, Blake, you know I'll shoot your ass if you ever try," warns Sal.

"Easy, tiger." Greyson catches her fist and playfully twists it behind her back. "You mess with my bro, and I'll take you down, lady."

"Sounds fabulous," sighs Sally with a dreamy expression in her green eyes. Everyone laughs, except for Greyson, who looks like he's considering following through with his threat. "Have a nice night, you two love birds."

Blake slips his hand over mine, and I love that for the second time today we are holding hands. The feeling reminds me of the first time we had locked fingers, running scared for our lives. His touch had me feeling so safe, and it sparked the exact same reaction now. "Where are we going then, macho man?"

"You'll see."

"I already told you, I don't like surprises, right?"

"You'll fucking love this one, I promise," his voice drips in sincerity, and I'm completely intrigued.

We climb further up the steep dust track, the night sky growing darker and my hand still firmly locked in Blake's. He's marching at a steady pace, but I'm losing rhythm and getting breathless now. He squeezes my hand. "Almost there, baby." It's not enough to encourage me, I'm really struggling now, and as usual he's sensed it, so there's no need for words. He scoops me up in one swift movement, and my arms land around his neck. "Close your eyes, no peeping," he murmurs softly. I scrunch them tightly closed and snuggle into his chest. He smells amazing, lime and spice mixed with the sweat of a hard day's work.

He carries me easily up the last few steps and places me down next to him covering my eyes with his hands. "Ready?" he whispers, breathless from the steep climb to the top. He releases his hands and we're standing side by side. I gasp in awe as I'm faced with the most amazing view below.

"We're on top of the world, Blake. It's breath taking!"

"See, I knew you'd love it." His eyes are dancing and I attempt to step forward.

"Woah there, be careful. It's a sheer three thousand foot drop to the bottom." He pulls me in closer, standing tall behind me. My back is against his chest and my head tucked neatly under his chin. We stand for the longest time drinking in the spectacular view below us. It's a clear night, and you can see the desert span for miles, with small make-shift towns scattered here and there lighting up the vast space. "This is how I feel when I'm with you, Candy, right on top of the world." I notice his hardness pressing into my lower back and realise just how much I've come to mean to him. I want to respond, to tell him how deep my feelings run for him, how crazy I am about his smile, how I fantasise about kissing him every second I am with him. But I'm choked. A tear rolls down my cheek, he turns me into his chest catching it with his thumb and stroking it up to my hair to tuck a loose wave behind my ear. Oh god, I'm losing it. I stand on my tiptoes bringing my mouth closer to his and lean in to place a bold but gentle kiss on his gorgeous lips. Before I reach him, his hot mouth crashes into mine caressing my tongue with his and grazing on my lower lip. He catches my tongue between his teeth gently and sucks. His kiss makes me lose my balance and I am forced to lower myself from my tiptoes. I look away coyly. "I don't usually kiss on a first date."

"I don't normally date," he replies with a cheeky wink. I knew it was the truth, Greyson had told me. He was a player and had been with more women than I can comprehend. Sal's warning niggles away like my inner conscious whispering in my ear. The niggles turn into flashing sirens with his next request. "Lie with me."

"Erm, Blake..." I stutter, but it's too late. He trips my legs out from underneath me, literally knocking me off my feet and catches me as he lowers us to the ground. He places his arms above his head like the cat that's got the cream and sighs happily. It feels natural to copy him and we lay next to each other as I realise his intentions are innocent.

"This is the real view I wanted to share with you." He rolls over, his arm covering my body, propping himself up on one elbow, his eyes roaming my chest before landing on my face. "Stay where you are, beautiful, I want to watch you enjoying the stars. Aren't they awesome? The sky's so clear up here, isn't it?"

"It's magic, Blake, like you could reach out and touch one." He glances up and we both see the brightest one fall from the sky and shoot over us. He lowers his lips to mine and kisses me tenderly once, twice, and I moan with desire.

Blake

*M*y lips are tasting hers, and the sexy moans that come out of her mouth are doing absolutely nothing for my raging hard on. I stop kissing her and look straight into her ocean blue eyes that are full of lust, with a hint of something else. Fear. She's scared I won't think she's attractive because of her burns. I don't want to draw attention to them, but I am desperate to reassure her. To me, she couldn't be more beautiful. Her burns show she cares enough to be here in the first place. I just wish she would believe me when I pluck up the courage to tell her, she's perfect to me. Every flaw, every imperfection is a sign of her vulnerability and a magnet to my dick, that I'm fastly losing the power to control. The girls I've known pretend to be strong, they're bolshy and overdone. Candice is the polar opposite, understated but stronger than most people I know, men included. Despite her undeniable courage, I'm overwhelmed with a fierce need to protect her, to never let anything or anyone hurt her again.

Stroking her face while looking deep into her eyes, I kiss her again and she doesn't shy away, matching me perfectly. I lick my tongue across her bottom lip seeking entrance into her mouth and she doesn't deny me. She opens up, and I tangle my tongue with hers, kissing her passionately with everything I have, trying to show her everything I want to say. She moans into my mouth, and my hands respond. I trace a finger gently up and down her sides and then a flat palm over her perfect round tit, which only makes her moan louder. I pull away sensing her anxieties. "Do you want me to stop, Candice?" She pulls me towards her by the scruff of my shirt and places her soft lips against mine, while shaking her head. My green light that she's okay with this, and I place myself on my side and lift her leg over my waist so my cock is pressing against her pussy and continue kissing her deeply.

She starts to grind her hips against me adding more pressure to my cock, willing me to go on. I trace my hand up her thigh and onto her bare ass, her skirt now up by her waist, pulling her gently onto my cock. I roll over so I am in between her thighs moving my hand up her top and kneading her breasts with my hands and pinching her nipples causing her to moan directly into my mouth. I run my hand down her stomach into her panties, gliding my fingers through her wet slit, and she is soaked. I push one finger straight inside her, she rubs herself against my hand. I push another finger in and start sliding them in and out of her pussy. She feels so tight around my fingers, I can only imagine she will feel like heaven around my cock. I feel her tightening around me, so I press my thumb against her clit rubbing it gently in circles.

"Blake...God...don't stop, it feels so good," she cries out.

I kiss her while telling her, "I got you, baby, let it go." I keep my strokes steady, never missing a beat as her pussy tightens and she comes hard around my fingers, and I keep going, letting her ride every last bit of her orgasm. "Do you want more, Candy? This is on you, it's your decision?"

She nods, still breathless and her quiet whisper follows, "I want all of you, Blake."

"You sure about this, Candy?" I don't want to hurt her.

"I have never been more sure about anything in my entire life, Blake. I need you like I need my next breath."

"But what about..."

"Shhh." She places a finger to my lips. "Please don't talk about them, don't let what happened to me ruin this moment."

The look of carnal desire in her deep, blue eyes only spurs me on, to make her entirely mine. "Then you have me," I tell her, before pulling my shirt over my head and unfastening my jeans. Candy slides her skirt and panties down her slender legs, but sits up slightly when I start to unbutton her top. Shit, she feels uncomfortable. I slow down, leaving her slightly covered by her loosely buttoned cotton white shirt. I want to rip it from her lithe body with my teeth but don't want want to push her. Taking a condom out of my wallet and placing it between my teeth, I rip it open and rid myself of my jeans. My cock falls into my waiting hand, and I pump it a few times watching Candice. She bites down on her bottom lip, her eyes full of lust and fixed on me. I slide the condom down my solid length, before making my way up her body with kisses. Planting them all the way up the inside of her legs, licking and nibbling until I reach her trembling inner thighs. I place a few more kisses up her and glide my hands over her toned stomach reaching her breasts. Her nipples turn solid beneath my fingertips and my lips are on hers.

We're kissing each other desperately, each of us needing more. I position myself, waiting at her entrance as she grinds down, slowly. My head dips slightly inside her it's like torture and pleasure, all at the same time. She lets out a soft moan of pleasure as I thrust my aching cock into the tightest pussy I have ever had wrapped around it. She feels like heaven. I pull back and push in deeper, filling her entirely for the first time. Her fingernails dig into my back and her body tenses up, breaking our kiss, It's obvious my length only just fits all the way inside her, that's why it feels so fucking amazing and I've not even moved yet. "You good, baby?"

"So good Blake," she smiles. As soon as the words leave her mouth I'm kissing it again. I slowly withdraw myself before sliding back in more gently this time, but the pace soon picks up and her hips are matching mine perfectly. She feels amazing wrapped around me. Each thrust has my cock swelling and her pussy tightening firmer around me. It's almost enough to push me straight over the edge. I slam into her harder and she cries out, the sound echoing around us in the night sky, and turning me on even more. I push myself up slightly, reaching down and padding her clit with my thumb.

"Blake, I'm gonna come," she pants before her body starts shaking and her greedy pussy tightens even more around my cock. I find my own release right there with her, still sliding in and out of her sweet pussy. I watch her enjoy every bit of pleasure until her orgasm has been and gone, and we are lying there in a hot flustered panting mess.

I place my forehead on hers, and we look into each other eyes, breathing in each other's air, knowing that our relationship will never be the same again. We stay wrapped up in each other, both comfortable in silence, until I sense I'm crushing her and roll next to her. We're both side by side again, and I feel her small hand reach out for mine. I wrap my fingers around hers and think how much she looks like a real life angel right now staring up at the stars. How blissfully happy she looks and how calm I feel. A far cry from my usual world where my mind is in constant overdrive, and I never get a minute to just breathe.

The daylight has completely faded now, and I notice goose bumps appearing over her soft skin. "Come on, let's get you back," I say as I stand holding my hand out to help her up. She reaches up and takes my hand before enveloping me in a hug.

"Thank you, Blake, for showing me that life can still be good even after the chaos."

I feel a lump forming in my throat...yes, Mr. Bigshot Laine, feels like he is going to cry.

"You deserve everything, beautiful," I manage to squeeze out before throwing my clothes back on.

I hold her hand in mine guiding her back down to camp, never letting go of her. I walk her back to her tent and plant a kiss on her forehead. "Goodnight, my angel."

"Nanight, Blake." She looks up at me like she has something more to say but shyly smiles and turns into her tent.

CHAPTER THIRTEEN

Candice

What was I thinking? Last night had literally changed everything, and now here I was pretending to be his girlfriend for a whole week. I've packed up a few bits, but only plan on taking hand luggage as the weather will be cooler back home, and I can pick up anything extra I need up when we get there. I pack a few of my fave t-shirt dresses, just in case. I wonder what he's thinking. Does he think we're together now, or is this all still a big game to him? He's a self-confessed commitment phobe, so I'm assuming he won't expect anything more just because we made out. It hadn't seemed like just a fuck, though, it felt like we really connected. Surely he knows how much of a big deal it was to let his body touch mine with my burn almost completely uncovered.

I can't understand why I don't mind Blake's touch when my

own feels so repulsive. I decide to try and not overthink this, and tell myself to be casual and just go with it. I don't want to ruin our friendship by expecting more. After all, it's not like I was ready to settle down either. I'm still a mess after what happened, in every sense of the word. Plus, I've only just really started travelling, there's so much more of the world I want to see, and I owe it to Marshall to see all of the places we had planned to.

"All set, sweet girlfriend of mine," his words melt me and goose bumps prickle my arms as I'm faced with the most alluring man I've ever laid eyes on. His faded denim jeans hang sexily from his hips, and even though his white t-shirt is loose, I can see his chest muscles and biceps bulging underneath. He's unshaven and tanned with piercing green eyes that are always searching, always trying to read me. It may not be a long term plan, but for one week, why shouldn't I enjoy being his girlfriend? After last night I feel like it'll be an easy part to play.

"Ready."

"Where's your luggage?"

"I travel light, it's only for a week," I shrug.

"Candice, that's not travelling light, your bringing nothing!"

"C'mon, I guess we can buy whatever you need in Harrod's," He says, nonchalantly.

"I'm not really a shopping kind of girl, Blake, I don't need much, and anyway, everything is always uncomfortable over my burns."

I surprise myself bringing it up as I never mention them to anyone. He doesn't even flinch, and that makes me feel normal again, I love the way he doesn't ever acknowledge my injuries like they're irrelevant to anything. He opens the door for me before walking round the cab and jumping in himself and we set off for the airport.

"Are you excited, boyfriend?"

"Not as excited as you should be," he replies, heightening my sense of adventure.

Ever since I was little and Dad flew me to Disneyland Paris to celebrate my high school exam results, I had loved to fly. And no matter how many times I flew, it never grew old. As we check in, he's carrying my luggage for me and holding my hand like we've been dating for years. He is really taking this whole role play thing seriously, I need to up my game.

"Your flight's been delayed by two hours, Mr. Laine, we apologise for the inconvenience. Is there anything..."

"Book us into the business lounge, and upgrade our flights to business class. That will be, all thanks." He flicks his credit card forward, and I just stand there, mouth gaping open. Did he really just speak to someone like that?

"Don't be acting like that when we're at dinner, Miss Embers. If you're my girlfriend you would be used to all this, remember."

I put on my best snobby voice and turn my nose up dropping my bag to the floor, "My bag, Mr. Laine. I'll be heading to the duty free, make sure my champagne's on ice."

He rolls his eyes, and I smirk as he quietly scoops up my bag and puts a hand on my lower back guiding me away from the check in desk where the assistant's mouth is the one gaping now. What must I look like with my scruffy bun and worn out flip flops.

"Thought you weren't much of a shopper." I laugh at his low, moody tone. Winding him up is too easy and so much fun. He follows me round the duty free guiding me away from my favourite Anna Sui perfumes and over to the Chanel counter.

"Ewww, it's too strong for me, Blake."

He laughs, "Okay, okay, I'll give you that, even as cheap and nasty as the bottles look, you do always smell like flowers and the ocean." Wow, he's noticed how I smell!

He picks up three bottles of the various Anna Sui summer fragrances and places them on the counter handing over his card. No one's ever bought me perfume before. It's really weird not buying it myself, and I kind of hate it, but I know he will be insulted if I stop him.

"Thanks, Blake, now your turn."

"Huh?"

"C'mon, what's your favourite?" I'm heading to the aftershave counters in the hope he follows, which he does.

"There's no way you're spending a penny on this trip, so you can get that idea out of your head right now."

"Just tell me what your scent is, I agreed to accept your gifts, you never said anything about me not buying you any?" He shakes his head and heads out towards the waiting lounge. "Just popping to the ladies," I say, and he looks confused. "Blake, I can go to the toilet on my own, or do you follow all your girlfriends to the bathroom?"

"I told you, Candy, I don't have girlfriends. I'll be in the lounge." I watch him walk away, the denim clinging to his gorgeous ass, I resist the urge to chase after him and grab it. As soon as he's out of sight I sneak back to the duty free, glad I listened to my mum's advice to keep my cards separate from my cash. I smell through the three most expensive aftershaves I can find, the second is his, I recognise it straight away spraying it on my wrist. I'm triumphant as I know he won't be expecting this! I get a little carried away and cover my whole dress in his scent before purchasing a medium sized bottle. I can't afford the biggest, it's super expensive, but this is Blake Laine, he doesn't do cheap.

The woman packages it up, and I make my way to the airport lounge smugly swinging my expensive bag that's just took a big chunk out of my rainy day savings.

He's pacing towards me looking hugely pissed off when he sees the bag. *Oh god, what if he tries to make me take it back.* I duck and attempt to charge past him as our flight is called on. He catches me in a headlock and starts tickling me frantically right in the crease of my neck. I'm laughing hysterically.

"Let me go!" I wriggle, but he's not budging. I beat on his chest between my laughter, and he finally lets me go to board the plane. "You're a nightmare!"

"Then don't piss me off," he growls.

"I'll try," I quickly fire back and slip my hand in his.

Even though he's upgraded us, these seats just aren't made for people his size. "You can take the aisle seat."

"Well, I'm not gonna fit in that one, am I," he says, pointing to the cramped window seat. I curl my legs up and lean into his chest, my head resting just under his unshaven chin. The plane engine roars, and by the time we tilt upwards and take flight, a few minutes later, I've pulled out my book, and he's looking bored senseless already. This is going to be a loooong fifteen hours. "What you reading, baby?"

"The newest in my collection, this is my second time reading it. She's my favourite author ever."

"Monica Robinson," her name sounds alien when his rough voice says it. I'm used to only talking about my books with my girlfriends. I read on as he falls silent before he interrupts me again. "What's it about then?" I instantly blush wondering how to describe the naughty, slightly kinky sex scene I'm just about to break into.

"It's difficult to explain, it's just a romance, really."

"I've heard about books like this all soppy and ultra-boring, the girls kisses the boy, the boy proposes, yada yada...yawn, the end." He did not just slag off my favourite book! He's eyeing me now looking curious, and he knows I'm annoyed. He raises an eyebrow. "Prove me wrong then, hand it over." I glance between him and the raunchy scene before me in my shiny new paperback. He holds his hand out. I'm done for. I place it in his hands, and he begins to read aloud in an over the top way to embarrass me. As the chapter unravels his voice grows quieter. "Oh my god, Candice, I can't believe you read this stuff. It's pretty full on." I can feel his hard cock straining under his jeans beneath my arm as I'm resting over him.

"Read on, it sounds even better coming from you," I keep my voice casual, daring him. He raises an eyebrow, and I snuggle in closer. He continues the whole chapter, whispering in my ear so no one can hear. It's like we're in our own little bubble, and I'm relishing every minute. Before I know it, I can feel myself drifting off into a light sleep, his hand gently stroking my hair away from my face over and over again. I can feel his heartbeat in my cheek still resting on his chest, and for a minute I'm not playing around, we're boyfriend / girlfriend, the real deal.

Blake

I carefully take the book out of her hands and read on a few more pages. My cock swells at the thought of being inside her, and I quickly close the book in an attempt to keep my cool. Her head is rising up and down on my chest as I breathe in and out, and her bun looks like it's pulling on her face. I unravel the bobble and let her long blonde waves flow around her shoulders. She looks so perfect, what the fuck am I doing? I can't give her the life she deserves. It's ironic, I'm filthy rich, but when I'm with Candy it's like I have nothing to offer. She stirs, and I stroke her hair, settling her again. She's covered in my scent, and it's turning me on. The air hostess comes round, and I barely notice her as I ordered two bagels with cream cheese, crisps, fruit and two champagnes. I grab Candice a water, just in case she doesn't feel like drinking when she wakes.

"Candy," I whisper in her ear. "Baby, we're halfway there. I've ordered some food." She blinks her bright eyes looking up at me before sitting up and shivering.

"Brrr, it sure is chilly on here." I take off my hoodie and wrap it round her.

"That's better, thanks."

"Did you want something to eat?" She's realised her hair is down, but doesn't say anything, just starts sweeping it back up into a bun again. We split the food, and I drink both champagnes as she sticks to the water.

"What's your family like?" she asks out if nowhere. I hate questions like this.

"They're okay."

"Oh, so you don't get on with them?" She asks sadly. "What makes you say that? I do get on with them, like I said, they're okay."

"What's your mum like? Will she be at the dinner we're going to?"

"Yes, she will definitely be there. She likes to think of herself as dad's manager," I smile. "She wouldn't pass up on sealing as big a deal as this one, when it comes to business she's a badass."

"She sounds really cool, what's your dad like?"

"He's everything you would imagine him to be."

"Overpowering and business like? A little scary?"

I laugh. "At times I guess he is, yeah. But not with you, he won't be. He's where I get my good looks and charm from." I say and give her my killer smile to drive the point home. Her face lights up.

"I can't wait to meet them."

"What about your folks," I ask, hating myself for not being honest with her about meeting her dad in hospital.

"They're great, they can be a little overprotective at times, but they just want the best for me, especially since losing Marshall."

"Do you bring all your boyfriends home?" She shakes her head, and her eyes drop like she's embarrassed.

"You'll be the first one." I shrink inwardly dreading how her parents will react when they see me.

"Do they know your bringing a friend?" At least, if she's already told them they won't be completely caught off guard.

"No, no way, I'm keeping you as a surprise," flashing me the sweetest smile to answer. I wonder if that's why they called her Candy...it suits her to perfection.

"Maybe you should just introduce me as a friend; I mean we don't wanna shock the crap out of them when they're already mad at you for leaving."

"How do you know they're mad at me?"

"Let me see," I say as I screw my face up pretending to think. "Only daughter is caught in a bomb explosion and then weeks later, ignores doctor's orders and flies back to the very place it happened. Hmmm, just a hunch." She laughs at me, but I can see guilt creep over her. "It'll be fine. I can charm anyone. I mean, just look at my biceps, your mum's gonna love me." She rolls her eyes, but not without checking them out, and I tense my arm a little tighter, wanting to impress.

The plane touches down, and my legs are barely there after being squished up in that tiny space for so long. Extra leg room, my ass. If that was business class I'd dread to see economy.

CHAPTER FOURTEEN

Blake

Jerry is waiting, as always, and greets me with a tip of the hat. He's staring straight past me at Candice, but I ignore him. He doesn't need any answers, she's my business and no one else's. I can tell she's a little uneasy at the sight of the Benz, so I shuffle up beside her in the cab, and take her tiny hand in mine. She's still wearing my hoodie and smelling like me. Why do I find that so enticing? She's like a miniature extension of me, and I feel so in sync with her, even after such a short space of time. It scares me, but I'd never let her or anyone else know that.

She's gazing out of the window, so I take the opportunity to drink her in. Her pale blue shirt dress matches her eyes and sets off her deep tan. Her legs are amazing, and her thighs are completely exposed as her shirt dress is tucked under her in the seat. My heart is hammering in my chest, my palms are sweating, and my cock is hard as a rock. Her girly scent mixed with mine invades my nostrils as we make our way to the penthouse.

"You okay, baby?" I ask her. She gives me a nervous smile and a nod of her head.

We pull up outside, and I thank Jerry, grabbing her bag and opening the door to help her out of the car. Maybe being a gentleman won't be so hard after all cos' the way she's looking up at me every time I do something for her has me wanting to kiss her feet and lay rose petals on her pillow at night.

The elevator is the longest ride of my life and the electricity and sexual tension I feel bouncing around us is undeniable.

"I feel it, too," Candice says, which shocks the crap outta me. We go through the double doors to the penthouse, and she gasps loudly, "Oh my goodness, I imagined it would be amazing, but this is just something else, Blake." She sounds just like her old self again.

"So, you like what you see. Do you, Candy?"

I say with a wink, and she blushes a deep shade of red and gives me a shy reply, "You know I do Blake."

"Would you like something to drink?" I ask while making my way to the kitchen and she follows close behind.

"A beer, if you have any." I grab two buds, and pass her one, making a mental note to thank my mother for getting the groceries in for me while we travelled back. "What d'ya wanna do tonight then? We could go out for dinner somewhere, or just stay in it's up to you?" I can see she's wiped out from the long flight and lack of sleep, but feel I should at least give her the option.

"I really don't feel like going out. I'm a little tired out, perhaps we can just stay here and chill."

A couple of hours later, and a few more beers too, we are happily talking away on the couch with some music in the background. Candy is relaxed, cuddled up in between my legs, and she seems so much more at ease being here. More so than I thought she would. Her back is resting on my chest, and I have never felt so complete. Having her here with me just seems right somehow. I just hope we can find a way to make this fucked up shit work because now I have had a taste of this sweet girl, and I don't think there is any going back.

Her hands have been moving up and down my thighs in a gentle motion for what feels like an eternity, and my cock is aching to be inside her. If this is her pretending to be my girlfriend, her role play skills are blowing my mind. Hmmm, role play, now there's a thought!

She leans up to reach for her beer, and my hands span her hips and turn her round so she is straddling me. "God, you are so beautiful, Candy. Do you have any idea how much I want you right now?"

She pauses for a brief second before she replies, "Take me then."

I put my hands on either side of her sweet face, and my lips so close to hers, but not quite touching. I wait for her to kiss me first and to my relief, she doesn't keep me waiting long. Her mouth tasting just as perfect as always. Before I know it, her tongue is tangled with mine. And god, we fit together perfectly. We both pull away breathless and panting.

"Not here, can we go to the bedroom?"

I don't need to be asked twice, I stand taking her with me as she wraps her legs around my waist, and I carry her upstairs. She traces her finger along my forehead, down my cheek and across my lips. Her eyes are taking me in, and her soft touch has me wanting to explode. I slip her finger into my mouth; catching it between my teeth and dragging it back out between them before kissing the end and placing her down on my bed. The sight of her in my space in fucking glorious.

I pull my t-shirt over my head in one swift movement. Her fingernails drag in a sharp straight line across my stomach as I undo the top few buttons of her shirt dress, exposing her bare breasts. I don't attempt to remove her dress, wanting her to feel comfortable with me, and safe to take things at her own pace. Sliding my hand inside her shirt, I cup her breasts as she lets out a low sexy moan that makes my cock swell. I trace my fingers down her body towards her centre. I can feel how wet she is for me through the fabric that's shielding what I remember to be the sweetest sexiest pussy. The need to be inside her is overwhelming. I shred her knickers in one swift movement, and she gasps feigning shock.

"They were my favourite."

"I'll buy more." I'll buy you them in every colour we can find, I think to myself. I glide two fingers through her wet slit. Fuck, she's drenched. "So ready for me to own that sweet pussy, aren't you, Candy."

"Hmmmm," is all the reply I get. I push one finger inside her then another, gently stroking in a come forward motion. She moans loudly, blowing hot breath into my ear, which only turns me on more, and my already throbbing cock is desperate for her.

I pull her closer to the edge of the bed, and she lies down in anticipation. Taking my jeans off, I release my cock into my hand and work it up and down, but the sight of her bare has me wanting to taste her.

I lick straight through her centre, caressing her clit with my tongue and give it a suck as her hips buck in the air, and she moans incoherent words. I continue eating her pussy like it's my last meal.

"Blake, please, I need all of you," she pleads.

"With fucking pleasure, baby." I reach to the side of the bed and grab a condom out of the draw, tearing the foil open with my teeth and rolling it on. I lean forward and rub the end of my cock through her soaking wet slit, and in one swift movement I thrust inside her. She screams out loudly. "Shit, Candy, are you okay?"

"I just need a minute, Blake." She holds still underneath me letting herself relax around me. "Okay. I'm good now." I move slowly at first, not wanting to hurt her. "Harder, Blake," she pleads. I lift her leg over my thigh and start pounding into her, over and over again, until I feel her slick walls starting to squeeze my cock. I know she is close. Thank fuck because the sight of my cock thrusting in and out of her, has me on the edge, and I can feel my own release not far away. She digs her fingernails into my back. "Blake, I'm almost...ahhhh..."

"Let it go, baby. I have got you, I will always have you." She comes hard, and I find my own release right along with her. I roll over onto my back taking her with me, so she is lying on top of me, both trying to find our breath. I gently stroke her back, my hands wandering underneath her sweat soaked dress, and I notice she doesn't tense up when my fingers almost reach her burns. After a minute, she looks up at me all flustered, her long blonde hair framing her perfect face.

"That was amazing, Blake."

"That was so much more than amazing, Candy."

We lay there together, holding each other until her breath evens out, and she drifts off to sleep. Shortly after she starts twitching. Soon, she's shaking as if she's terrified, and I dunno what to do for the best. Some of the lads suffered with night terrors during my first tour of Afghan, and we'd always been told not to wake them up as it can cause further trauma. I can't just lie here and watch her suffer. The bomb must have affected her more than I thought. After all the fucked up shit I'd experienced in Afghan, I forgot how scary it could be to those who weren't living and breathing it. Her soft skin has turned clammy, and I can feel the sweat turning her hair sticky. My stomach twists, and I do the only thing I can think of and start singing softly.

"With eyes like the ocean and a heart made of gold, you wanna stay forever and watch her grow old. She kisses like fire and Embers is her name. She'll spark a glow inside you that'll turn into flame. From the moment I saw her, I knew what she was, my angel, my second chance sent from above."

I don't know where any of it came from, but she stirs before mumbling something I can't quite make out, but I swear she just said, "love you." Oh shit, did she just say love you? Now what? Surely she couldn't have fallen for me in a few short days. My body's frozen stiff underneath her. I'm speechless at the thought that this beautiful woman in my arms might love me. I don't deserve it; she's way too good for me. She's fucking perfect, and I'm... Well, I'm Blake Laine, London's most eligible bachelor. I don't do crap like this. I'd warned her when I met her, I don't talk to women, I just fuck them. So, why with Candice did I suddenly feel like there's so much I want to say?

Candy

I wake up realising where I am and smile stretching out to throw an arm over his gorgeous body. It falls flat hitting the cold sheet where he was. I sit up in the middle of his massive bed and throw off the duvet in a huff, blowing my hair upwards out of my face moodily. It's the middle of the night, I want to be in his arms, and every second I'm not is a second wasted. I tiptoe to the doorway and can't hear him in the bathroom, so creep further towards the stairs with the luxury cream pile carpet cushioning my steps. His voice drifts up the stairs, except it doesn't sound like him at all. He's pissed off, and his tone is cold and hard. I know I probably shouldn't, but I'm curious now, so I lower myself and take a seat on the top step feeling sneaky and a little guilty.

"Which part of I'm not interested do you not understand." Silence. "Whatever fuck ups have gone on before, get it out of your head." He sighs heavily, I can almost see the frustration in his deep green eyes. I wait to see what's coming next. Nothing. Oh no, he must have hung up, I run on my tiptoes and dive back into bed trying my best to look like I'm fast asleep. My mind's racing as he sneaks back in beside me, and there's a tension between us that wasn't there before. He stays over on the other side, lying on his back, and I hate the distance that he's put between us. Still pretending to be sleepy I roll over and curl my back into his side. He instantly relaxes, throwing an arm over me, and I circle my hips back rubbing up against him as he turns into me to let him know I'm awake. His reaction is instant, like I knew it would be. He lifts my leg so my thigh is on top of his own and with no underwear to get in the way, he's inside me within seconds. He withdraws, swirling his wet head around my most private part, the emptiness he leaves has me in a state of desperation.

"Don't tease me."

"Say what you want, Candy."

"You, Blake, all of you," I moan. He smooths a flat palm over my stiff nipple before gently squeezing and pushing himself inside me with a deep moan of sheer pleasure. It's different than earlier, slower and steadier. Although my bodies exhausted, he's in full control, and he withdraws, rolling me onto my back so he's on top of me and thrusts into me again. I grab a fistful of his hair, and his face crashes over my ear where he whispers, "You feel fucking amazing." His hot breath has my body squeezing him in tighter. My legs are wrapped steadfastly round him, and he grabs my ass lifting it up, tilting my pelvis towards the ceiling. His next thrust tips me over as he slams deep into me before we both collapse, and he's covering my neck in sloppy wet kisses.

"Jesus, baby, you're so fucking perfect."

He's crushing me a little, so it's bitter sweet when he rolls off me. He pulls me in close, taking a handful of my hair, moving it up onto the pillow and kissing the back of my neck softly. He inhales deeply. "You smell just like me."

"Sexy then," I reply.

"Seriously sexy, baby girl." I drift into a dream sleep almost forgetting about the shitty phone call I overheard.

When I wake up it's like a Deja vu as I find myself all alone again in his giant feather down duvet. Instantly grumpy because he's not here, I raid his wardrobe and grab a t-shirt that's crisp, white and freshly ironed. I take off down the hall, and this time I can't hear him anywhere. As soon as I reach the monochrome living area, the fresh air hits me and the sounds of a busy London city below. The sight of Blake with his back to me pulling himself up into a tight chin up in his balcony doorway had my temperature soaring. He's wearing a skimpy pair of black boxer shorts and nothing else. Every muscle tenses and ripples as he lowers himself up and down over and over. I step forward and can see for miles. "Great view," he laughs.

"The best." He raises an eyebrow looking me up and down. "I see you found yourself an outfit."

"You don't mind, do you?"

"Baby, with those legs and that smile, you can take every item of clothing in my wardrobe and keep it. I actually think it looks better on you than some of your own t-shirt dresses. The same but shorter...perfect."

I giggle, "Sooo, what's the plan for the morning?"

He falls to the floor and starts a fast round of press ups. Is he for real, after last night I have zero motivation and could quite happily spend the day relaxing here, looking at the amazing view, or Blake...or both.

"Well, much as I would love to throw your ass back in bed and fuck your brains out for the morning, I usually like to grab breakfast early and beat the crowds."

"What do you eat?" I'm looking at him like he's some kind of fitness god who couldn't possibly eat anything other than avocados and spinach.

"Sausage on toast with a load of ketchup." I can't work out if he's joking or not, but love the way he taps my ass as we head back inside to dress. He grabs a shower, and tempting as it is to jump in with him, the whole bathroom's steamed up, so I know he's got it hot. My stupid burns aren't anywhere ready for coping with hot water yet. I can just about manage a cool bath, so I steer clear and throw on one of my own t-shirt dresses, red today. I'm feeling bold.

I pull the hem so the creases wrinkle out and slide on my flip flops making a note to thank Rainy for my nude shellac that's lasted way longer than it was meant to on my toes. I add a silver toe ring and my usual silver links bracelet and scrunch my hair high on my head. It's unusually bouncy today as I've slept with it down, so my bun is loose with lots of the waves falling out and framing my face. I don't bother with makeup, but slide some of my cream under my dress and over my burns. I shimmy into my loose cotton panties and wince as they skim across my charred bum cheek. They are more like men's boxers really, but I can't deal with anything tighter right now. I shudder at the thought of a tight g string.

Even though he's showered and dried, and I've simply thrown a dress on, he's ready before me and looking a little impatient as I come down the stairs.

"Red."

"You like?"

"Stunning." He smiles at me approvingly. "Now, are you ready for five-star treatment?"

"Oh please, babe, I was born ready." We take the elevator, and I notice the security guard nods to Blake as we walk out of the hotel, he's holding my hand again, and I feel like a like a princess.

"Did you call a cab already?"

Before he can answer a spanking new black BMW pulls up in front of us, and he opens the door for me.

"Jerry," he says with a nod.

"Morning, Blake. Morning, Miss."

"Candice, my name's Candice." He doesn't reply.

"Harrod's," Blake commands, and we're off.

I'm lost in my own world staring out of the window. Even though I only live a couple of hours away, I hardly ever come into London, and I definitely should more often, it's amazing. We pull up at Harrod's, but Blake pulls me in the other direction.

"See ya, Jerry." Blake nods, and I give a little wave. I don't think I'll ever get used to having a driver.

"I thought we were shopping?"

"And I thought you were hungry? C'mon, this place does the best breakfast in London."

We're heading down the side of Harrod's and winding through the back streets where there's no cars and only pedestrians. The tiny café he leads me to, is crammed full, and I see someone leaving a table for two in the window, so I quickly grab it from them while Blake queues up.

He looks kind of awkward in this tiny place. He's at least a foot taller than everyone else in here, and I can see the waitress eyeing him up as she pours our coffee. The walls are covered in fake bricks, and there's a really quirky feel about the place. I read the positive quotes written in graffiti while waiting for him.

'Make today awesome, so yesterday gets jealous.'

Well, I'm definitely off to a good start with that! He sets down two juicy sausage toasties, ketchup oozing out of them, two coffees and a large tub of fruit with two spoons. I watch him sink his teeth in taking a huge chunk out of his and decide there's no polite way of eating this, so I do the same. His face breaks into a smile as ketchup oozes right down my chin, and he wipes it away for me growling as he takes an even bigger messier bite out of his own. He has me laughing, and my inhibitions fall away. He takes a spoonful of pineapple and holds it up for me to bite. I feed him a strawberry, which he holds between his teeth before leaning towards me as if he's going to kiss me, pressing the strawberry to my lips and pushing it forward into my mouth with his tongue.

Who knew fruit salad could be sexy?

CHAPTER FIFTEEN

Blake

I have been sitting in the VIP shopping experience in Harrod's women's department for the last three hours. The first hour and a half I spent answering emails and making a few calls, but that changed as soon as Candice started trying on different outfits.

I'm captivated watching her each time she appears from behind the screen. Every new outfit looking better than the last as she poses playfully and twirls around, seeking my approval. To me, she would look fantastic in anything but these dresses she has been trying on are something else.

She's bagged copious amounts of shirt dresses, no doubt to team with her beloved flip flops. I'm pleased the assistant has talked her into trying on some dinner dresses, too. I notice there are no jeans or pants. In fact, since the bomb I've only ever seen her in dresses, which suits me fine as it means easy access twenty four seven. Especially, as she so often forgoes underwear.

Just as I'm starting to wonder what's taking her so long the curtain pings back, and she steps out in a pale blue dress that hangs off her with so much elegance she looks like some sort of Greek goddess. Her hair is piled high with sparkly decoration holding it off her face.

"What do ya think?"

I stand and make my way over to her and hold both her hands taking the sight in before me.

"Candice, you look stunning."

"Really, Blake? You don't think it's, ya know, too much?"

"Nope, not at all, baby. This one seems like it was made just for you. It's perfect." I plant a kiss to her lips before she turns around and heads back behind the curtain. I know she is taking all her clothes off behind it, and the thought of her standing there, just a few feet away, in nothing but her panties has my cock instantly hard.

If it wasn't for the shop assistant helping Candy to change and the fact my girl loves to be as loud as possible, I would have her pinned up that wall and would be fucking her into next week right now.

'Ding,' my phone pulls me from my dirty thoughts, and I see it's a text from Jason.

Heard you're back in town, bro. Here to save the day again. See you @dinner. Don't fuck this up.

You missed me then, Bruv? U better put the phone down and get ya self a date you're running outta time ;)

Whose ass have you bought out this time?

Speak for yourself; my girls amazing, the folks are gonna love her. Bring on the competition Jase uv got no chance.

Whateva, Blake. We'll see.

I shove my cell back in my jeans pocket eager to get back to my girl when it pings again. Fucks sake, I thought this conversation was over, has he got nothing better to do.

My body tenses as I see the name flash up, and I turn away from the changing room consumed by guilt. TIFFANY. What the fuck does she want now? Was I not clear enough on the phone earlier? The words have me on edge:

C u @dinner, Blakey Baby X

Fucking great. Like I haven't got enough shit to deal with trying to close in on this deal, now I've gotta deal with Tiffany Parker and her melodramatics.

She better not try anything in front of Candice as I've got no qualms about dropping her ass on the line and letting her daddy know all about how much of a slut his precious daughter is. Trying to make a name for herself in the business world, one blow job at a time.

I can't believe I'd crawled back to her. Sure she is hot, but I'm fully aware she's a bitch to the core.

She hadn't always been, though. She was a decent person before all the money went to her head, and she learned she could make more money by spreading her legs. As a kid she'd been pretty cool and kinda fun to chill with. I can see why she thought we had somthin' going for a minute.

I need to set the girl straight. We ain't never gonna be nothin', she's only ever been an easy lay in shitty time, and that girl who'd made me smile in high school was long gone. She was quickly replaced with another faceless, slut I'm not interested in.

"Pssst," the shop assistant waves me in, and Candy peeks around the curtain.

"You know I'm not much of a shopper, but now we're here, and the lady, Denise, is showing me some underwear I think I could cope with. Am I okay to get underwear too?"

I kiss her on the forehead not wanting to invade her privacy. She watches on, her blue eyes wide as I hand Denise my card.

"Charge whatever she wants to this, yeah." I wink to reassure her I really don't care about what she's buying. It might be expensive to some, but it's pennies to me. I'm actually glad to have someone to spend it on for once; most of my cash just sits in savings and investments.

"I've got some calls to make, Candy. Just text me when you're done, I'll be waiting in the car with Jerry." She rolls her eyes at me. I didn't even stop to think she might want me to wait with her, god, I suck at this relationship stuff. Regardless, I don't offer to stick around as I really do need to get down to business while I'm back in London. I do land a kiss on her forehead in an attempt to soften the blow.

"I won't be much longer." However, I know the girls here are trained to make you spend big bucks, and as much as my angel is feigning boredom right now, even she will be forced into some fun by the assistants and their crazy enthusiasm for draining my bank account one pair of shoes at a time.

CHAPTER SIXTEEN

Candice

A few hours later, I sit on the end of the guest bed carefully patting myself dry and smooth on my creams, noticing most of my burns are scabbed over now. I'm starting to feel positive about the slight improvement.

Blake's just got in the shower, so I know it won't be long before he's ready to go. I'm not rushing for anyone.

It's been months since I got dressed up, and if it's a fancy dinner, then I don't want to look out of place. The better job I do of convincing everyone I'm perfect for Blake, the more effort he will put into his performance as boyfriend of the year tomorrow.

I turn the volume up on my cell while Jlo's 'Love don't cost a thing', pumps out, and I can't help singing along.

I feel carefree and happy for the first time in ages. I slick on some mascara, highlight my cheeks with a strobe stick and finish with a new nude matte lipstick. I lift my boobs up giving myself an amazing cleavage then sigh dropping them back down again.

I'm annoyed, I still can't wear an underwired bra but glad they're no bigger, so they don't sag. I opt for braless and slip into my dress. It's a black cami number that I managed to sneak in without Blake seeing. I know he's expecting me to wear the blue one, but I love catching him off guard. I have a feeling not many people take him by surprise, and it seems to be one of his favourite things about me.

The material is loose enough to not irritate my burns but tight enough to show off my figure. It's not my usual style, but I know Rainy would have chosen it out for me, she is the ultimate little black dress fan.

My tan is glowing, and I slip into some black barely there stilettos and throw over a chiffon black kimono with heavily embroidered flowery edges. I uncurl my rollers and long loose curls tumble past my shoulders. I was planning on an up do but this is even better.

I have no idea what Blake's usual type of woman is, but I can imagine it's something like this. I twist around in the mirror.

Okay, so maybe they would be with more makeup and a bra, but still not far off!

I shimmy into my loose undies, but you can see the white edges peeking out.

"Ready when you are, Miss Embers," he shouts up the stairs. I slip them off, deciding no one has to know and grab my clutch making towards the stairs and closer to my boyfriend for the night. I hear him draw a sharp intake of breath when he catches sight of me.

"Candice, you look breath taking."

"Thank you, I see you've tried to make an effort," I tease as he fiddles with his left cufflink. He looks so expensive and sexy in his navy blue suit and white shirt against his deep tan.

It's not even what he's wearing, it's the way he carries himself a mysterious aura of raw, hot scented manliness. He takes my hand and twirls me around checking out every inch of me.

"My little firecracker's blazing tonight...I think I'm coming down with something, maybe we should stay right here?" His deep green eyes look hopeful, and his dark stubbled jaw is tempting my inner nympho.

"Five-star treatment, you promised! I haven't got all dolled up for a night in. In fact, I'm looking forward to being wined and dined after weeks of canteen meals at the centre."

"Fair play, if anyone deserves a decent meal, it's you. C'mon, Jerry's already waiting."

He locks up, and the tension in the elevator is almost unbearable. What is it with him and elevators? I'm going to need to start taking the stairs at this rate; it's all I can take not to throw myself at him right now.

He seems quiet and a bit subdued as we walk to the car, and I'm a bit disappointed when he doesn't hold my hand. It's like he's disappeared, lost in his own thoughts. I selfishly want to pop his little bubble and sap all his attention for myself again.

"You sure you can pull this off with my parents? I mean, my dad will fall for your good looks straight up, but my mum's a little harder to please."

"You think they won't like me?" I try not to look as bruised as I'm feeling.

"Of course, they'll like you, they're just not used to sassy woman. My mum might have a hard time believing I've fallen for someone like you."

He thinks I'm sassy? I can't help asking the obvious, and as usual blurt my thoughts out without thinking.

"And what do you think, Blake, could you fall for someone like me?"

His eyes darken, and my hopes shatter. I look away to lighten the mood, but the silence hangs over us like a black cloud.

He speaks first, his tone low so Jerry can't hear. "I already told you, I don't fall for women, Candy, I'm emotionally unavailable."

Emotionally unavailable, I repeat in my head, what does that even mean? I lean my face right up to his neck and whisper in his ear daringly, "Liar."

He frowns. "I said no sassiness tonight, I'm introducing sweet cotton Candy, not hot like fire Miss Embers." He touches the end of my nose playfully, diminishing the awkwardness between us.

I move away dramatically, sliding to the other side of the car. "You know it's funny, you saying you wouldn't fall for me, as if you would actually stand a chance with me, even if you were interested."

He looks amused. "I'm quite the big playa round here, you know." He laughs. "You're in London now, baby, these are my parts. You're just a tiny fish swimming amongst the sharks."

"Well, let's hope your parents don't bite," I say seriously, and we both laugh. The mood is light again as we pull up outside the restaurant, Scarpetta.

Mmmm, I just love Italian, at least the food will be good. It certainly makes the company less daunting, and I mean company in every sense of the word. Suddenly, Blake isn't just mine anymore. He's Blake of Laine Corporations, and as soon as we step out of the car, I'm photographed on his arm.

Rainy is going to die if this makes the papers. I can just see her amber eyes flashing now as she spots me in a gossip column somewhere. The thought has me grinning, and I can't resist a quick pose as the camera flashes again, this time a little closer than I would have liked. Blake pushes it to one side.

"Back the fuck up, or I'll shove that camera up your ass," his voice is low but aggressive enough for the pap to quickly shuffle backwards.

I wonder again just how much this gorgeous being is used to getting his own way. The hostess that greets us is testament to that, and I slip my hand into Blake's subtly, but my glare doesn't leave hers the whole time she's speaking. He may only be mine for a few days, but I've never been a good sharer, Marshall would vouch for that!

Blake

$\mathcal{I}$ place a hand at the small of Candice's back and guide her through the tables, following the hostess to our table for the night. I see mum and dad looking fabulous as always sitting beside Tiff's parents, Susan and Matthew Parker. Next my eyes fall on Jason, who's sitting with his arm around the woman I have dreaded seeing since the other week. Tiffany. Our eyes meet, and she smirks looking straight back at Jason, and she starts kissing the side of his face trying to wind me up. It doesn't work, I don't give a shit about her.

"Mum, Dad, this is Candice," I say while giving mum a kiss on the cheek and shaking my dad's hand with a slap on the back.

"Ooh, Candice, we are so happy to finally meet you, sweetheart. I am Elaine, and this is my other half, Jonathan." My dad gives her a kiss on the cheek, and my mum practically squeezes her to death.

"Its, great to meet you all, too," Candice says enthusiastically.

I go on to introduce her to Mr. and Mrs. Parker, then the bit I was dreading. Jason and Tiff. Jase is way over friendly, standing to hug her and kiss her on the cheek, which I soon put a stop to. Tiffany is her shitty self, blanking Candice apart from a slight nod, which makes me feel a whole new level of guilt.

I contemplated telling Candice about Tiff, but thought better of it. I mean, I wasn't actually with Candice at the time, right? I question myself as we sit down, knowing it's bullshit. I've belonged to Candy since the day I laid eyes on her.

We're seated right next to my parents, and the waitress is over with a bottle of champagne while another waitress is taking orders for food from around the table. I don't miss the fact that Tiffany hasn't taken her eyes off Candice since we arrived. She better not say as much as a single impolite word to her.

I'll give it to Tiff, she looks hot as hell in a floor length red dress, but compared to Candy she's non-existent.

"What are you fancying to eat?" I ask her as she studies the menu. I hardly ever bother reading them and toss mine on the table knowing I'll have the steak or the special and a cold beer.

"I'm not sure yet," she says quietly, looking a little out of place as she realises she's the only one looking at the choices. Everyone else has obviously eaten here before. Hats off to her, she could have easily just closed the menu and ordered, but not my sassy ass, she slowly carries on reading until the waiter returns and approaches her first.

I glare at him, warning him, *keep your fucking eyes to yourself asshole.* He gets the message, stepping back and standing a little more upright and formal than before.

"I would like the bagna cauda for starters please, followed by carbonara, and I'll take cannoli for dessert please."

"Wow, a girl that likes her food. I'll take the same," Dad says with a smile putting Candy instantly at ease.

Tiff and Mum both order salads without dessert. Like most woman in London's social scene, they're probably scared of putting on a few extra pounds or eating messily in public.

"So tell us, how did the two of you meet?" Mum looks genuinely interested. I let Candice take the reins, and hopefully she will be able to relax if she gets chatting a little.

"Oh, we were working together, Blake..." I bang my knee into hers under the table, I don't want every fucker knowing about my knee injury. Thankfully, she smiles towards me letting me know she understands. "Blake started working on the same project as me a few months ago, and we sort of hit it off straight away. He wouldn't stop pestering me for a date, so I eventually gave in, and here I am."

"I've never known you to pester, Blakey." I knew Tiffany wouldn't be able to suppress the green-eyed monster, goddammit.

"Blakey?" Jason looks at her, obviously bruised.

"Oh sorry, honey, slip of the tongue."

But Candice knows her game, and I watch the realisation that I've shagged the girl sitting with us and that everyone around the table probably knows. It hit her like a late-night tube pulling into Euston Station.

"If you'll excuse me," she stands, and I jump up with her pulling her chair out. "Which way is the ladies?" she whispers quietly, and I show her, watching her hair bounce around her shoulders and tight ass dancing as she walks away.

Every inch of me wants to follow her and wrap those long legs around me making sure she's okay. Making her understand Tiffany Parker is completely irrelevant, and then fucking her senseless in the cubicle. Instead, I sit and watch as Tiff excuses herself and follows her. I die a little at the thought of her talking to Candice about us.

It feels like they're gone for an age, and by the time they return, I'm aching to get my girl out of here. I know Tiff will have filled her head full of shit, I've just gotta have enough faith in Candy that she will see her for what she is.

The meeting is in full swing now, and I focus my attention on the Parker's who seem tense and on edge, compared to my parents who are at ease in each other's company.

"So, what are your plans post sale, Marty?" Dad slyly assessing how committed the Parkers are to going through with the deal.

"Well, the odd game of golf isn't going to hurt."

Susan rolls her eyes at Mum, trying to muster some female solidarity. She won't find it there. My mum's very much of the mind-set, 'if you can't beat them join em', and has come to enjoy a game of golf as much as the men in the family.

Two sons and no sisters has meant she's mastered living in a man's world perfectly. Unlike spoilt Mrs. Parker who is clearly dated in her outlook on a women's role in the business world.

"You okay?" I mouth to Candy, when I eventually catch her eye. She just stares at me accusingly. *Oh fuck. Not good.* I try and place a hand on her thigh, but for the first time when I've touched her, she brushes me off making me feel like the smallest guy in the room despite being easily the tallest.

She bends down, pretending to fix her shoe and whispers,

"You should have told me you've fucked her." She snaps back up to the table with a smile on her face and plays along with the meal for my sake, which only makes me feel even worse.

"So, do you have any real career plans for when you've finished volunteering?" Tiffany smiles sweetly, pushing Candice. She's fucking obsessed, what's she playing at.

"Oh, this and that, I'm much more interested in hearing about all your achievements in the business world. Blake's told me so much about you and your journey to success." Tiff looks dumbfounded.

Wow, touché Candy. I smile at her, she still looks pissed at me, but there's a softness in her eyes telling me she's starting to see through Tiffany's fake ass.

She doesn't stop there, making sure Tiff knows she's not some dumb blonde to be messed with and turning me on with that hot fire burning in her eyes.

"But more importantly, how did you and Jason meet? You two make such a sweet couple, you look just great together."

Jason's eyes narrow, and I place a protective arm around my girl.

"We've know each other since we were kids, that's really all there is to it."

"Ah, childhood sweethearts, that's awesome." She's pushing their buttons now, playing them at their own game, only harder.

"Not quite," I mutter, and the conversation is dropped.

Dad prods Martin on a few more formal matters. Tiffany throws a few more digs at Candy, and Jason consumes way too much champagne and doesn't take his eyes off my girl, all fucking night.

Time to get outta here.

"Father, it's been a wonderful evening. Mr. and Mrs. Parker, it's been a pleasure as always doing business with you, and for the record, I think you're making the right decision at a good time. But I wouldn't expect anything less from the best."

"You're a real tycoon, Blake. I expect great things from you in the future."

"Thanks." I shake his hand and kiss Mrs. Parker on the cheek before saying bye to my parents and taking hold of Candy's hand, preparing for what I know is going to be an awkward and uncomfortable rest of the evening.

Back at my apartment, neither of us has said a word to each other since leaving Scarpetta, and again with this girl I find myself outside my comfort zone. I'm not one for conflict anyway and would normally have made my apologies, dropped my date off at home and be in some low key bar drinking away the stress by now. Instead I'm watching her undress wondering if she's left the door ajar to tease me, or if it's in invitation.

I agonise as she pulls each strap over her shoulder and lets the skimpy black dress slip down easily over her tiny waist. The fabric skims her peachy sweet cheeks, before pooling at her black stilettos. Damn, her silhouette is fucking divine.

The realisation that she's been naked under her dress all night is such a turn on. I'm sure my dick is going to bust right out of my jeans any minute.

She grabs my white t-shirt from earlier off the bed, throwing it over her head, and I swear she looks even sexier than she did in her little black dress. I need to be inside her so bad.

Screw Tiff for pissing off my girl, and screw Candy for letting her get under her skin. A surge of rage rips through my veins turning my blood hot. The tension between Candice and I coupled with the bottle of champagne has my anger in overdrive.

"Candice, I…"

"You should have told me."

"Oh, and what exactly is it you think I should have said?"

"I dunno, Blake, something…anything."

"Oh sure, cos'… by the way, the girl I've been shagging might be there draped all over my fucking brother. Sure, that would have gone down a storm."

"Shagging when, Blake." Her question catches me off guard, most girls would have broken down crying hearing I've been screwing someone else, but she looks passive. Her wide baby blues staring at me blankly, awaiting a response.

"Does it matter? We're through, she's nothing to me."

"So, you do your best to charm the pants off me in South Sudan then what, as soon as I'm out of the picture you press speed dial and hook up with some...some nothing?" I wince at the ugly truth and know there's no point denying it.

"It wasn't like that, Candy. She was just there."

"You used her. Oh. So, are you using me?"

"Of course not, it's a completely different situation, and you know it. What we have is real, and everything else is...well it's shit."

She opens her mouth to speak again, but I continue, cutting her off, needing to make this right.

"Candice, you listen to me. NOW. Yes, I've fucked women before you. Everyone knows that about Blake Laine, the guy from Laine Corporations. I used women to pass the time in an empty life of money and alcohol, but that's not me anymore, angel. I promise. Since you came into my life, all you've done is make me better. Not just my leg, I'm talking about me. I'm a better person because of you, Candy. Everyone can see it. When I signed up to the army, I never thought I'd see the shit I did, and I was fucked up when you came along. Maybe I wasn't ready for settling, but I am now. Jesus, I settled up there on that mountain top when I claimed you for my own. Don't you dare deny that what we've got..." I step closer continuing, "tell me that this," gesturing between us, "isn't real."

She's upset now, rather than angry. Her beautiful blue eyes glisten with a layer of unfallen tears. "I'm sorry, it's just hearing all the details like that, knowing you hooked up while I was in hospital. It's just a bit much. I know we weren't exclusive back then, but even so."

"What details?"

"Tiffany, she told me everything when she followed me into

the bathroom earlier. Sounds like an amazing night and way more than just nothing."

"Candice, I don't know what the fuck she told you, but I doubt any of it was the truth. There was no amazing night, we fucked, and that was it."

"Nice."

"Sorry, I know it's not good to hear, but that's all I ever did before meeting you. I told you back in Bor, I don't have relationships with women, at least I didn't until you."

Her voice softens slightly, "So, are we in a relationship then?"

"Of course we are."

"And we're exclusive?"

I step forward stroking her flushed cheek. "I'll never do anything to hurt you, Candice, you have to know that."

"I do, that's why I'm still standing here."

"Practically naked."

"Yeah, I..." My mouth crushes into hers, our tongues colliding in a hot and heavy kiss, and I can't help pressing my ready swelling into her stomach. I take a fistful of her blonde waves tilting her head back slightly and pulling away.

"And sexy as hell." This time it's her mouth on mine, and any anger I felt before melts away as I'm numbed to any sensation other than her mouth engulfing mine.

"Take me to bed," she moans into my mouth.

"With fucking pleasure," I growl and spin her around leaning her over my bed and lifting my t-shirt to reveal her firm round buttocks and her sun kissed smooth skin.

"I want to see you, angel, let me put the light on?"

"I...I can't, Blake, I just...I place a hand between her thighs, spreading her legs and cupping her centre.

"Shh, it's okay, you don't need to explain." I roll a condom down my raging hard on, and after a few strokes of her pussy, I'm pushing inside her as deep as I can.

"I want you to know..." I pull back and thrust back in harshly. "...you're fucking perfect."

She moans sexily, and I withdraw pumping myself before pushing back inside her hitting her top wall. I'm so deep.

"One day I'm gonna fuck you in broad daylight." I continue slamming into her, but pausing when I'm inside letting her tight muscles work my cock, driving every word home. "I'm gonna watch this ass grind on me, and I'm going to..."

"Aaah, Blake..."

"Love every fucking second of it..."

"Blake, I'm so close..."

"Let it go. I want to watch you come for me," I say in a low growl. For the first time, I place flat palms over each of her ass cheeks, one silky smooth and the other bumpy and uneven. She's grasping for it now, pushing that sweet pussy back up onto me over and over again. When she feels my hands over her burns she screams out in pleasure, and I watch the shape of her reaching her orgasm, claiming it for her own. I smile to myself as my sweet girl collapses forward in exhaustion on the bed, and I lay down beside her hearing her gulp back a sob.

"Baby, what's up? Did I hurt you? Are you okay?"

"It's...I'm fine...it's just when you touched me, you know...there, I could feel it."

"You felt it?" She's laughing through her tears now.

"I did, Blake. I really did."

"Fuck, that's...I'm so happy for you, angel."

Her voice quietens, "You're the only person who's touched me there. I haven't even touched myself there yet."

"Well, we gotta put that right."

I take hold of her hand and guide her fingers to her lower thigh tracing one finger further up towards her side. I can feel her body tensing up as we reach the patch of charred skin underneath my t-shirt she's still wearing.

"You can do this," I will her on, wanting so much for her to see herself the way I see her. Perfect.

I trace her finger in small circular motions over the bit of burnt flesh that spreads near to her stomach, but she flinches before even reaching it.

"It's okay, Candy, we'll get there...you've just got to get to know yourself all over again." Still holding her hand in mine, I follow the trail from her stomach to between her legs and guide her to rub over her slit. She doesn't pull away.

"We can start here," I whisper into her neck placing heavy kisses on it, not caring if they leave a mark. I push her fingers forward and watch the way her back arches in pleasure knowing she'll be extra sensitive after her heavy orgasm. "That's it, baby girl. Work yourself for me." I pull my hand away pumping my solid erection that's still aching to find release.

I can hear from her quickened breathing that she's picking up the pace and has found her rhythm. "You ready for me?"

She mumbles some incoherent response before surprising me by taking a hold of my cock and pulling it towards her entrance.

"Fuck, Candice, you're soaked." She's throbbing around me,

and I lean forward thrusting into her while kissing her at the same time. She feels amazing and sinks her teeth into my bottom lip as we come undone together. I collapse on top of her still connected at the mouth until our kisses slow down, and I roll to the side of her pulling her in close ready to spoon the fuck out of her all night long.

I feel her chest rise and fall against my own, and her breathing drops to a calmer, dreamy pace as she finds sleep. I lie awake, stroking her hair for a while and wondering what will come of visiting her parents tomorrow considering it's not the first time.

I've never met a woman's parents before, aside from Aimee, but that was different. We grew up together, her folks were practically family. Candice's parents were a whole different ball game. No amount of charm could overlook the fact that he's warned me off and with good reason. I've completely disrespected him, and he's not going to appreciate me turning up at his house a few weeks later, to be introduced as Candice's boyfriend.

Just as I'm about to give into the darkness and find peace for the night, her body starts jerking and shaking against me.

She's mumbling something I can't make out. "My head...get her out...run..."

I hold her as close as I can, but I can't stop the demons in her head from tormenting her, and it frustrates the hell outta me.

I stroke her hair, quietly whispering, "I got you, angel. I've always got you." I remember how my voice settled her last time, so I sing a little bit of Ed Sheeran's, 'Thinking Out Loud', and she eventually settles back down.

CHAPTER SEVENTEEN

Candice

*W*e pull up at my parents' house, and I cringe inwardly as my dad spies the expensive car I'm stepping out of. He hates anything flashy, and even though Blake and I are still figuring things out, I really want my dad to like him as much as I do. I catch him looking at me through the window, and I can see the disappointment in his eyes. I can tell he's still mad at me for leaving. He soon flashes me a smile though, that's dad. I always win him over in the end. Mum comes hurtling towards me and crushes me forgetting about my side, and then she's on Blake hugging him, but I don't miss her disapproving look at the car as Jerry drives away. Just like dad, she can't stand anything over indulgent.

"I've missed you so much, Candy."

"Mum, it's only been a few weeks."

"You look so well," she says remembering and stares at my side awkwardly.

"I'm okay, Mum. The sun's done me the world of good."

"Pleasure to meet you, Mrs. Embers." He holds out a hand to shake.

"It's Joan, please call me Joan." She turns to me shaking her head in amusement at his formality. "C'mon, let's head inside and find your father." I can tell she's mad that he didn't come out and meet me on the porch.

"You should have told us you were going, Candice," dad's tone accusing. "We could have handled it, you know, even if we didn't like it."

"I didn't wanna break your hearts, Dad. I just have to be out there to sort my head out, and the sun really has helped me feel better. I've been getting loads of fresh air to my burns." Blake places a hand on the small of my back protectively.

"Blake," Dad nods. That's weird, I haven't introduced him yet. He must have heard us talking before we came in.

"This is my dad, Stu." Blake shakes his hand, and an uncomfortable look passes between them. I ignore it. "Blake's someone I met when I first went to Afghan, and he was there when the bomb went off. He technically saved my life."

"Well, then we owe you everything," my dad says and slaps him on the back.

"I just did what I'm trained to, Mr. Embers, you owe me nothing. Your daughter's friendship means everything to me. She was worth the save," he jokes attempting to lighten the mood. Mum's looking at the two of us back and forth.

"So, you two are together now?" Trust Mum to come straight

out with it, I can thank her for that unique quality. I dodge the question and attempt to change the subject.

"Shall we eat? I can't wait for some home food."

"Well, we didn't know we were expecting a plus one," she shoots me her best annoyed look. "So, let me shuffle a few things round before the guests arrive."

"Guests?" Blake and I speak at the same time.

"Well of course, guests, Candy. Your Aunty's been really worried, and Stephan's dad is away. I couldn't see him without a hot meal on a Sunday." I blush as Blake smiles at me sickeningly, he's going to enjoy this, I can tell.

"Play nice," I whisper as we enter the dining room, and mum flaps around seating everyone.

Now that he's here, it's really strange seeing him sitting at the table in the home where I grew up. I wonder what he's thinking compared to his fancy dinner last night. I'd pick this any day over all that fakeness.

"Stephan, you're up here next to me today."

He's eyeing Blake suspiciously but can't resist teasing me.

"Nice to see you've been working hard out in South Sudan, Candice. I can see you've been real busy out there," his voice dripping in sarcasm.

Blake looks less than amused, his tone deathly flat, "We're two weeks ahead of schedule, and your right, Candy is one of the hardest working volunteers out there. She's amazing, actually; you should be really proud, Mr. Embers.

"Stu, it's Stu, and we are both very proud of our girl, aren't we Joan?" he replies and squeezes her hand.

I can tell Stephan feels small and awkward. I actually feel a little bad for him. His usual banter made our Sundays more interesting growing up. I need Blake to understand, he's no threat, he's like a cousin to me.

"Stephan's signed the deal for a second garage," boasts Mum. "He's doing amazing things for our community with both businesses doing so well."

The doorbell rings, phew saved by the bell!

"Raineeeee, I've missed you billions! Let me take a look at you." I squeeze her shoulders and hold her in front of me like I've never seen her before. She's such a beauty.

Oh my god, I've barely told her anything about Blake, and now she's here and is about to meet him.

"Get ready for the most awkward dinner of your life. Mum and Dad are still trying to set me up with Stephan and Blake's here!" I barely finish my sentence; she storms past me into the dining room.

"Blake! I can't believe you're here," she excitingly says pulling him into a hug. "It's so good to meet you, I've heard so much about you." I cringe as he looks at me knowingly.

"All good, I hope?"

"Obviously, you know Candy, she's an all or nothing kind of girl. If she didn't think you were awesome you wouldn't be sitting here."

He beams, a full dazzling charm smile, and I can see Rainy fall straight under his spell. There's an awkward silence between everyone that I feel the need to crack as quickly as possible.

"Blake's helping at the centre for the next few months, it's really coming together, and if you could see the kids...Rainy you just have to visit. It's not like the schools over here, these kids are desperate to learn. Their English is really coming on. It's amazing, I can see why you like teaching so much."

"I've just finished my first uni placement for summer. I was helping the additional needs class. It's been pretty full on, but I've learned loads."

Stephan speaks up, "That sounds really cool, Ray. If you're in need of a summer job, I've just opened my second garage and could do with a helping hand on the admin side of things."

"Actually, I have put my name around, but there's nothing much out there at the minute. So, I might just take you up on that."

"Great job with dinner, Joan. Candice was right, you really can't beat home cooked food."

"You're welcome, Blake, glad you enjoyed it." She looks happy about the compliment, and I like that he's making the effort with my parents.

I might moan about them, but I know I'm really lucky to have them both, especially still together.

"Now, who's gonna help your momma with the dishes?"

"I'm in," and Rainy volunteers, too.

"Just us girls then. You might as well clear off lads, there's a pack of beers cooling outback when you're ready."

Blake looks a little peeved to be leaving my side and also at my mum for telling him what to do. I can tell he's struggling with her forward personality, but he smiles at me patiently and follows the others outside.

Rainy shocks me by asking, "What happened to Stephan these last few months? You could have warned me, Candy. He's a total babe."

"Ew don't," I reply. I can't think of him that way. Seeing him all muscly and with his haircut, it just doesn't seem like him until he starts with all his usual banter.

"He sure loves winding you up, doesn't he, Candy?"

"He always has, muscles or no muscles, he's still just the same snot nosed kid next door," Rainy laughs.

Mum cuts in, "Never mind Stephan, how much are you into Blake, then?"

"Truthfully?" The answer comes surprisingly easily, "I think he's amazing, Momma. I'm in awe of his constant hard work at the centre, and he's really helped me feel better about myself since the fire."

"Well, he seems really nice. I must admit, when you pulled up in that monster of a car, I thought he'd be stuck up with his head in the clouds, but he comes across as fairly down to earth. Can I ask, is he Blake Laine as in, the Laine Company?" *Oh god, she's not gonna like this.*

My voice is small in reply, as if trying to avoid answering, "Yes, Mum, that's him."

She looks upset, her head lowers attending to the dishes, but I know she's not done.

"Honey, I have to ask. You have thought about this, haven't you, I've seen his reputation in the papers."

"He's not like that at all, Mum. He's sweet and funny and different than any other guy I've met. I really like him." I don't need her permission, I'm a twenty four year old woman. So, I don't know why I feel like I'm seeking it.

Aunty Julie chips in, "Every leopard can change its spots,

Candy. As long as he's looking after you, which he seems to be. Then ignore all the other shit, it's yesterday's news."

Rainy nods in agreement, adding, "He's clearly smitten with you, it's written all over his face."

"You think so, Rayray."

"Babe, the day I find a man who looks at me the way Blake looks at you, is the day I propose. Leap year or not, I'll be down on one knee."

I'm laughing now, and Mum's swatting her arm with the tea towel.

"Stop it, Rainy, I can't even stand the thought of it. What would your mother say!"

"I'm just saying, you only find that sorta love once, Mrs. Embers. If it comes my way, I'm gonna grab it with both hands."

It tickles me the way Rainy still talks to Mum the way she did when she was five years old. I can tell sometimes, that's the way Mum still sees us, too. She ruffles her hair.

"Rayray, I'm sure when the times right, all your dreams will come true. Any man would be lucky to have you on his arm. Come on, let's go enjoy the gorgeous weather while we can."

Mum slips an arm through mine, and Rainy winks at me, our thoughts synchronised. Mum's dropped the Blake issue for now, meaning, she will definitely come around to the idea in the end. Whatever the end is. Considering we don't exactly know what's going on ourselves, I'm not going to lie. I've got completely caught up in him.

I'm starting to feel scared for when the week is up, and we are back to normal life, back at the centre. Has this whole thing been a whirlwind romance that we've both got carried away in? Can we make this work despite his army life, and my travel plans? It would be a challenge in the long run, but so worth it. I don't think I could give him up, even if I tried.

His eyes meet mine as we join the others out on the front porch. This place never feels any less magic than when I used to sit out here as a child. It's dusk, and the reflection of the sun sinking is captured in the water.

Out of habit more than anything, Stephan chucks me his hoodie, and I slip into it without thinking about what I'm doing. Blake's glare darkening, he looks like he's about to blow. Even Stephan, who is usually oblivious to the feelings of others and cares very little about what people think, notices his reaction.

"Chill, Blake. It's just a hoodie," I say in a muttered breath, but everyone's noticed the tension.

Stephan speaks up, "I get the feeling you think I'm after Candice, bud, but let me assure you, there's no competition here. Candy has been one of my best mates since, well, forever, and there's no way in hell she has ever looked at me the way she does you. We might have kissed when we were about thirteen, but from then we both knew that we were just mates. So, you can relax on that front."

Blake looks as though he's digesting the information that we kissed once. I'm hoping he doesn't even try and compare this to our dinner with Tiff.

His expression relaxes, and he smiles at Stephan, before replying, "If she says you're cool, then you're cool, bro."

My eyes dash between them. I've no idea how Stephan's going to react, he's not great with new people at the best of times. He reaches forward and chinks his beer against Blake's.

"Thanks for saying that, Stephan. If you're one of Candy's friends, then you're one of mine, too."

Mum and Dad look slightly broken. Dad speaks first looking like he's going to throw Stephan out on his ear. "You kissed him at thirteen?" he scowls at me.

Rayray falls about laughing. "Not a snog, Mr. Embers, I saw it all. It was only a peck."

He visibly relaxes, sitting back in his chair. "You really never liked each other like that, in all these years?" Mum looks hurt.

"Sorry, Mum, but Stephan's right. Much as he annoys the crap out of me, he's one of my best friends, and that's all he was ever going to be."

"Anyway, she's not my type," he teases.

I quickly shoot back, "And the sixth member of One Direction isn't mine." He flips his cap backwards flashing a peace sign.

Blake smiles and comments, "This is getting interesting, would you care to enlighten us all on what is your type, Candy."

"Don't you dare, I don't think your father can take much more," Mum laughs.

And just like that, friends are made and laughter fills the night as we sit and joke late into the evening until the air turns cold. Dad keeping the wood burner lit, and Mum keeps the beers coming.

This night reminds me of so many others I've spent out here, overlooking the peaceful river Windrush. Despite how much I love South Sudan, home is definitely my favourite place to be. Especially, with Blake sitting by my side. Everything feels so right, and I forget about my burns for a whole night, and I'm my old self, only happier.

Blake

I could probably sit out here all night. I'm feeling so chilled, but the air's cooling, and the sight of Candice in Stephan's hoodie is still irking me.

No wonder Candice's parents bought this place, what an investment. I'll bet it's worth a penny or two now that the markets boomed. They'd found a gem with a view that rivals my own balcony overlooking the city.

Her parents seem great, the real deal, like my own really. Stu clearly dotes on Joan and vice versa. It's a simple life, but I can see why Candy has turned out the way she has.

She's always noticing the small things, and money doesn't appear to matter to her. She never seems affected by expensive things, despite my best efforts to impress her. I know she's just as happy sitting here or taking a walk in the park. That's one of my favourite things about her. I notice she unravels her bun letting her hair fall about her shoulders and blow in the wind. She's never looked more fuckable. Her cream t-shirt dress exposes her long, tanned legs, and the sequin flip flops leave her feet almost bare.

I imagine them rubbing against my thighs the way they do when she's wrapped around me. I give her a look and secret smile that suggests I'm ready to leave, selfish I know, but I want this girl to myself.

She takes the hint, her sweet voice saying bye to everyone while embracing them all, including Stephan, in huge tight squeezes like she's never going to see them again. Stephan hugs her back, but I'm pleased to notice he doesn't hold on to her too long and pats her back the way I would with G. They share a weird hand fist pump thing that pisses me off but makes Candy grin, so I try and shrug it off and let Rainy take over. She's an over hugger, too.

What is it with these people, they clearly had no concept of personal boundaries.

I attempt to shake their hands, but now they're all on me. I can't tell if her dad's being genuine, or if he's just trying to please Candice. He's a hard one to read, but I sense he's still got his reservations about me. And rightly so, as I open the door for her, and she steps into the backseat of my BMW, I question what I can offer a girl who deserves the world.

Have I made a mistake bringing her to London and letting her into my world? Just a few days ago we were both so clear that we didn't want anything serious. Now we've agreed to be exclusive, but what does that even mean? Can I really be what she needs? Maybe her dad was right all along, I'm gonna end up hurting one of the only girls I've ever really cared about.

Demons aside, the thought of her not coming back to my place tonight crushes me. I'm starting to crave her company, and whenever I'm not with her, I'm obsessing about what she's doing, who she's with, whether she's safe. There must be a way I can commit to her while still fighting for what's right for our country.

She throws her arms around me in the back seat. "Thanks so much for coming with me tonight, Blake. I had the best time."

"Me too," I reply hugging her closer and hoping she doesn't notice my cocks hardened at her sweet touch.

She's quiet on the way home, and I remember she's still healing. She's probably overdoing it, and I suddenly feel like shit for letting her.

"How about we just slum it tomorrow, gorgeous?"

"Slum it?" Her eyes looked up at me inquisitively.

"Yeah, you know...just veg out for the day."

"Now that, I would love to see, but I've said I'll meet up with Rainy for a girly day. You don't mind if we take a rain check, do you?"

"Of course I don't, I just worry about you doing too much, too soon."

"That's so sweet of you, Blake, but I'm fine, honestly. More than fine, actually. Since I've been here with you, I've barely thought about what happened."

"So, I'm a good distraction then?"

"The best." She smiles at me, and I wrap my fingers around hers thinking how small they are compared to mine.

We reach my place only to find the elevators broke again. "For fuck sake, does this piece of shit ever work?" I joke with the concierge.

Candy looks up at the stairs letting out a sigh, she looks exhausted. I scoop her up.

"Blake, what are you doing," she squeals. "Put me down. You can't carry me up nine flights of stairs."

"Watch me." She doesn't struggle, and I run up the nine flights like it's nothing, which compared to my standard army training, it is. I keep her in my arms while unlocking the door and drop her straight into my bed. I don't give a crap how tired she is, I'm taking her right now.

I can see the heat and lust in her eyes as I start to take off my belt. She stops me suddenly.

"Let me, Blake."

"With pleasure, angel."

She fumbles with my belt, but it's soon off, and she unfastens my jeans shuffling them down my legs, freeing my rock hard cock. I step out of my jeans and pull my top over my head, so I am standing there completely naked, in front of my angel.

She takes hold of my cock, sitting herself on the very end of the bed with her legs spread over mine. She licks from the base to the tip, giving it a swirl around with her tongue. I honestly think I could come right now at the sight of her hot mouth wrapped around me.

"Fuck, angel."

She smiles up at me through them long beautiful lashes and repeats exactly what she just did; only this time she puts near enough my whole cock into her mouth.

I let out a deep moan as I feel myself at the back of her throat, letting her know how good she feels. I tilt my head back.

"Fuck, baby, I think my cock was made for your mouth."

She continues licking and sucking and begins stroking a finger over my balls in a come to me motion. *Shit, I'm losing control.*

I pull her dress up, for the first time revealing most of her naked body and she doesn't seem to care. I love her growing confidence around me and can't wait for the day when I can take her fully exposed.

I pinch and rub her nipples, kneading her breasts until she

moans loudly. The sound sends a rippling vibration through my cock that has me losing control.

"Okay, enough. It's your turn," I say with a wink as she leans back and up onto the bed. I climb up with her, in between her legs as I run my tongue straight through her soaking wet slit and clamp her swollen nub between my lips, sucking hard.

"Arrrrrgh, Blake. Fuck!"

I rest my hand on her lower stomach to steady her bucking hips and continue eating her pussy. It tastes so good. I feel her tense as I thrust two fingers inside her.

"Yes, Blake, yesss." She is so loud which only turns me on more.

I continue to suck her and thrust my fingers until she's yelling, "Fuck, Blake, I am going to come."

I'm still not stopping as she is screaming and coming all over my fingers. I turn her around so she is bent over on all fours, and I thrust forward, straight into her drenched pussy.

"Fuckkkk."

"Baby, you feel so good, I am going to fuck you so hard, do you want me to?"

"Yes," she moans out.

"Tell me. Tell me you want me to," I demand.

"I want you to," she says softly, and I grab onto her hips thrusting and pounding into her over and over, exploring her breasts and pinching her nipples. I watch her sweet ass grind up and down my length and can feel my release is close. Moving my hand round her, I begin circling her clit while slamming into her mercilessly.

"Shit, Blake...Fuck. Fuck!"

Squeezing and tensing herself around my cock, we find our release together, and I collapse onto the bed taking her with me. I pull her in close, kissing the side of her neck lazily.

"Candice."

"Ummhmm."

"I want you to be mine."

"Okay." She murmurs sleepily as she dozes off. I will be continuing this conversation with her first thing tomorrow, I think to myself. We've played around with the idea of a relationship before but never properly agreed to anything.

Now I've experienced what a life with Candice could be like, there's no going back for me. If this is what love feels like, then I think I'm in it.

I need to be with her more than I've ever needed anything else, before. She needs to know that I am serious about this. About us. Relationship doesn't seem the right word for what I am feeling.

I don't want to just be with her. I want to devour her, to completely consume her, until she forgets everything that has gone before and I am all she knows.

CHAPTER EIGHTEEN

Candice

"Morning, angel." As usual he's up before me, looks like he's already completed his fitness regime and is now standing before me in nothing but a pair of black boxers. He's holding a tray with a tiny arrangement of flowers he's picked off from downstairs, croissants and a tall glass of fresh orange. Without bits. How does he know me so well?

Damn him for beating me to it, I want to surprise him one of these days and get up earlier, maybe I'd even stretch to a workout on the balcony. Then again, probably not!

I consider him for a minute as he stands patiently holding the tray and beaming at me with a yes-I'm-amazing-I-should-be-your-boyfriend smile, and I notice for once, he looks kind of vulnerable.

He's tried to wow me and impress me the whole time I've

been in London, but it's moments like this that knock me for six. Quiet intimate moments I'll never forget that have me daring to think the commitment phobe could want something more.

"Morning. What's the special occasion?" I ask as I wriggle myself up and prop the pillows so I'm sitting rather than star fishing. I grab a bobble from the bedside table and throw my hair up in a bun.

He places the tray down on my lap then looks like he doesn't know what to do with himself.

"Sit with me then, I'll never eat all these," I say pointing to the stack of croissants in front of me. He doesn't sit, he just stands tall, looking sort of official aside from the nakedness.

"The special occasion is that: 1. I have a beautiful woman in my bed. 2. I slept next to her all night without fucking her, which brings me to 3. Candice Embers, to hell with playing games I want this to be my everyday normal. Sleeping next to you, waking up with you in my arms. I'm all in. I want you to be my girl."

I nearly choke on my croissant.

"You do?" I eye him suspiciously searching for an ulterior motive but knowing deep down there isn't one. I can see the genuine want in his eyes; it's there every time he looks at me.

I blurt out my answer without even thinking, "I want you, too, Blake." I place the tray on the side table and throw off the duvet covers. "In every...single...way."

I roll onto my stomach lifting my hips slightly off the bed, an invitation. He's on me in seconds. He's instantly hard and doesn't waste a second, thrusting straight inside me in one swift move. Thrusting forward and hitting my favourite place over and over sending me dizzy with ecstasy.

"Say it, Candy," his words rough in my ear. "Say you're mine."

"I'm yours," I scream out, and he slams into me with brutal force making me scream it again. "Yours. Blake."

"Fuck, I love it when you say my name."

"Blake," I repeat panting...needing him...wanting him to take me over. He pulls back and hesitates, growling.

"Give it to me, angel," before driving forward. His juices mixing with my own in a hot wet mess of sexiness. He collapses to the side and pulls me into him, and we lay there for a good while with him still inside me.

"I can feel you pulsing on my cock, baby."

I squeeze my inner walls tight around him.

"Be careful what you wish for, missy. I could go again in seconds."

I consider it, but my eyes spy the bedside clock. *Shit, Rainy!* Time for me to get up.

I couldn't visit the city without a girly day, and I literally cannot wait to spend some time with my bestie. I jump up and head for the wardrobe where he's made me a space and had my few outfits pressed and hung up.

"What's got you smiling like it's your birthday?"

"I'm just looking forward to seeing Rayray, it's been ages since we had a proper girly day."

"You won't miss me at all then?"

"Nope!"

He pretends to look hurt.

"Okay, well, maybe a smidge."

"You going shoppin', angel? What d'ya wanna buy?" he looks genuinely interested.

"Hmmm, more t-shirt dresses, maybe?"

"Your nuts, don't you ever wear anything else?"

"Well, everything else annoys me. Before the stupid bomb all I'd wear was my jeans and denim shorts." My mind wanders to my burns again and a familiar rush of disappointment flushes through me. As usual, Blake is quick to distract me and pick me up again.

"Turn around angel, I wanna see that beautiful ass one more time before I have to get up."

I spin round playfully and twerk in his direction, laughing. He grabs my buttock and bites down hard, but not enough to hurt me.

"Ouch!" I yelp whacking him with the pillow, he grabs his before crashing it down over my head.

"You've wrecked my hair, that's it now, Mr. Laine."

"Oh, my girl's got that fire in her eyes again." He begs for mercy, and I assassinate him with my pillow until we both run out of breath laughing.

It's tempting to stay put and wrestle him until he's back inside me, but I need to run the last few weeks past Rainy in private and get her take on everything. She always knows what's best for me. Better than I know myself at times and second only to Sal, who has come to mean so much to me during our time at the centre.

Blake whips out his credit card, "Right, my little angel, I'm letting you go, but only if you promise to treat yourself. I promised five-star luxury, and I can't have you selling your story to the tabloids, saying you had anything less than the best."

"Did you really just say that? It's a good job I know when

you're joking, or I would finish you off altogether." And I throw my pillow his way.

"I've already texted you the pin, keep it in your head, and delete it before you leave. I'll call you as soon as my meeting finishes."

"Meet back up for tea?" I ask hopefully.

"Whenever you're ready, princess. This is your day, go enjoy it." He knows what I'm thinking.

"And don't you dare refuse. We made a deal." I throw him a confused look.

"I don't remember signing anything? How did we make the contract binding again?" I tease. He doesn't need asking twice, his mouth is on mine in seconds, and his kiss sends fire through my body.

"You're the best," I announce without any inhibitions, throwing my arms around his neck. He kisses me softly on the forehead.

"Have a good one, baby." And with that he heads for a shower and calls out, "Candy, I forgot to say, you've got Jerry for the day. He's meeting you in the lobby at nine."

I roll my eyes. Does he ever stop organising for like, five minutes?

I use the en suite to get ready. I'm not bothering with make-up, just a smoosh of lip gloss, oversized sunnies, my nude t-shirt dress, converse and denim jacket.

With my black leather rucksack, I look like a full on tourist. I redo my bun and shout, "See you later, Mr. Laine. I'm off to the Daily Mail to sell my story."

"Make sure you get a good deal on me. I'm worth it," he shouts after me.

Jerry is the perfect chauffeur and escorts me from the elevator to a black four by four with red leather interior. It's gorgeous, and it screams luxury, like everything Blake owns.

"I'm sitting up front today. Well, at least, until we pick up Rainy."

"As you wish, Miss Embers."

"I already told you, it's Candice." He drives without words, looking overly serious. I think he's annoyed that I've sat in the front.

"So, have you always been a chauffeur?"

"For the last ten years." I'm considering him, he looks about fifty.

"What did you do before?" He sighs as if talking to me is really bugging him. "I was a bodyguard."

"Wow, cool, did you look after anyone famous?"

"Yes."

"Aren't you gonna tell me who?"

"No."

"Okay." We continue in silence for the next few miles. "So, how long have you worked for Blake?"

"Ten years."

"Wow, you must have seen a lot driving him round for all that time." His face lightens a little.

"He's like family, Miss."

"I had a feeling you are a big softy under that hat or yours." He snaps back to his serious face then surprises me by shaking a finger at me.

"Don't you go telling anyone."

"Your secrets safe with me," I reassure him.

We pull up at Rainys, and she hurtles towards the car as excited as I am that we've got a whole day together. She's been working so hard between uni and part time jobs, she's barely had a day off since Christmas. "Oh my goooood," she screeches.

"This car!"

"It's gorgeous, isn't it?" She shrugs.

"I mean, I'd obviously switch the interior to pink, but I guess I could make do with it."

"So, where shall we go? Blake gave me his credit card for the day, so we can afford to treat ourselves."

"Whaaat! Show me. Show me right now." I pull his card out.

"Woah, Candy, this is just crazy. He really just handed you his card for the day?" I feel a little embarrassed; this is completely out of the norm for the two of us. I can tell what she's thinking already.

"Make overs?"

"You're on! Jerry, can you please drop us at Luxe? It's the small salon on the corner, we'll direct you." He nods and speeds off towards the village high street. It's not flashy like the ones in London City, but Ange and Mel are the absolute best hair dressers, bar none. "I know it goes without saying, but just in case, you never know who's listening Rayray, so can we keep the whole credit card thing between us?"

"Obvs," she replied, and we burst through the door.

"Can you fit us in, Ange, we're after the full works?"

"Then you've come to the right place, ladies. Sit down and

Mel will fetch you some mocktails. We have a new juice machine now."

"Oh, we're not driving today." She raises an eyebrow shouting after Mel.

"Gurrrrrl, turn those mocktails into cocktails, we're going all out today, doll face."

I'm instantly relaxed surrounded by all our home comforts, with my best friend. We had our prom hair done at Luxe, and I remember talking about coming back together when we were grown up and getting ready for a double wedding.

A pang of sadness hits me as I remember Marshall's wedding day, he was so young. I try not to kill the mood and stay cheerful. It's been ages since we had some quality time together, and I want to enjoy every last minute.

"I'll have some highlights and a curly blow, please," I say to Mel who's already teasing my hair. Rainy pushes hers forward, checking the lengths before deciding.

"I'll have mine blown straight, but no colour for me. You know I'd never suit anything other than my red."

"You'd probably never cover it if you tried, baby. You've had that gorgeous colour since you were a grasshopper, and if you don't stop calling it red, I'll have to shave it all off. It's summer auburn and that's, that."

"Sorry," laughs Rainy. "I forgot my hair has a season."

"Everyone's does. Look at Candy's blonde, it's cold as ice on a winter's day."

"I guess so." Rainy stares at me like I've suddenly turned into a snow queen, and I laugh taking another sip of my cocktail. Strawberry daiquiri, yum.

While I wait for my colour to take and Rainy's hair to be straightened, we both have matching French gel nails on our fingers and toes. By the time we're ready to leave, we both look and feel like Hollywood superstars, and I almost cry when I look in the mirror. She's done a beautiful job of my hair, and with the burns on my face all healed up, for once I feel pretty.

Jerry pretends not to notice, but I see the trace of a smile on his lips as we step out of the salon and back into the car. The fresh air takes hold as the effect of the cocktails has us feeling giddy and excitable.

"Where next?" I ask Rainy.

"It's a Wednesday, so shall we hit the flea market and do the vintage shops up that way."

"Perfect." I knew she would think so, and I love that we are so similar, she's never been a big spender either.

Memories of Saturday shopping trips in our early teens flood back to me. Our parents would give us five pounds, and we would always come back with some new top or kooky piece of jewellery.

We spend the rest of the morning meandering through the hustle and bustle of Bourton on the Water markets, and wind up full of bags of goodies in a little tea shop that must have recently opened. We grab a window spot and decide on afternoon tea for two from the menu when a familiar face steals my attention from ordering drinks. Someone standing across the market place, at least I thought I recognised him, but when I try and look closer, he's disappeared.

"That's weird, I thought I just saw Blake's brother over in the market, but there's no way he'd be round these parts. He wouldn't even know a place like this existed."

"Must have been a doppelgänger, babe." Rainy shrugs.

The waitress brings over the cutest three tier cake stand filled with tiny triangular sandwiches and different types of cakes.

"This looks too good to eat," I say, taking a minute to admire it all.

"Nothing's too good to eat," voices Rainy, popping a mini cupcake in her mouth, and eating it in one with a silly grin on her face.

"So...Blake. Tell me everything." I smile, finally being able to offload is such a relief. I don't hold back, giving her the whole story of how we met in Bor. What it's really like in South Sudan, how I felt the first time I saw him, that night on the cliff top. Every. Single. Detail. And as always, she listens wholeheartedly without saying a single word until I've poured everything out in the table.

"Wait, he gives you his credit card and asks you to be his girl?" I nod confirming the hottest gossip we've shared in ages. "And you said yes? Even after Loser Luke and Dickhead Damien." We're both laughing at the two worst attempts of dating in history.

"I didn't even have to think about it," I confess. "Gah! I really like him, Rayray. It's like, when I'm with him the world stops turning and it's just the two of us."

"Awww, my girlies found her beaver."

"My what now?"

"Your penguin. Your other half. Your soulmate."

"Maybe, but why a penguin though?" "Because penguins mate for life. When they find their true love, they never leave them."

"You think I love him?"

"Do you think you don't?"

"Shit, this has all happened so fast, I haven't stopped to think what I feel about him. I'd never even been in love before. How would I know?"

"Girl, you love him. I saw it all over your face when I walked into dinner at your mum's the other night."

"You did?"

She pours another mug of tea, nodding.

"I did." She sips her drink. "He loves you, too," she says simply.

"You think I could be with someone like him, for good, I mean like, stay together? I'm so different to his world." She looks unimpressed and gives me her best pissed off face.

"Don't you dare be talking like some tramp, you're a catch, Candice, and you know it." She knows what I'm worried about. "Babe, with them legs and boobs, he ain't gonna be lookin' at your side." She stuffs a mini cupcake into her mouth.

"What about the press, what if his family don't like me?"

"Screw anyone else, this is about you an' your man."

I try one of the finger slices as she stuffs in another cupcake. She's right as usual, and proves, yet again, why she's my best friend.

Blake

*R*iding up front with Jerry, I wonder what she's up to with my credit card and fire her a quick text reminding her to delete the pin. My dad would completely freak out if he knew I'd just given a girl I've only known a few weeks access to my private account. That's where we're different. Despite what he thinks, I really don't give a shit about the money. Jesus, I doubt he's even given Mum access to his accounts after thirty plus years of marriage. Knowing Candy, I bet she won't wanna spend much anyway. I smile and shoot her another text.

Hope my girl's spending ;)

I shove my phone away needing to get my head in the game. We pull up outside, and I make my way indoors taking pride in the smart, expensive surroundings. Everything's black and gold and every surface is the finest glossy marble.

I take the elevator to the top, and ignore the assistant outside, stepping into my dad's office and noticing there's no one else here or in the boardroom through the glass wall next door.

"Hello son, how's it going?" He offers me a handshake, and I pull him to his feet, shoulder touching over the table, I pound a fist to his back.

"Hi Dad. It's going good, thanks. Where's the motley crew?"

"Coming at eleven. I wanted to talk things through with you first. We gotta be careful with this one. Parker and I go way back, and despite what you think, even I wouldn't go as far as to screw a friend over. Well, a decent one anyway."

"Wow, is Jonathan Laine going soft in his old age?"

"Old age, you cheeky bugger. I'll have security escort you out if you carry on like that."

"Let them try," I joke and he breaks a smile.

"Seriously though, sit down, son."

I take the seat opposite him, and he continues, "You know how your brother always feels like he's not part of the family?" I don't even bother responding, but I know he notices I've tensed up. "I want him to think he's sealed this one for us. It's important he knows I trust him. But like I said, I'd be stupid to fuck with Martin when we're both on the brink of retirement. Who else am I gonna hit the golf course with?"

"So, what's the plan?"

"We've got the meeting today to finalise the details, dinner to shake hands on it and then the signing of the contracts next week."

"Sounds like you got it all mapped out, Dad. You sure you need me in on this one?"

"Course, son. I keep telling you it won't be long until Laine Corporations is all yours. I need you to know the way everything works. I'm not taking any risks. I..."

"Built this baby up from the ground."

I finish his sentence for him, the same old line I've heard a thousand times before. It irks me that dad paints himself as some kind of business genius busting a gut to get by in a small town with a working class background. It wasn't too far from the truth.

My grandfather never had much money, but his shrewd business sense made a success of the few security companies he set up. By the time he retired early to travel, he had worked enough that the Laine family were easily in the middle class circuit, with a number of steady contracts and wealthy clientele.

He'd lived simply, leaving a tidy sum for my dad to start up with, and he'd followed in his father's footsteps making good choices at the right times before Laine Corporations was born.

The usual feelings of guilt flash up as I reflect on how little enthusiasm I have about the fact that one day I will be left to run the business. Meaning that any bad decisions would be made under my dad's watchful eye and the scrutiny of the press.

"So, Jason should be here in ten minutes, closely followed by Parker. Jase thinks we're signing contracts today and celebrating at the meal on Thursday."

"You're gonna put on this whole facade just so Jason thinks you trust him?" I look my dad straight in the eye, but he looks away in an attempt of avoid the question.

"Would you, son? Would you trust him?" The answer is obvious and in need of no response. "Exactly," he continues. This way he will finally feel like part of the family, it's one of our biggest deals to date.

"Well, it would be if we were actually making it."

I can't help but state the obvious, although Dad pretends not to hear and continues, "We sign contracts and toast champagne to celebrate Jason's success, and boom. He might finally feel like I'm proud of him, and the sense of belonging might just be enough to stop him from making shitty decision after shitty decision."

"I doubt it, Dad, he's been on a path of self-destruction since…"

"Don't, son," he cuts me off. "Don't speak about your brother that way. I know you might not agree with the way I go about my business, but it is just that, mine. Blake, when it comes to raising my kids and signing deals that affect their future, I expect you to respect my decisions."

I realise I'm clenching both fists in frustration and feel like a teenager being told off for truanting from school. I want to tell my dad that no matter what attempts to make Jason feel a part of our family, he never will. Not because he is adopted, but because he's a selfish bastard without any idea how to have a successful relationship with anyone other than his drug dealer.

"So, can you please clarify as this is a little confusing? Are we taking down the Parkers, or are we not?"

"We won't need to, son, I'm making more than a decent offer. Martin said it himself, he's ready to retire, and he has no heir to hand the business down to."

"But what about Tiff, is she not going to cause any trouble?"

"You think he'd be that stupid as to hand over his life's work to that bimbo?"

"It is his only daughter, Dad. And she wasn't always bad."

"Tiff will do just fine with the pay-out I'm giving them. Martin would rather we get rid, and go out on a high. So, you'll go along with it?" Dad's face red in frustration, and as always, more of a command than a question.

Before I get chance to ask just how he thinks he's gonna con Jason to sign a contract that is effectively meaningless the elevator pings and in walks my brother. He heads straight for Dad giving him a fake ass hug, and then nods at me.

"Blake."

"Jason."

There's an instant awkwardness between the three of us. A silent mood that enters with him and lingers in the room, like the smell of rotten sewer on a hot day.

Dad speaks first, "So, shall we run through the agenda?"

"Don't worry, Dad, I got this." He's close enough that I can detect more than a hint of stale alcohol on his breath. Great, he's half fucking cut.

"Okay, son, I trust you. If you're happy everything's in order, then I'll run with it."

"You got the contracts drawn up?"

"Sure have, son."

"Let's have a look then."

Oh god, not good...I need to distract him from having time to examine the documents in any detail and realise they are essentially full of shit.

I risk darkening the mood further by blurting out, "Ya think a certain someone will be in attendance today, Jase?"

"What the fuck are you on about?"

"I heard Martin's trying to teach Tiffany the ropes, so I'm guessing he might bring her along."

"So."

"So, you two looked pretty cosy in Aspen. I saw the pictures; you don't expect me to believe you two just bumped into each other."

"None of your fucking business," he growls at me. Distraction successful, but a whole new problem given the look on dad's face and Jason's level of alcohol intake prior to our meeting.

"Boys, I know you'll appreciate how hard I've worked on cinching this deal, so if you'll escort me to the boardroom and we can talk business." He's deflecting, and all three of us know it, but out of sheer respect we follow him in, neither of us saying a word. I glare at Jason, I might be keeping a lid on it for dad's sake, but he needs to know how much of a scumbag I think he is.

Martin enters and aside from his assistant he's alone. A wave of relief washes over me, grateful that I don't have to deal with Tiffany and her petty digs for the next few hours. As the entire meeting is one big charade, I try and switch off, paying just enough attention to nod in agreement in the right places.

"Jason will run through the contracts with you." Martin skims through, he must think a lot of my dad to be going to all this bother.

"It's a great deal, the way the industry's going you'd be forced to downsize in the next couple of years anyway. You're selling at the right time."

Jason attempts his sales pitch, but gets a shock when Martin replies a few moments later, "Bullshit."

"Excuse me?" Jason looks confused, this is getting interesting, surely he wouldn't blow the whole thing up so late in the game?

"I call bullshit," Martin repeats. Nobody speaks for an awkward few seconds. "This is no pound shop, Jason. You drive a hard bargain, almost as callous as your father, you're a Laine through and through." His scowl lifts to a sly smile, and the colour begins appearing in Jason's ghost white cheeks. He thought he'd lost the whole deal, and for a minute there I almost pitied him, *almost*.

"Hand me the pen. I'll sign, but it's with a heavy heart. I've put the best part of forty years into that place. I hope one day you two will be in the position your father and I are in."

"Oh, they will be, Martin, I've been showing them the ropes since they were tall enough to climb into the boardroom chair."

"They've learned from the best."

"Thank you, Martin, we've appreciated your support all these years."

A few more pleasantries and the contracts are signed and exchanged, and it's only when we all stand to leave that the expression on Jason's face turns black. His eyes narrow and he tilts his chin erupting into a vile, tinny laugh. "Now, I'm calling bullshit."

"Excuse me?" Martin looks confused. What the hell's he up to now, he's probably more pissed than I'd originally thought.

"You think I'm that stupid? What, you thought I'd believe you'd sell first time, no questions asked?" He rips the contracts down the middle throwing them at a pale Martin before turning on Dad. "And you, you thought you'd fake a deal for me cos' you don't fucking trust me to do a real one, cos' why? Because my names not Blake, and let's face facts, he's your real son, isn't he Jonathan. I'm just some damn screw up you tried to save."

"Son, it's not like that. I'm sorry, I just…"

"Save it, I don't wanna hear another second of your bullshit. You're right, I'll never be part of the family, but the joke's on you, *DAD. You* adopted me, you took me on as your own, which means I get half of it fucking all, and there's jack shit you can do about it." He laughs even louder now, like some evil hyena from a Disney movie. I'm about to tear him apart when Dad flushes beetroot in anger.

"GET OUT!" he booms at the top of his voice.

"Don't worry, Dad, I was going anyway. I think champagnes in order, care to join me, *bro?*"

I grab his scrawny little throat and punch him straight in the face. His nose bloodies instantly, and his balled fists bounce off me like ping pong balls. With my hand still firmly gripped around his neck, I march him to the lift and throw him in. He falls into a cowering mess in the corner like the little piece of shit he is.

"You're not worth it, you screw up. Get the fuck outta here, or I'll show you what a Laine is really fucking made of." The lift closes, and I hope to god that's the last I see of him for some time, or fuck knows what I'll do to him.

CHAPTER NINETEEN

Candice

We finish up our afternoon tea and move away from the markets towards the vintage shops. I can't shake the weird feeling I'm being watched.

"Look, Candy, it's still here, let's go inside." Rainy is jumping up and down outside The Velvet Box, a little jewellery shop that we always dreamed of going into. As kids, we used to stand in the window picking out our favourite sparkly pieces like a pair of magpies. The shopkeeper would always give us a little wave. The bell rings as we enter.

"Hi, can I help you." The little old man turns to face us and realisation dawns on his face. "Have you two been here before?" he asks.

"We've never been inside before, but we did always look in

through the window," I answer, feeling slightly embarrassed; surely he wouldn't recognise us after all these years.

"Of course you did, I would recognise that red hair and your little blonde sidekick anywhere. You two were always together. That's special that you've kept your friendship all these years." We both smile.

"I can't believe you remember us!" We're stepping *inside* today, not just window shopping. A sterling silver heart shaped pendant filled with pale pink pearls catches my eye. There's one in a shell colour, too.

"Oh, Rainy, check these out, they're gorgeous."

"Um, I don't really feel comfortable spending Blake's money on myself, it just doesn't feel right. I don't mind the odd treat, like lunch or our makeover, but buying things like this feels different."

"You could probably buy the whole shop with Blake's card and he wouldn't even flinch. But let me guess, you're not going to?"

"Not a chance, I'm quite capable of earning and spending my own money," I reply.

"I hope he knows how lucky he is to have you, Candy."

"We'll take these, please. They're lovely." He lifts off his glasses to look at them closer.

"Yes, they are, a local designer new to the market...she only popped in yesterday, but I snatched them up and ordered a few in other colours. I'm glad you've found something you like, ladies." He smiles as he wraps them in tissue paper for us and swipes my debit card through.

"Now that we've finally made it in here, it seems a shame not to have a peep at the kind of rings we used to dream at in your window displays."

"Aha." He winks, tapping the side of his nose. "We hardly get any expensive stuff in, nowadays, with the bigger stores developing, but I still like to dabble in the odd find. Now, if it's special you're after, let me get my newest delivery out of the back, you'll love it."

He vanishes to the back of the shop and quickly returns with a tray of antique looking jewellery. My eye is drawn straight to the oval blue sapphire in the middle. It's set on a platinum band with clear diamonds running along the band on either side and surrounding the clear, bright blue jewel. I allow my imagination to run wild for a few minutes, I can picture Blake placing this ring on my finger and my heart bursting with happiness.

"Try it on," Rainy encourages me, so I do. It fits perfectly, and against my petite hand and glowing tan it looks exquisite. I'm in love!

"It suits you. I picked it up on my travels, but can't bring myself to part with it yet. This is exactly the kind of piece my wife would have chosen."

"I hope whoever buys this one deserves it. It's a beauty, and I'll bet your wife was, too." He looks distant, but his lips smile.

"That she was, girls, that she was."

He disappears with the jewellery, and the doorbell rings again as someone else enters. When I notice it's Jason I feel instantly on edge and I didn't miss the huge black eye he has coming on. He walks straight over to us reaching and putting his arms around me from behind the way Blake would, which makes me feel uncomfortable.

"Well, well, you're not wasting any time draining our families well-earned cash, are you, Candice. Maybe you're better than I first thought."

I break out of his arms, the hairs on my own are standing on end, and my chest is racing faster. How dare he put his arms around me? I try and brush it off, maybe he's just being friendly.

"You don't like being held, Candice? That's a shame, I thought we had a moment back at the restaurant."

"What are you doing here, Jason?"

"Following you."

Rainy is staring at him furiously, she's taken an instant dislike to him.

"And why would you be doing that." She steps in front of me putting herself between us.

"Maybe I want a bit of what Blake's got."

"And maybe you should back off," Rainy growls protectively. I'm thankful because I have no clue what to say to him. I just know that his presence gives me chills, his breath smells stale, and I want to get away from his as quickly as possible. I try and maintain politeness, it is Blake's brother after all.

"Jason," saying his name brings a sickly feeling in the pit of my stomach. "I'm with Blake, and nothing's going to change that."

Rainy looks mightily pissed off and confronts him, "I assume you're not jewellery shopping, so why don't you go back to wherever it is you came from, and we'll forget this conversation ever happened."

"It was worth a try, I thought we had something, that was all, you two need to chill the fuck out."

As he turns to leave he brings his face closer to mine and breathes harshly into my ear whispering, "This isn't over."

I'm shaking from head to toe, and I've turned stone cold.

"What a freak."

"Yeah, he's pretty intense, isn't he? He was like that at the dinner, too. He touched my leg under the table with his foot, but I didn't say anything, thinking maybe it was an accident. It happened twice."

"Watch yourself with him, Candy. There's something really creepy about the way he looks at you."

"I know, I'd thought the same." The shopkeeper returns with what I'm guessing is a photo of his wife, but he sees me looking pale.

"Everything okay, Miss?"

"Yes, I'm, I'm okay, thanks." I need to get out of here. I feel like his eyes are still on me.

"We'll be back when we're next in town," Rayray told the shopkeeper, thanking him for showing us around.

"Good luck to you both, girls, stick together and you'll come to no harm."

What an odd thing to say, but he's right, we always have stuck together and whatever trials and tribulations have hit us along the way, we've always come out on top in the end. We're unbreakable! I slip my arm through hers and take a seat on a corner bench facing the market square.

I text Jerry and am grateful when he pulls up in front of us within minutes. My sides aching with all the walking, and we collapse into a heap on the back seat while Rainy chatters on about all our market buys.

"This scarf is just everything," she exclaims whipping a flamingo print chiffon scarf out of her bag and throwing it round her neck. "You wouldn't get one of those in any department store!" She laughs. "Keep your fancy shmancy shopping, Mr. Laine. Bourton Markets will always be our fave."

I laugh as she puts on a snooty voice and adjusts her scarf in a bid to look posh. We pull to a halt outside her parents place, just up the street from my mums. I'd pop in, but I'm pooped, and I know she has her WI meeting later, and Dad will be fixed on one of his impossible jigsaw puzzles enjoying the peace.

"Until next time, gorgeous one." She gives me a big squeeze.

"I'll keep texting when I can, but don't be worrying if you don't hear from me, the signal is awful round the centre."

"I won't worry now that I know you've got your own personal bodyguard, and I don't mean you, Jerry."

He quickly looks away, but I can see he's concealing a smile in the rear view mirror. He jumps out and carries Rainy's shopping to her door, which I think is really sweet, and we head to Blake's place at maximum speed.

It's a bit weird that I'd hardly heard from him the whole day, he usually bombards me with messages when we're apart. Maybe he was just busy, or maybe he needed a break from me, and now I'm waiting at the elevator about to surprise him.

What if he thinks I'm being too full on. Ah well, I'm here now, if he looks awkward I'll just ask Jerry to drop me back at Mums for the night. I'm sure he won't mind.

The lift takes forever, as always, but I have zero motivation to carry all that shopping up nine flights of stairs. So, I just stand here, waiting.

That's when I see her out of the corner of my eye. A young woman, polished to perfection attempting to run down the stairs in her tiny red stilettos and matching red pencil dress. She's beautiful...and crying. My instincts tell me to keep watching, so I do, my eyes glued to her, until I realise, it's Tiffany. Then I hear his voice.

"It doesn't have to be like this, Tiff."

"Screw you, Blake, screw you both."

Oh god, she's seen me. I look away, not knowing what to do. She gives me a death stare through her bloodshot teary eyes and storms off. He doesn't follow her, and I know he hasn't seen me. The lift pings, but I don't get in. I just stand there, wanting to run away but needing to get some answers. I turn and run out of the apartment block and away from all things Blake, past Jerry and his stupid expensive car, and past Tiffany on them ridiculous red high heels. I ignore the security following me to give me my shopping back. I don't need it, I just have to be alone to decide my next move. It starts to pour down, and I slip into the bus shelter over the road from his apartment, seething. I can't believe I ignored everything I knew about his lifestyle and his reputation with women. I'm feeling small for overlooking everything I knew about him just because 'it felt right'. What even was that? A feeling, probably lust, just like all the other girls before me who he'd wined and dined.

I don't care if I shouldn't, I feel cheated. Has he planned this? Was there even a business meeting today, or was it a ploy to get rid of me so he could bed Tiffany. Damn, I hate that woman. I bet she's not got any flaws like me.

How could I have believed someone like him could ever fall

for someone as damaged as me? Even before the fire, I couldn't have competed with her. She's groomed and full of Botox, and her hair is long and glossy, like her legs. I take one last look up at the apartment and make my decision.

I'm walking away.

CHAPTER TWENTY

Blake

J'm furious and pacing up and down my apartment feeling like a caged animal. I swipe a fist across the fireplace and let the ornaments crash to the tiled floor, smashing to pieces. I don't even flinch at the sound.

Needing some air, I throw the double doors open and lean against the balcony with my head in my hands, grabbing my hair in frustration. How dare she come here? How dare she think that a few dirty fucks when I've been wasted meant that I want her? She was obviously more crazy than I had originally suspected.

I don't know what, call it a force of nature, but my head is drawn to the bus in front, and I watch it pull away. Shit. Candice.

That's my girl, just sitting there alone, crying and vulnerable, and I'm all the way up here. I run almost faster than my legs can carry me, tossing security my keys as I pass. "Lock up the penthouse for me, Will." He looks shocked, but I've no time to explain. I reach the bus stop, but she's not there.

I shout her name instinctively, "Candice." I notice her speeding up through the crowds and walking in the opposite direction to me. The sight hits me right in the chest. What's she playing at, I know she's heard me. It's raining hard, and I'm fucking soaked when I reach her.

"Where the hell are you going, angel. You'll catch a death walking around like this." She's sobbing, and it's stressing me out. "What's happened, whatever it is we'll get through it together. I'll help you, if you just explain.

She scowls at me, and even I ain't stupid enough to realise that she's upset. What I don't know, is why. Let's get you back to the apartment and dry, then we can talk. I pull her into me. "C'mon, please." She pushes me away glaring at me accusingly.

"There's nothing to say, Blake. I saw her with my own eyes."

Fuck. My heart sinks, I don't insult her by playing dumb knowing she'll see straight through it, and I'll risk losing her forever. "I told you before, she's nothing to me, Candy. You gotta trust me, angel, I'd never do anything to hurt you. I promise."

My voice cracks in desperation, and she must hear it as she fires back,

"Five minutes...I'll give you five minutes to explain, and then I'm leaving. You're saying you wouldn't hurt me, but you already have. I was gone, for what? A day and you've already had her round at our. Your place?"

"It wasn't like that, c'mon I'll take my five minutes." And I practically bulldoze her back up to my apartment. "Sit please,

Candy, and wrap this round you." I pass her a throw. She's soaked through but doesn't take it.

"I'll stand." I've never seen her look so mad, but really, I know she's just upset and it kills me, I need to make her understand.

"Candy, she just turned up here. I didn't even know she knew where I lived, she's barely even been here before."

"Spare me the history."

"Listen, you're right. I do have a history? Dammit, doesn't everyone? But it's not one I'm proud of, angel. You need to know that. You're the best thing that ever happened to me."

"Save it, Blake. I don't need one of your shitty chat up lines. They might work on girls like that, but they won't work on me. I said five minutes, but I've heard all there is to be said. I'm not staying for you to convince me and yourself that you're ready to settle down. You were clear straight from the off you weren't looking for anything, and I get that."

"Fuck, Candy, will you take a breath."

"I'm leaving before either of us gets hurt."

She turns to walk away, and I grab her shoulders in desperation.

"You have to stop punishing me for my past, angel, please. I said I wasn't looking for anything, that doesn't mean you didn't come along. I really don't know why she came here tonight, she knows she could never compete with you."

"It's not about that, Blake. It's the fact that she was in here, in your apartment, you let her in and obviously listened to what she had to say. That's not just fucking."

"Maybe I should have been clearer with you. Tiffany has

always had a thing for me, we used to be friends, before...well before life got in the way. We grew up together."

"So, she's not, nothing then?"

"She is now. She changed, the money and lifestyle, it all went to her head, and by our late teens I didn't even recognise her anymore."

"The business industry is a hard one, Candy. It takes no prisoners, especially Martin Parker, and he's almost as much as a tyrant as my dad."

She looks up at me, tears streaming from her eyes, and I take her mouth for my own in a harsh kiss that leaves us both breathless. When I pull back she says nothing but bravely lifts her soaking wet t-shirt dress overhead standing fully naked in front of me. Revealing herself to me for the first time, and she's fucking perfection encapsulated. Her nipples stand solid, and she's shivering from the cold.

I pick her up as she wraps her legs instinctively around my waist and carry her over to my black leather sofa using one arm to pull my soaking wet top over my head. I sit down with her now straddling me, tilting her chin with my fingers so she is looking straight at me. Her sparkly eyes are dull and sad.

"It's only ever been you, angel. I don't see anyone else, just you. I want you to believe me, please. I want you to move in with me." She looks shocked.

"Blake, you don't know what you're saying."

I press my finger to her lips to shush her. "Yes, Candice, I do. All of this," I say gesturing my hand around the apartment, "I want to share it all with you." Placing a kiss to her mouth, then her neck, I continue working my way down her body. "I want to go to sleep with you every night." I move my mouth, kissing between her breasts, then her nipples. "I want to wake with you every morning." I want to spend my life with you," is the last thing I say before I clamp my teeth down on her nipple, and she grinds herself down on my throbbing erection. "You like that, baby? You like the feel of my teeth sinking into your nipple?" I already know the answer as her eyes are alive with need and her breath has become heavy.

I lift my hips as she rises onto her knees, just enough so I can push my erection free from the soaking wet jeans I still haven't bothered taking off. I settle back down onto the sofa and lower her towards me so her pussy is resting right over my cock. I wrap my hand around her slender neck, pulling her mouth down to meet mine. Sharp currents of a force resembling electricity flows through our bodies, and I'm kissing her with all I have as she shamelessly rocks her hips, gliding up and down my erection. I swear I could come any second.

"Oh god, Blake."

"You like that, Candy?"

"Mmmm, yes, I so do," she barely breathes out.

"You ready to take me now? To own me like only you can, Candy?" Looking at me curiously, she bites down on her bottom lip and gives me a nod. I rest my hands on her hips waiting at her entrance. "Then take me, I'm all yours."

She glides down as I thrust up and screams out as I fill her with my cock. She feels fucking amazing, slow and uneasy at first, but I reassure her running my hands over her whole body. The sight of naked is doing all sorts of crazy things to my senses, and I guide her sweet ass up and down, until she finds her rhythm.

Soon my girl is slamming down onto me, taking me...owning me, and fuck, she looks like a real goddamn angel. Her blonde waves framing her face and falling at her perky breasts.

"Ahhhh, Blake," she cries out on another deep thrust.

"Feels so fucking good, doesn't it, baby."

"Mmmhmm," she moans while biting her lip. I can feel how close she is, and I'm almost there, too. Padding her clit in slow circles with my thumb, I can feel her about to come apart, her sweet pussy tightening around my cock.

"Come for me, angel." I start thrusting harder and harder. She screams out, clamping down hard on my cock as she climaxes and milks the cum from me in the process, taking everything I have. Our bodies feels so sensitive as we ride out the last of our orgasm together, neither wanting it to end. I pull her down towards me, both gasping for breath, and she rests her head on my chest. I sit stroking my fingers up and down her spine until we have both found our breath again. I'm still in awe that she's letting me see her naked. I know it's a massive deal for her, and I want her to know just how gorgeous she looks.

I pick her up effortlessly and take her to the ensuite, turning the shower on and walking with her still wrapped around me. We step into the huge shower space, and I place her on her feet and press a kiss to her lips. "I want to wash you, angel." She lets out a nervous giggle.

"Um, you don't have to do that, Blake, I can do it myself ,you know."

"I know, but I want to."

I grab the body wash and squeeze it out before lathering it up in my palms and using my bare hands to wash my girl. The cool water is a welcome change to my usual steaming hot showers, and I enjoy taking in every inch of her nakedness. I avoid rubbing over her burns, but make the point of skimming over them gently, a silent message that they don't bother me one bit. I finish up washing myself too, and we dry off before climbing into bed, and I cuddle her into me in our favourite position.

"So, will you move in with me, angel?" She looks up at me confused.

"Blake, I thought you were just saying that?"

"Baby, I would never say something didn't mean. I want you here with me."

"Can I have a little time to think about it, please?"

"I place a kiss to her head. "Of course you can, angel, I want you here because you want to be, not because I badgered you into it. Oh, by the way, how would you feel about coming to my parents place with me tomorrow?"

"Sounds great, Blake, I'd love to," she says with the biggest smile on her face.

I've never took a girl home to Mum and Dad before. Sure, they knew Tiff and I had a thing once, and they'd always hoped me and Aimee would eventually see sense and settle down together. Aside, of course, from the endless press reports and stream of pictures online of me 'dating' a whole platoon of women. Some were true, others not so accurate. Some downright insulting and enough to see my mum to an early grave, but none important enough to introduce to the real Blake.

Strangely, I'm not nervous about the prospect of letting my parents get to know Candice, as I know they will love her just as much as I do. I watch her crash out, starfishing across my whole bed and admire her blonde waves loosely flowing around her.

Why she wears that ridiculous fucking bun, I'll never know. But I kind of love the fact that when she does wear her hair loose, it's nearly always when she's alone with me. A little piece of her that's just for me. I wrap my fingers up in it as she curls into me for the night.

CHAPTER TWENTY-ONE

Candice

I wake to find him on the balcony, pumping iron as usual. I grab a bagel from the kitchen and lie across the corner sofa to watch him. "You wanna join me, princess."

"I'll stick to my bagel, but thanks." I wave my bagel at him and catch a few crumbs as they fall out of my mouth. He grins at me, hitting another chin up effortlessly.

"So, you never got round to telling me, did you have a good time with Rainy yesterday?"

"It was fab, Blake, we had the best time."

"Did you buy much?" He lowers himself before lifting himself up and over the bar again. God he looks sexy. I watch his arm muscles crunch tightly as he holds his body weight and the way his fingers wrap around the bar make me wish they were gripping me.

"What, sorry?"

He laughs at me, and I feel my cheeks blush pink. "Shopping, yesterday, did you buy anything good?"

My mind flits back to yesterday and a shiver passes through me as I recall the way Jason had appeared in the jewellery shop.

"I ran into your brother, actually."

"What, Jason?" he asks, getting breathless now, and I notice beads of sweat starting to jewel over his forehead.

"Yeah, he was in The Velvet Box. It's a little jewellers in the village. Rainy had me trying engagement rings on for fun, and he just sort of appeared."

"What, in the jewellery shop?"

"Yeah, it was a bit weird, actually."

He drops from the bar, giving me his full attention.

"Weird, in what way?"

"It was nothing major, he was just...well he kinda came onto me." I don't tell him the full extent, knowing he doesn't get on with his brother already, I don't want to make things even worse. Jason's words play over in my mind. 'This isn't over.' What could he have meant by that, he was probably just trying to give me the creeps.

"I'll fucking kill him." Blake's jaw is clenched, and his eyes narrow in anger.

"It was no big deal, maybe he was just being overly friendly."

"He'll be overly friendly with my fist when I see him. I'm going for a shower." He storms passed me, and I don't follow him, letting him have a minute to cool down. He can be a real hot head at times.

I get ready, and by the time he's finished and dressed, he's back to his usual relaxed self.

The drive seems to take ages, and we pass the time chatting about our families. Well, mostly me chatting, he just listens and asks questions about mine rather than telling me much about his. I love the way he's so interested in me, but I prefer it when he gives a little bit of himself, too.

I can't wait to find out more about him and his family life, everything about this confident, but private man intrigues me. I want to know everything there is to know about Blake Laine, however, I feel like whatever I find out won't change my feelings for him.

The more time we spend together, the more my guard is coming down and I can't see a reason to say no to moving in with him. In fact, living with him these past few days feels like the most the natural thing in the world.

We hadn't drove far outside of the city before we arrive in Oxford, and the high rises are left behind for wider roads with cleaner air and houses where trees line the streets in neat rows. Jerry pulls in outside Blake's parents' house, and I draw a long breath, nothing could have prepared me for this. It's enormous and set behind security enabled gates. We drive up the gravel path to a grand white gothic style manor house from around the eighteenth century, I'm guessing.

"Oh my god, is this where you grew up, Blake?"

"Yeah, baby, but if anyone asks, I'm a city boy through and through," he says with a wink. I'd never even been in a house this grand before, it looks like a postcard! I notice the flower filled hanging baskets and yellow fresh flowered wreath on the door, obviously Elaine had an eye for colour. The whole garden is filled with roses.

"It's beautiful."

Elaine runs out towards me giving me a hug before I get chance to say hi. She's dressed in a tiny golf skirt and looks a bit like she's stepped out of the pages of a playboy magazine. Except way more classy in her fresh white tennis pumps.

"Your dad's out the back, son. He's setting up for a game with the weather being good. Hope you don't mind, Candice."

"Oh, call me Candy, all my loved ones do."

"Wow, well okay, Candy, that's real sweet of you." Blake grins at me. "I'm guessing you mean a game of golf by the outfit."

"Why, do you think it's a bit much? I just like to get in the zone, it makes it more fun."

"You could never be too much, Mum."

"Well, I've never played before, but I'd love to give it a try."

"Ooh, I was hoping you'd say that. I got you an outfit just in case! C'mon, let's go change." She pulls me away, and Blake just waves as he disappears to find his dad. The house inside is even more stunning, and there's fresh flowers everywhere making it smell delicious. Elaine shows me into one of the guest room where everything is white and daisy related. Lying on the bed, there's a baby pink polo shirt style dress with matching visor and sneakers.

"I guessed you were a size four at the meal, but I ordered a six, you know..." She glances at my side, "So, you can be comfy. Blake told me about what happened to you, Candy. I'm really sorry." She looks genuinely upset for me. God, I hate talking about my burns so much that I can't think what to say back.

"I'm getting better every day, he's really helped me."

"Always was one of the good guys, my Blake. Takes after his father. Can I talk to you, Candy."

"Of course." She sits on the bed and pats the space next to her, so I take a seat too.

"I may be over stepping the mark here but I just wanted you to know, I haven't seen my Blake this happy in a very long time. I didn't think he would find happiness after his best friend died. I'm really glad you've came into his life."

"He never mentioned his friend died, I'll bet he's seen so much in the army."

"She wasn't in the army lovely, Aimee was his closest friend since he was tiny, and she died in her late teens after a long battle with leukemia."

She stands and takes a small photo frame from the cluttered sideboard, passing to me. Looking down, I see a young Blake smiling up at me, with his arm wrapped around a pretty brunnette wearing oversized glasses. They both look happy, but I can see a sadness in Aimee's dark eyes. "Wow, they look so happy."

"They were, they were inseparable, right until the end. He was by her side through the whole thing, It broke his heart...Anyway, I've probably said too much. I just wanted you to know, I'm glad you're here." She pats her eyes as if wiping away tears and changes the subject before I can figure out anything to say.

A smaller frame catches my eye at the back of the sideboard, Elaine turns to see what I am looking at. She passes me another frame from the collection, and I take a closer look. It's a black and white, baby scan of twins. "That's Blake and Logan at 17 weeks, he was a twin, you see."

I don't really know what to say, his Mum has caught me off guard by being such an open book. She is so different to Blake who is a lot more reserved and private. "He never mentioned a twin."

She answers in a quiet voice. "He won't have love, Logan was born sleeping."

"I'm so sorry for you all." I lean in and wrap my arms around Elaine, trying to give even a tiny crumb of comfort to what must be a world of pain.

She stands up and shakes out the skirt, laying it back down on the bed beside me, abruptly changing the subject. "Anyway, I imagine you hate anything with a waistband, so I knew you wouldn't want a skirt."

"It's perfect, thanks Elaine." Help yourself to any toiletries from the ensuite, darling, and I'll see you downstairs."

"I won't be long."

"I'll have Jerry light us a barbecue for later, it looks like it's going to be a scorcher."

She disappears, and I'm left alone with a room full of trinkets and pictures all in white ornate frames. There's a lot from when Blake was little, most of them in different sports uniforms. His smile and the cheeky glint in his eye haven't changed. Then I see his baby photos, he's a little podger! I throw the dress on sliding the visor over my messy bun. It's loose enough not to bother my side but shorter than I'd normally wear, especially to meet someone's parents for the first time! I make my way back down the winding staircase and outside into the sun and run straight into Blake. His eyes nearly fall out of his face.

"Nice dress," he murmurs.

"Thanks, sexy." I smile.

"Ugh," he groans as I skip past him, and he taps my ass.

"Later, angel."

He catches me up taking my hand, and I whisper back,

"Is that a promise, Blake?"

He looks exasperated, and his parents break the tension.

Jonathan greets me casually,

"Hey Candice, good to see you again, girl. Are you ready to get your ass kicked at golf?" Blake rolls his eyes.

"I should have warned you, he's pretty competitive when it comes to family games."

"That makes two of us," I reply looking straight at Jonathan, and he playfully slaps Blake in the back.

"Woah, son, where did ya find this little firecracker?"

"She came straight from heaven," he says as he throws me his dazzling but smug 'I'm-the-best-boyfriend-in-the-world-and-you-know-it', smile. I let him have his moment, he is an amazing boyfriend, after all.

We share a golf caddy, and Elaine and I climb into the back letting the men take over the driving. I'm surprised by how interested Elaine is in the centre, and the kids we've been working with. She didn't initially seem like the maternal type, but she's nonstop questions about it.

Blake cuts in, "My mum's quite the fundraiser, isn't she Dad." Jonathan turns to me and rolls his eyes looking more like an annoyed father, than a CEO of an international business, by the minute.

"Oh, yes, my Elaine loves to throw a good party. I just wish she didn't have to use my house as a bloody gala venue so often. I hate all those bodies crammed into my living room." Crammed in! I looked back towards the massive house and grounds and can't imagine how even a herd of elephants would be crammed in so much space.

"Oh, stop it, Jonathan. You never complain when the champagne's flowing, and you're always one of the first to donate, you big softy." The way she approached him made me smile, despite all the grandeur of Lakeland House, it was clear that the two of them were genuinely in love and a perfect match for one another.

It makes me wonder why Blake was such a commitment phobe when I met him. Surely he wants to find someone to love the way Jonathan does Elaine. She reaches forward and squeezes his shoulder affectionately. In some ways they remind me very much of my own parents.

"You know you should think about a fundraiser for the Peace Centre, Candice. It sounds like a great cause, and I know lots of people would be interested in donating. International causes always do well, in my experience, as people want to help out without actually having to travel to the country themselves."

"And put themselves at risk," his dad's voice full of frustration. I lean forward and throw my arm around Blake's neck defensively.

"It's a really good idea, Elaine, and definitely something to think about, thank you." I smile politely.

"Great idea, Mum, you offering to help out?" He turns and winks at me.

"Of course, Blake, I'll support in any way I can, just let me know what you need. It'll be good to have a friend to collaborate with, I'm usually surrounded by men."

A friend! She likes me, thank goodness I've made a good impression.

We pull up and Blake jumps out just before we're stopped and lifts me down from the caddy, his hands gripping my waist. I forget our company at the feel of his touch and throw my arms around his shoulders. He plants a soft but brief kiss on my mouth before lifting me higher and twirling around. His parents ignore us and begin to unload their golf clubs. Blake sets me down.

"C'mon, you can use mum's clubs, they should be just your size."

"Blake," I hiss under my breath, "I've never played golf before."

"Well, let's hope you're a fast learner cos' my folks are the competitive type." He senses my nerves and takes a pink handles club from the bag.

"I've got you, angel. I told you, I've always got you." He stands behind me, his arms covering mine and my backside pressed tightly into his crotch. I feel him instantly harden under me and the firmness of his touch has my mind roaming.

"You make a start, Mum. We're gonna take a few practice shots first."

"Ready, baby?" I nod but am way out of my depth here, I've never even held a club before. He pulls our arms back and down to touch the ground just behind the ball.

"Okay, so just let gravity drive your arms forward and aim a little higher."

"Okay." I've got this, how hard can it be? I swing high and stump my club straight into the grass chipping the earth up and throw my club in frustration. "I can't do it," I pout, not caring if I look like a sulky teenager.

"C'mon, one more try for me?"

"Okay." He picks the club up for me again pulling my hips into his and running his hands smoothly up my arms leaving a trail of goose bumps behind, before gripping my left shoulder.

"Don't overthink this, angel, let the power come from the shoulder, and don't swing to high." He stands back, and I can see both his parents watching me, 'no pressure' I think to myself. I draw the club back and do everything he showed me, the ball flies in the air.

"Fore," Blake shouts, and I watch as it flies way out of sight. "That's it, Candy, well done, baby."

"Oh my goodness, I did it." I jump up and give a little celebration dance, which stops abruptly when I notice Jonathan and Elaine are still watching.

"Great shot," Elaine shouts encouragingly, and we join them for my first game of golf.

Blake

I catch up with Mum in the kitchen and grab an iced water to cool off.

"She's just lovely, Blake. So genuine, I got a really good vibe about her as soon as I saw her. It's in her aura. She's even won ya Dad over!"

"Thanks, Mum, I've fallen for her big time. I just wish I could have saved her from what happened. I would do anything to take her pain away, she's been so brave."

"She's probably stronger than you think, Blake. Us women usually are."

"I know, Mum, I just wish she could see how perfect she is. All she sees when she looks in the mirror is a bunch of burns."

"And what about you, son, what do you see?"

"A future, Mum. My whole future. I didn't realise how lost I was until I found her."

"You weren't lost, son, you'd just experienced more than most. Losing Aimee hit us all hard, she was a special girl and so is Candice."

I'm just glad you guys have had the chance to get to know her and that you like her. Are we okay to use the guesthouse later? We might as well crash after the meal to save us the journey back to London."

"Course you are, son. Keys are in the cupboard, I'll see you at dinner."

I don't waste any time. I know Candice won't be long getting ready, and I really want to keep this a surprise until after dinner. I shower and throw on a white Armani shirt with Hugo Boss jeans and my Gucci boat shoes. Casual but smart enough to let her know I've made an effort.

I'm soon seated in our entertaining dining hall, the one Mum would have us sit at all the time, if she could get Dad to agree.

A huge chandelier compliments tall silver candle sticks, and the low lighting sets an intimate mood. The room is too big for just the four of us, and I notice Sandy our maid clearing away an extra plate, meaning Jason's let Mum down again. I'm relieved he's not here, I don't want him letching over Candice anyway.

"It's just this way, Ma'am," I hear Sandy showing her into the hall, and I'm taken aback by the sight of my angel in the floor length blue dress she'd bought at Harrod's. The one that makes her look like a Grecian goddess. She has a little more make-up on than usual, and her eyes are shining like huge crystal blue sapphires. I walk over and kiss her lightly on the neck. Her smell of sweet summer berries sends a tingle straight to my cock.

"Did anyone ever tell you, you're the most beautiful girl in the world?" I whisper and she smiles.

"Oh, one or two times for sure," she lies, and I gesture for her to take her seat as if she's a royal princess.

She's chatting easily with Mum and Dad and even sharing a few laughs which is completely unexpected. They seem to love her and watching her smile light up the room, it's easy to see why. Her hairs swept up in a loose bun with strands falling free from her face and a silver hair slide to match silver crystal blue earrings. I focus on the way her eyes change and dance as she talks and notice the way her lips part slightly when they rest. I'm completely captivated by her.

"Didn't I, Blake?" Suddenly all three of them are looking at me, awaiting my response, and it's clear I haven't listened to a word she's been saying.

"Yeah, baby." I smile and am relieved when the conversation quickly moves on to my mum's love of art and Candice is in her element having someone to discuss her passion with.

Personally I don't see how talking about how modern artists and the internet are killing art culture can piss anyone off, but Candice is just as riled up as Mum. I shift my dick under the table which is making its own attempts to respond to Candy, who looks hot as hell when she's mad about something.

I drop a not so subtle hint in the form of a huge yawn and put a hand on Candy's leg under the table, signalling I'm ready to go. She ignores me and continues in her deep discussion with Mum, and Sandy dishes out hot apple pie for dessert. It's my favourite, so frustrated as I am, I sit a while longer and enjoy watching her lick the cream of her spoon after each mouthful. I pour her another glass of prosecco and notice she's looking a little tipsy as the night goes on.

"Are you trying to get me drunk, Blake?"

"Of course not, Candice." And she smiles at me and hiccups.

"Sorry, everyone, I'm not really used to the wine."

"It's a special occasion, sweetie, don't you apologise. It's always a good night when my handsome boy comes to stay over, and especially this time, since he's brought you along."

"We never thought we'd see the day," Dad chips in.

"To a perfect night." Mum raises her glass and we cheers before Candice whispers, "Stays over?"

"We're gonna head off for bed darlings, I'm up early for hot yoga."

"Thanks for tonight, both of you. You've been so welcoming."

"Welcome to the family, gorgeous," Mum says winking at me and sauntering out of the room, her chiffon layers trailing after her like an Indian ambassador.

"Oh my god, welcome to the family," I mimic.

"Way to play it cool, Mum."

"Night kids," Dad disappears after her like a lost puppy and ten miles away from the chief exec of Laine Corporations.

"So, do I get to sleep in your old bedroom tonight, Mr. Laine."

"Not quite, Miss Embers, come with me," I lead her outside. The light breeze causes her dress to swish, and strands of blonde hair dance softly around her sweet cheeks. We walk down the twisting garden path lined by hedges that make it seem as though we're in our own world.

"Oh my god. Blake, what is this place, it's breath taking," she gasps on sight of the glass summer house.

"So are you, Candice." I sweep a strand of hair away from her face.

"Dance with me."

"What? Here?"

"Right here." I lift her gently by the shoulders and kiss her before pulling her into my chest and wrapping my fingers around her dainty hands swaying us gently back and forth. I hum a made up song out loud and twirl her around. She's clumsy, giggly and slightly giddy from the wine.

The rain comes from nowhere and we ignore the first few drops lost in each other's arms, but it soon makes itself heard splashing down in bucket loads and soaking us wet through. She lets out a squeal, and I pull her hand guiding her into the glass summer house.

"Did you do all this, for me?"

She looks taken aback and it strikes me that she had probably never dated anyone like me before. She clearly likes surprises, despite telling me she doesn't in the past. I can tell from the way she's gone quiet and a little subdued.

"I wanted to give you this, I pull the small box from my pocket and hold it out to her." Her mouth gapes wide open, panic in her eyes but also a look of excitement. From the look on her face she wouldn't say no if I did propose here and now, I can't say it hasn't crossed my mind either. I'm almost out of self-control around this woman, almost, but not quite.

"Blake," she gasps, opening the box and laughing. "I thought you were gonna ask me to marry you, silly."

"Not yet," I reply watching the realisation of how deep my feelings for her run sink in. "It's my apartment key, angel. No pressure, but like I said, if you wanted to move in, it would be cool with me."

"Cool with you, hey? So you're saying you don't mind if I'm there or not, tough guy."

"No, I'm trying to say I want you, Candice, everyone knows it. Most importantly..." I step closer to her taking her hands in mine.

"You know it." I toss the key and box down on the bed taking a deep breath, and she kisses me before I can catch my breath. I pull away needing to tell her those three little words I'm so desperate to say, but she doesn't let me, her hands roaming my chest under my shirt, turning me rock solid under her touch.

"So, is that a yes?"

"Yes." She laughs between kisses, and I scoop her up throwing her gently onto the bed.

CHAPTER TWENTY-TWO

Candice

$\mathcal{N}$o one's ever done anything like this for me before, and I can't believe Blake's thought of all this. I hugely underestimated his ability to sweep me off my feet.

The glass summerhouse is stunning. A huge bed in the middle covered in white bed linen along with fresh rose petals that he's sprinkled all over it. The heavy rain covering the walls make the place feel private despite anyone being able to see in, if they were around. Blake has literally filled the place with vanilla scented candles, and the low lighting seems to blank everything out. Everything except from each other.

His wet shirt clings to his broad chest, and I trace the curves of his abdominal muscles with my eyes. His eyes are hungry in anticipation and a surge of confidence tingles through my whole body. He's created magic tonight, and I need to feel his skin on mine, all of him. So, I do. All night long he completely worships me, taking me over and over again until I'm wrapped up tight in his arms completely spent. His smell and touch are overwhelming my senses as he pulls me in tighter.

"Do you feel it, Blake?" A question that needs no answer except for the deep passionate kiss that follows telling me everything I need to know. I close my eyes and drift off into the kind of sleep that only comes with a feeling of contentment. I've fallen hard and fast for Blake Laine in the last few months, but that didn't change his reputation of London's most notorious fuck boy. My head's telling me to slow down and be cautious, but I snuggle in a little tighter knowing it's way too late for that.

The sound of the rain wakes me a few times, and it's almost two in the morning now. Most of the candles have burnt out, and Blake's heavy breathing tells me he's fast asleep. His arms are still around me, bodies pressed together and if feels like heaven. So, I don't know why I can't shake off this creepy feeling that someone's watching me. I roll over to my side and watch the raindrops slide down the glass panes and the gorgeous garden beyond.

Blake was so lucky to have grown up in such a fab home, and the garden area reminds me of my own home by the lake. It might not have been our garden, but we had all shared the lake growing up, so it felt like it belonged to each of us. I remember digging up mud pies with Stephan and him threatening to throw me in during the summer months. My eyes begin to feel heavy and start to close as I dream of home.

I catch sight of something in the hedgerow and struggle to gain focus through the dark. Oh my god. It's Jason. He's right there looking in on us, the next load of rain falls from the roof and when it clears enough to see out again, he's gone.

Blake sighs dreamily and rolls over. I wrestle with myself, but decide I can't wake him, he's too settled. Why am I freaking out so much anyway, it's only Blake's brother, it is his home after all.

Maybe he was just walking back after a heavy night out. But why would he be looking in on us? Maybe he didn't know we were here and he was just checking who was staying.

Goosepimples appear all over my arms and legs, and I realise I'm shaking, but I look at Blake so content and decide to try and sleep off the horrible gut feeling that something is wrong.

I wake to find Blake mid press up on the luxurious sheepskin rug next to the bed on the floor.

"Morning, gorgeous," his breath hot and heavy.

"Don't you ever take a day off?"

"Nope." He jumps to his feet and wearing only boxers I admire his chiselled physique. It should be illegal for this guy to ever wear clothes!

"You ready for breakfast, angel."

"Sure am, we've got a plane to catch, remember."

"How ya feelin' about flying back out, you think they managed okay without us?"

"I'm excited to see everyone, especially Sal. Julie will have held everything together, she's quite the control freak, as you've seen." We get dressed, and I scoop my hair up into a messy bun which Blake scruffs up playfully.

"Don't mess with the hair."

"Ooh, what you gonna do, Miss Embers?" He messes it up again, and we play fight all the way back to the breakfast table.

Elaine's still in her tight yoga attire sitting in front of a fruit bowl, while Jonathan is tucking into a full English. I pray I look good in Lycra at her age, her body is like a twenty year old supermodel.

Without warning, last night flashes back to me in a horrible memory of his blank expression starting back at me in the dark of night.

"Is Jason not joining us for breakfast, then?" Blake looks a bit surprised but Elaine's answer has my thoughts reeling.

"What gave you that idea? Jason's out of town, honey, he won't be back until next weekend."

"Oh, I...nothing, I just had a feeling he would be here."

"No, darling, not this time."

We finish up, and I can tell I'm being a lot quieter than last night as Elaine keeps asking me questions and I'm firing back with one word answers.

Had I really dreamt the whole thing? I'd been so sure his face was right there, so vivid in my mind.

It's later on in the day sitting in a packed Heathrow Airport when I broach the subject with Blake over coffee.

"What did you think of my folks, then?"

"Ah, they are just gorgeous, Blake. Really, I can see where you get all your charm from now." He grins flashing a set of pearly whites like he's straight from a toothpaste advert.

"This is going to sound kinda strange, but last night, while you were sleeping, I just couldn't settle. I was tossing and turning and when I looked out of the summerhouse..."

Oh god, there's no way of saying this that doesn't make me

sound like a total weirdo, so I spit it out fast, "I saw your brother in the bushes."

"Woah, slow down, angel, what the fuck are you talking about?"

"Your brother was at the summer house, it was like two this morning."

"Well, what was he doing?"

"It looked like he was just staring at us sleeping, through the glass." My whole body has tensed up as a result of the huge knot in my stomach that's twisting and tighting as I explain everything to Blake. Great, now that I've said it aloud, it sounds even more freaky than when it was in my head.

"And you're sure it was Jase, you weren't just dreaming or having a nightmare or something?"

"Honestly, Blake, he was right there, I saw him."

"Okay, it's okay. Don't worry, there must be a simple explanation, he was probably tanked up and didn't want Mum to know he was home so he stopped by the summer house to crash there."

"Maybe." I shift uncomfortably.

"How about we call him and get to the bottom of it? Would that make you feel better, angel?"

"Yeah, I think so. I mean, I guess it might help." Blake flips his phone and presses the loudspeaker symbol.

"Hey Bruv, how's business?" His voice even sounds disingenuous down the line.

"Yeah, I'm all good Jason. What were you doing at home last night?"

"Home, as in Mum and Dad's?"

"Yeah, why were you creeping about in the early hours?"

"I don't have a clue what the fuck you're on about, bro, I'm in Miami for the week. You wanna get out here? There's daisy dukes on every corner, might help loosen you up a bit."

"I'm good thanks, see ya, Jason." Blake ends the call abruptly, and we board our flight back to Juba to finish what we started.

"See, nothing to worry about at all, he's not even in town. It must have been a dream or a reflection or something."

I don't say anything, I still have that crunching feeling in my tummy when we're talking about him. Despite the long flight, neither of us say much. Nothing like a long flight for brooding time. By the time we're in descent, I've labelled Blake's brother as a rapist, axe murderer and sex addict who gets his kicks from spying on others in the act. All of which can't be true because, as he confirmed, he's not even in the same state for the week.

CHAPTER TWENTY-THREE

Candice

*T*he plane pulls into Juba and, as usual, the airport is utter carnage. Even the locals want to get the hell out of here and to a place of safety. It's so heart breaking seeing family after family queued up, each trying to catch a flight to a new life where they don't have to worry where the next gunshots coming from.

Blake drapes an arm around my shoulder protectively and guides me through the crowd and out into the scorching heat. Is it spoiled that as we sit in the taxi bouncing around with no seatbelts, I'm wishing Jerry was here with the BMW and air con that would allow a taste of cooler air instead of the open windows that don't even muster up a breeze?

I can't tell if Blake's just as excited to see everyone as I am, but both his legs are bouncing up and down like they always do when he's anxious or a little on edge. He's probably itching to get back to work and catch up with Grey.

It's been an intense few days with just the two of us and being with the others gives us something else to focus on. It's a chance to take a step back and decide if we are ready for this, the last week has been a complete rollercoaster. We've somehow jumped from not committing, to moving in together, and I'm not quite sure how it all happened, but it feels so good. I jump out of the cab and run straight towards Sal on sight of her.

"Oh my god, Sal, I didn't realise how much I missed you!"

"Well that's lovely, isn't it?"

"No, I mean, it's so good to see you."

"It's good to see you, too, babe. It's been pretty boring with just me and Julie doing the rounds. Wait 'til you see what's been happening." I look around.

"It looks like a whole lot has been going on, this place looks amazing!" "That's not all, we have a surprise for you, c'mon."

She grabs my hand, pulling me towards the rear of the centre. The kids are all lined up outside with a huge handmade banner that reads, 'Welcome to our School', in brightly coloured paint. There're tiny handprints are splashed all around the edges.

Tears prick my eyes, and an older lady nods her head and runs to the front of the group shouting, "One, two, three," and all the children throw their hands in the air, bursting into the cutest version of 'Twinkle Twinkle Little Star' I have ever heard. Their little fingers are wriggling above their heads, and their bodies are swaying and moving to the rhythm they are creating.

I can't find words as they come to an end, so I give them a big round of applause and notice the rest of the team are gathered around me clapping too.

Sal takes hold of my shoulders from behind, turning me to meet an older Sudanese lady whose eyes are shining with pride.

"This is Nameera, she's going to run the school. She's travelled from Taiz, which is miles away. She's had a tough old journey but left as soon as she heard about the Peace Centre and hasn't looked back. She speaks fluent English as her grandmother worked in England for a while, years ago."

"Pleased to meet you, Candy, you have an amazing class of children here. I hope you don't mind me taking over."

"Of course not." I hug her, and all the kids cheer running to over to us excitedly. Aliya taps me on the shoulder.

"Miss Nameera made me her helper, Miss Embers, and guess what?" She flashes her infectious grin at me and doesn't give me a second to guess, instead continues excitedly, "She has a morning class just like yours."

"Wow, Aliya, that's amazing news. She is very lucky to have such a good helper." I hug her close, and she treats me to another toothy grin before skipping off to find her friends.

"You've done an amazing job, Nameera. Thank you so much."

"Your friend, Sally, has helped a lot, too. We're really going to miss her."

Miss her? "Why, where are you going?" I ask Sal, a sense of panic washing over me.

With the centre all finished, I have no idea where she will go now, and I'm not ready to lose her. Although, the centre looks perfect, and I'm so pleased for the early finish and that the children can keep on attending school, I have a distinct feeling of 'what next'. The thoughts are unsettling me.

"Are ya gonna miss me too, Candy? Now my head's gonna be stuck in books, since I've been accepted onto a fine art course."

"Wow, Sally, that's fab! I'm so proud of you. Well done, you clever clogs. How did you keep this a secret for so long?"

Sally laughs at my reaction before she says, "Do you think ya can put up with us being neighbours again?"

"You're joking? Your course is in England?" She's nodding happily.

"Gloustershire College, to be exact."

"No way. Oh my god. That's right by me! This is so cool." I'm crying again. I'm an emotional wreck lately. All I do is cry.

My cloudy eyes meet with Blake's, who's watching from the side lines. He throws me an 'I-love-you-smile', and I'm overwhelmed with feelings of happiness and completeness.

I must be the luckiest girl in the world right now, and whether we've said it or not, or whatever he thinks of us, I know in my heart of hearts that I will forever belong to Blake Laine. He is my everything, and the look in his striking green eyes tells me I'm his.

We spend the next few weeks helping to finish up the health centre and Sal, and I spend my most of my time with Nameera, helping her get to know the children. Blake and Greyson are able to focus on decorating the centre and adding the finishing touches, as the rebels appear to have backed off, for now.

There have been no more shoot outs in the local area, for

weeks and the locals now have a safe place they can take ownership of and start to rebuild their community.

It's not long before we're ready to leave, and I'm excited that Sally will be coming back to England, too. I can't wait to introduce her to Rainy, and take her around all my favourite places in Bourton-on-the-Water. I just know they are going to love each other!

Blake's quiet on the last day, I know he doesn't agree with Greyson's decision to is stay out here. He has tried everything he can to convince him to come home with us and take some well deserved time off, but Grey is having none of it.

I finally feel like it is time for me to let myself move on from Marshy, and start a new chapter of my life. With Blake by my side, I have somewhere I belong and no longer feel as though I need to be here, to be close to my brother. Marshall will always be with me and the pain of losing him will never fade, but allowing myself to move forward feels good. He would have wanted me to follow my heart, rather than my head and would have told me I'm stupid for hesitating to let myself love Blake. I smile to myself as I can almost hear him telling me that Blake is the lucky one to have me in his life.

When I get back to England, I need to find his wife, Evelyn and make sure she is coping. It had been over a year since I'd heard from her and we used to be so close. The last rumour I heard was that she had moved to London but I am determined to find her and make her realise that she is allowed to be happy and have a life after my brother, it's what he would have wanted for us all.

Blake

Four weeks later

*W*e've only been back in London for a week, but the Peace Centre feels like a million miles away from the luxury of my apartment. Today will be our first day apart since we came home and I'm not looking forward to it one bit, but I need to put some hours in a the office to help my dad cinch the Parker deal.

Back in England, life has been a whole lot better. Especially now that Candice has moved in with me. She seems happier too. Her nightmares have been relentless and never give her a night off, but they seem more manageable now. I think she's taking some control back, and she's learning to expect the initial horror scenes that flashback unwelcomingly.

She is always able to get to sleep easier when I'm here. Probably due to the sheer exhaustion as I haven't been able to leave her alone. The sight of her in my bed at night is so hot, and waking up next to her each morning has me wanting her more every day.

I know better than to wake her up during an episode as the doctors say that could trigger a panic attack. So, I just stroke her back gently, and her body always responds to my touch. She snuggles in tighter and eventually the bad is overcome by good, and she sleeps undisturbed and safe in my arms.

I wake first, as usual, and slip out from underneath her. I've been slacking on my workouts the last few days. I head out onto the balcony and take in the impressive view of London's skyline in all its morning glory. The sun is still rising above the tall three storey buildings bringing a peaceful feeling to a city full of chaos.

I pump twenty chin ups with ease and flip some old school Usher on my IPhone, dropping to the floor and clapping to the beat in between push ups.

I get the call while she's upstairs taking a bath.

"Serg."

"Blake, we've got somethin' in the pipeline. I'm gonna need a few of my best men, can't say too much at the min, but can I count you in?"

"Am there, boss, have you spoken to Greyson?"

"Not yet, but I know he'll be in, too. Thanks, Blake. Is that knee of yours back to full health now?"

"Yeah, all better, Serg. Just the last few physio session to complete."

"We've got a few weeks yet, keep on top of it, and I'll be in touch with the details ASAP."

"Speak soon, Serg." I hang up wondering what I've just gotten myself into. If Greyson's there then I'm sweet. We make a solid team and can quickly train any newbies to follow in our footsteps. Shit.

My thoughts turn to Candice. Would she be okay about me leaving? She knows this is what I do, surely she wouldn't expect me to give up who I am to be with her. I'll have to sit down and properly talk this through, it's the first time I've stopped to consider how this is going to work. The main thing is, I want it to.

I wander upstairs, and my cocks twitching when I discover the bathroom doors unlocked. I enter and am instantly hard at the sight of my girl lying under the oily, cool water. I wish I could take her burns away, so she could use bubble bath and all the other girly things she deserves.

Her eyes light up as soon as she sees me. I'm mindful not to invade her personal space, so using all my willpower, I take a seat on the sink top.

"So, what's my angel up to today, then?"

"I'm gonna pop in on Mum and Dad then Rainy's meeting me for a girly day."

She seems to have forgotten her usual shyness and sits up to wash her hair revealing the most perfect rounded tits I've ever laid eyes on.

"I'll do that, I can't just sit here talking to you. I won't be able to resist you, and you know it."

I take the shower head and gently rinse the suds out of her hair letting it flow down her back. She lets out a relaxed moan as I work my fingers into her scalp. I gradually move the shower head along her shoulders and around to spray the warm water directly over her boobs.

I flip the switch. "Ahhh!" she squeals out as the ice cold water hits her nipples, making them stiff and hard.

I lean forward and bite down softly on one of her nipples sucking hard while spraying the other with ice cold water. She throws her head back in pleasure, and I flip the switch back to hot, moving the shower head under the water and close to her abdomen. Still fully dressed, I slip my arm into the water and reach down and cup her pussy before moving the shower to spray the hot jet straight onto her clit.

"Blake," she gasps out in surprise at the sensation, and I enter her with my fingers circling her inner walls, so wide and wet. I looked up to see pleasure seeping from her exquisite features, her wet hair matted and slicked back away from her face. Her lips are parted, and the room's filled with steam, although I'm careful not to let the water get too hot, or touch her where it would hurt.

"That's it, Candy, ride my fingers," I coax.

"Mmmhmmm." Shit, I'm so turned on at the sight of her that I swear my cock is going to explode. I move the heat and pressure of the shower head so close to her clit, it's practically touching and her hips buck in ecstasy.

"Give it all to me, baby." And she does. Riding out her orgasm in a wave of delight that has me needing to be inside her.

Standing only to rid of my clothes before I jump in the oversize tub with her, her face looks all flustered and completely fuckable. I sit down and pull her onto me, my cock sliding between her pressing right on her centre causing her to let out a moan. I take hold of her hips and guide her up and down my rock hard length, the sensation doing nothing to keep my building orgasm away.

"That's it, angel." Lifting her slightly, thrusting into her sweet pussy, even deeper.

"Fuck, Blake!" She feels so perfectly tight wrapped around my cock with water splashing everywhere. I silently thank the designer of my penthouse for installing this wet room.

"This view," I moan out at the sight of her riding me. Feeling like I am going to explode, I reach up and pinch her nipples, twisting them lightly. Her pussy tightens in response, squeezing and clamping down around me.

"Fuck, Blake, that feels so good." Sliding my hand around her neck and pulling her mouth onto mine, it feels as though she is kissing the air from my lungs. I continue my assault of her pussy thrusting harder and harder never breaking our lips apart. Reaching down and circling her sensitive spot with my thumb tips her over the edge, and with the next few thrusts we come apart in complete sync. Our bodies as one. Her ocean blue eyes locked on mine as we both fight to catch our breath.

CHAPTER TWENTY-FOUR

Candice

$\mathcal{J}$erry drops me outside my parents' house, and I pause for a second on the doorstep, allowing countless memories from my childhood to come flooding back to me. I let myself in with my key, like old times. It's Saturday morning, so I know they'll be in, Mum always cooks pancakes on Saturdays.

"Candice, is that you, honey?"

"No. I'm a burglar."

"Very funny. Get in here, girly. I've missed ya lately. Tell me you're staying for breakfast?"

"Of course I am." Dad pulls a chair out for me without looking up from his paper, and I take a seat going straight in with the big question skipping the chit chat.

"So, what do you think of Blake?"

Mum stops what she's doing. "Does it matter, sweetie."

"What do you mean, of course it matters, I really like him, Mum."

"I can tell, that's why I'm saying, it won't make any difference what we think, honey. If you like him, and he makes you happy, then nothing we say will make a difference. But, for the record, we think he's lovely, don't we, Stu." Dad pretends not to have heard.

"Dad?" He sets his paper down sighing.

"I don't wanna be the bad guy here, Candy, but much as I like Blake, the reality is, he's a soldier, and army boys never stay. I don't wanna watch you get your heartbroken, darlin'."

"He won't hurt me, I trust him. He won't leave me, either. I know it might not be forever, and I think about what happened to Marshy all the time. I know he could get snatched away in the same way at any time, but I don't care. I'd rather have everything with him for a short time than nothing at all. I think it's the real deal, Dad." I say, needing him to understand how serious I am about this. Dad places a hand over mine.

"There is no thinking involved when it's the real deal, Candy. When you know, you simply know. So, like your mum said, it really don't matter what anyone in the world thinks. If you're happy, and it feels right then you have to let your heart take over. The way I did when I met your mum and the way Marshall was with Evelyn. There's no second guessing involved. Love is only ever love, and if you're in love with this man then we would never stand in your way."

"He's right, Candy. All we ever wanted was for you and Marshall to be happy."

We all go quiet, the mention of my brother has everyone thinking about him. We miss him like we only just found out we lost him. I hug them both, one at a time, before sitting back down for breakfast, which is delicious, as always.

"What are you up to today, then. You not seeing Rainy as your back in town?"

"Of course I am. Actually, I've had an idea about doing a fundraiser, you know, for The Peace Centre. Mostly for the education side of things, I'm hoping to keep the morning school I set up going as some of the kids can't get to school in the day. They're too busy looking after their siblings, some are even working."

"It breaks your heart, doesn't it, Stu. I think a fundraiser is a great idea; let me know if there's anything we can do to help."

"Thanks, Mum, I will. Rainy's coming with me to look at venues today. I'm gonna rent somewhere out, and maybe have a charity auction, if I can get some of the local businesses to donate."

"That sounds perfect, I can start putting the word out when I'm doing my deliveries."

"Thanks, Mum."

"I'll be there, too, kiddo. Just give the details to your Mum when they come up."

"That's brill, Dad." I kiss him on the cheek before stepping outside where Jerry is still parked up waiting for me. I tap on the window, so he winds it down.

"I'm walking over to Rainy's, so you might as well go and do whatever else you do, take some time off or something." He looks at me like I'm speaking in another language.

"Even you must veg out sometimes, Jerry." I laugh.

"I'll be on standby, call me if you need me," he replies. He doesn't wait for a response, quickly winding the window up and speeding off.

"Bye then," I mutter through the glass, waving. He nods, and I give up with him and skip off towards Rainy's house just a short walk away along the river.

I catch sight of her sunbathing in a bright pink deck chair at the front of her house. She waves like mad when she sees me. I speed up a bit, and she jumps up to hug me.

"Hey Candy, you're looking gorgeous, as always."

"Thanks, Rayray. Speak for yourself, have you been working out? Your legs have disappeared." Her denim cut offs are almost indecent, and her legs look so shapely a twinge of jealousy overcomes me. It's been months since I worked out, but I'd never really needed to, I was always on my feet and our diet was minimal at the centre. I'd definitely made up for it since I've been back home. The amount of steak and fries Blake has fed me is unreal.

"So, a fundraiser?"

"Yes, I've already rang two places. I thought if we check them out this morning, and then we've got the afternoon for lunch and shopping."

"Perfect," she replies.

"Oh, and they're all here in Bourton, so I thought we'd ditch Jerry for the day and walk."

"Poor Jerry." She giggles.

"It's another gorgeous day though, isn't it? Let's eat lunch outdoors and pretend we're in Paris or someplace exotic."

"You're crazy." I laugh, and we head away from the river and into town.

The market place is packed as usual and full of the smells of fresh cooked foods and homemade bath products. We find the first place easily enough, but as we head towards it I get this weird feeling in my gut and I can't seem to shake it off. It's like someone's watching us. Teccina's is run down, and I can't picture any event has been held here in at least the last twenty years.

The next place is better. Jak's bar. It's a small cocktail bar, down one of the quieter side streets. It's a bit out of the way, but it's clean and modern inside.

"What do you think, Rayray, is it a goer?"

"I think we've found our place...Is it in budget?"

"Two hundred pounds over," I frown.

"Get Jack back in here, leave it to me." And as if right on cue, Jack reappears from the cellar.

"So, what dya think ladies." Rainy winks at me pulling out her phone.

"We think it's great, we just need to do the maths...Oh shoot."

She drops the phone and bends right over in front of Jack, shamelessly taking her time to bend down and pick it up. She pauses with her peachy ass in the air before spinning round and bringing herself face to face with his wide eyes and shocked face.

I can't watch, this girl cracks me up. I'm trying not to laugh as she bites her bottom lip before letting out a heavy sigh.

"The place is so great, Jack. Is is it yours?" His chest puffs out, she's playing him like fiddle.

"Yup, built it up from nothin' last summer."

"It's just, the event…" she unzips her hoodie revealing a huge amount of cleavage under a tight white vest top. "It's a charity night, you see. We were hoping you could give us mate's rates to help us out?"

His eyes are completely fixed on her chest, and I swear I just noticed his jeans shift slightly. I hold in my laughter as much as I can.

"Well, if it's for charity I can knock one hundred off. That any good?"

"You've got a deal. Thanks, Jack, pleasure doing business with ya."

"Anytime, babe, always happy to help."

"We'll be in touch with the details," I say as we hurry out before breaking down in fits of laughter outside. I squeeze my boobs together mimicking her pout.

"Oh Jack, we were hoping for mates rates." I jokingly say, and we fall apart laughing again.

Now we've moved away from the main shopping area and into the backstreets, and I'm reminded of the character in my home town by the graffiti covered walls.

"Would you look at this, some of this stuff's amazing."

"If you ask me, it's a bunch of kids with a spray can, but if you say it's good, I'll take your word for it."

"Mind if I hang on and take some photos, it's been ages since I've seen anything this good."

"Go for it. Shall I grab us a sandwich and meet ya in the square?" I'm already snapping away working my way further down the side of the building not wanting to miss anything.

"Thanks, Ray, see you in a sec."

There's something really painful behind the work. I'm guessing they've been sprayed by a girl as they're huge roses with intricate leaves, but everything's in black and white aside from the green thorns. The contrasts unreal, and I know I can Photoshop these and make them 3D with my new app. I've been dying to try it out. I stretch up to try and reach some of the higher stuff and notice a shadow appear in front of me on the wall.

Before I can react my phone goes flying out of my hand, and I'm shoved at full force into the wall. My forehead takes the impact and my knees crumble to the ground. My vision's blurry from the hit, but I throw my handbag away from me and attempt to cry for help, nothing comes out. I try to look up, but the sunlight dazzles my eyes, so I close them again, tasting blood that must be falling from my head.

I try to crawl away assuming whoever it is wants my phone and money, both of which they now have. Then what feels like a scratchy hessian sack is placed over my head, and I'm picked up.

I kick and scream as much as I can, but I'm right down the alley. I assume no one hears me because nobody comes, and I'm being placed in a vehicle next. I can hear the engine running when they put me in. "Help!" I scream but there's no response, only silence.

The material feels like it's tearing the skin on my forehead off, and everything I've been taught about survival situations flashes into my mind, but I can't act on any of it because: 1. I can't see. 2. The vehicles moving that fast. I'm being thrown from side to side with more force than I can handle.

I try and kick the tail lights out, like I read in a 'how to' emergency guide once. I've stopped screaming now as the sack's stealing my oxygen, and my chest is tight in panic. I feel like I can't breathe, and everything inside me is screaming get the fuck outta here, fast. We must have been travelling for what feels like hours and I'm still kicking when the doors open and someone grabs my legs dragging me from the car.

CHAPTER TWENTY-FIVE

Blake

*W*e've been trawling the local shops of Bourton on the Water all morning, in the hope of finding something unique for my girl.

"I'm just going to do it, Grey. Candice isn't one for all the mushy stuff, anyway."

"Don't be so easily fooled, bro. All chicks are into the mushy love stuff."

"Well, it won't even come to that if I can't find a decent ring to ask her with." Grey looks around spotting a tiny jewellers directly opposite us, over the market place.

"Keep the faith, bro." He reads my sceptical expression throwing the, "Don't judge a book by its cover," cliché at me.

I wanted something rare but not cheap or tacky, and I'd be surprised if there was a single diamond in this joint, but I step inside all the same. I'm impressed by the way the bell rings as we enter bringing an old school charm to the place.

We're greeted with a friendly smile, and it's obvious this jeweller knows a bit about business and the importance of the customer's first impression. Something tells me not to underestimate the old guy polishing silver behind the till.

I notice that although most of the pieces are Swarovski crystal, pearl and gemstones, the designs are rare, and I easily pick out three pairs of earrings that have Candice written all over them. A pair of moonstone ovals with a silver daisy dropping underneath. A set of freshwater pearls held in a lotus blossom twisted from white gold. And a pair of purple amethyst drop earrings, which are sparkly and long enough to be a statement piece, but modest enough for my girl to enjoy wearing.

I watch as he gift wraps them up in individual little boxes, another carefully thought out touch that doesn't go unnoticed, and I make a mental note to myself not to try and buy expensive things in a small market town. The two concepts are chalk and cheese. A bit like Grey and I standing here in our Armani jeans and Ralph Lauren polo's against the jewellers green corduroys and fleece jumper.

"You found everything you're looking for, sir?"

"Unfortunately, not," I admit. "I was looking for a ring."

"Any particular kind, sir?"

"It's Blake." I offer a handshake, which he meets with a firm grip. I'm not sure if he recognises me or not, if he does he doesn't give anything away.

"So, you're looking for a ring, you say." I nod.

"Wait here," he orders before disappearing into the back of

the shop, Grey rolls his eyes stepping outside, but I decide to hang fire, more out of courtesy than curiosity. He returns with a small box.

"This one's from my personal collection, I've been keeping a hold of it, but for the right lady, at the right price, I'll consider selling. He presents a huge blue sapphire with the clearest cut diamonds running along the band.

"White gold?" He looks offended.

"Platinum."

"I gotta admit, old man, I wasn't expecting you to pull this out of the bag!"

"You like it?"

"Actually, yeah, I really do."

"It's an Edwardian antique...2.5 carat, and you won't find clearer diamonds in any modern piece." He's marvelling to himself through a small magnifying glass rather than attempting to sell it to me. He doesn't need to, the piece sells itself anyway.

"It's perfect, I'll take it." He eyes me suspiciously.

"This girl, the one you're planning to ask, is she the love of your life?"

"She sure is. She's amazing."

"Okay." He nods.

"I know that look...used to have it in my own eyes." He places a hand on my shoulder. "Look after her, son."

"You can count on it," I reassure him handing my credit card over. I tuck the small boxed ring safe in my pocket and step out into the busy sidewalk.

G is chatting up some blonde waitress over at the market cafe. He never misses an opportunity! I listen in as I approach them, the blonde looking spectacularly pissed that I'm about to interrupt them.

"And this is my pal, Blake. So if you wanna bring a friend, I'm down with it."

"No need for the friend. I'm spoken for, but I'll take a black coffee no sugar, thanks." She rolls her eyes and sets about making my coffee.

"So, are we calling it a day. You know I've got your back, bro, but shopping isn't really my bag."

"I got one." I tap my jeans pocket like I'm carrying the world's best kept secret."

"No way...in that old place. Well now, what did I tell ya? I'm a fucking genius, ain't I?" I take a sip of my coffee, not giving him the satisfaction of being right, but he's not letting it slide that easily. "Come on, admit it, I'm the bomb! You wouldn't have even gone in there if I hadn't made you."

"Check it out." I pull the box out flipping the lid open and flashing the bright blue jewel in front of him.

"Oh my goooood." The waitress drops the coffee she had been about to serve me dead on the floor, and both G and I laugh out loud at her mortified expression.

"You think she'll like it?" I ask her holding the ring box open for her to see.

"Is it real?"

"Course it's real, what do you take me for?"

"Oh, I'm sorry, I just, I ain't never seen such a gorgeous jewel before, its huge! Wow. She's a lucky lady." Grey pats me on the shoulder.

"Damn straight she is. I can't believe you've gone and bought a fuckin' engagement ring, Blake, I never thought I'd see the day."

"Me neither, but if Candy wants me, then I'm all in. You know I don't half ass things, G."

"With Jason being the way he is, I feel like it falls to me to ask, you sure about this, bro? Like, marriage is a big deal, it's you know legal and all that shit."

"She makes me happy, Grey. For the first time in so long, for the first time since."

"Aimee," he chips in.

I repeat it back, "Aimee." It's probably the first time I've said her name without feeling physically sick.

"She must be one hell of a chick to tame my main man."

"She's fucking amazing, and you know I'm gonna be needing a best man, right?"

"Woah, woah, there." He nearly spits his coffee out. "You want me to, like, stand up, and be all official an' shit."

"Who else would I ask?"

Greyson beams at me and throws his arms around me pounding his fist into my back.

"You know I'll do it, thanks man. I, ya know, appreciate it. A whole day of you calling me the best, jeez, I wouldn't miss it for the world."

"Don't push it, G."

"Alright, I gotta split, bro, Am seeing the folks today, gotta pay them at least one visit before we head back out to the centre."

"Enjoy."

"Oh, that I will, you can't beat home food, can you?"

"Nah, I'll give you that, G, especially your mum's apple pie."

"See ya."

I shoot Jerry a text to pick me up. I've got the whole afternoon to myself so I decide to head into London, and put a few hours in at the office.

My dad is always saying I don't spend enough time there, and I know Candy will be another few hours yet. The traffic is fairly light, and we reach Regent Street in just under a couple of hours. Jerry drops me right outside, and I take the elevator up to my office, catching up on a few emails before surprising my dad.

I check his calendar and notice he's free before calling our favourite pizza place and ordering him a huge pizza, loaded with all our favourite toppings. I continue working through my emails until I receive a text to confirm it's been delivered. A few minutes later, I burst into his office and watch his face light up on sight of me.

"Son, you ordered our favourite. What are you doing here?"

"What, can't a guy have lunch with his old man?"

"It's good to see you, Blake. Come on lets gets stuck in, I'll never eat all this."

The pizza box almost covers his desk and I take a seat, tucking in to the best pizza in London, just like old times. When I was a kid, dad would always bring us into the office and order take out food together. It was our little secret as mum hated any kind of junk food, and would have gone mad if she'd have known.

When my dad was relaxed, there was no one better to spend time with, its just a shame it couldn't be like this all the time. He's a certified workaholic and while I respect him for his commitment, I wouldn't trade places with him for all the world.

CHAPTER TWENTY-SIX

Candice

a cold hand covers my mouth before he grabs my hands behind my back with his other hand. I'm too terrified to make a sound. My instincts kick in, and I bite down hard.

"Fuck, you little bitch."

That voice, I recognise his voice from somewhere. He pulls his hand away only to wrench my hands tighter up my back and slams his knee into my stomach. I fall to the ground and everything grows quiet. He carries me, kicking as hard as I can, in an attempt to break free and then drops me to the ground.

I recognise that scent of citrus and weed, and my gut feelings are confirmed as I lay here, my cheek pressed to the ground. I know he's still nearby as there have been no footsteps since he doubled me over. I frantically try to place him.

Mustering everything I have, I attempt a calm tone. My erratic breathing and uncontrollable shaking making me voice sound alien, even to me.

"Jason, I know it's you. You don't have to do this..." Silence. "Whatever has happened with Blake, I'm sure we can work it out. He is your brother, after all."

"Arrrrgh!" A sharp kick in my side causes me to yelp out. "Jason please." He takes the sack off my head, and my eyes struggle to adjust to the light, even though it's dim in the room. It's dusty, but it looks like an old bar of some kind.

A slap stings the side of my face, and a blindfold is placed over my eyes. Jason yanks it tightly around my head. I think about all the shit my brother would have endured during his time in the army. Like, Marshy, I'm made of stronger stuff. I'm not just going to give up that easily.

I gag as a wide piece of tape is slammed over my mouth. Panic fills me at the sensation of the air being snatched from me, and my nostrils struggled to adjust and take in enough oxygen to keep me from passing out.

"Oh, we can sort it out, you fucking whore. We *will* sort it out." My breathing is shallow now, and the pain in my side immense. My burns are still healing, and I feel like I'm ripping apart at the seams. "Tonight, I take what's mine. Fucking brother. You think a brother would screw me over the way he has. NO Candice."

A loud crash, I guess he's kicked something over behind me.

"Eighteen years of this bullshit. Me in the shadows pouring blood into the business while he, what, shags around and fucks off to the army for years at a time." Even in my terrified state a knot twists in my stomach when I hear 'shags around.' As if reading my thoughts, he answers my burning question in a way that rots me to the core.

"You're wondering why you're here aren't you, Candice, or is it Candy he calls you?" Bile rises up in my throat as my name passes his lips.

"You, my girl, are Blake's most cherished possession, and that makes you mine. It's all mine. First I'll take you, then his share of the business, then his father."

I scream out as he removes the blindfold, and I come face to face with the most terrifying pair or thunder cast eyes and twisted face I have ever seen. I screw my eyes shut, I can't bear to look. Seeing him this way was realisation that he meant what he planned and to follow through with his threats, and the thought filled me with dread.

"Open your eyes, bitch." Another slap. He rips the tape from my mouth.

"Blake," his name escaping my lips in a broken cry.

"Oh, I see you want Blake, do you? Everyone wants a piece of Blake, don't they Candice? Well, I think that's a great idea. Let's get him on the phone. He clicks his fingers, and for the first time it dawns on me that we are not alone. A familiar outline makes its way towards us.

"Tiffany," I gasp, more confused than ever. I thought she had squared things with Blake.

She hands Jason an IPad and shows me Blake's name across the dial page saying in a cold tone, "You're up, bitch."

The IPad is held in front of me, and I know if he answers this is going to kill him. I am desperate for him not to pick up and avoid the horror that this will cause him, but equally frantic to see his face. He's my only hope, but god knows how he will find me. Even with the blindfold off, I have no idea where I am.

"Candy." his face freezes in terror, his eyes loaded with questions, but knowing there's no time. "Stay calm, angel, I'm on my way."

"Blake, I don't know where I am," I wrasp, close to tears, but still refusing to give in to them.

"It doesn't matter where you are, who the fuck has got you, Candy."

Before I can reply, Blake is snatched away, and my panic heightens instantly as if losing sight of him is losing hope of ever getting out of here. I know my chances of escaping unscathed are slim, so I need to be clever about this.

My strength is restoring after the kicks to the floor, but I won't let them know that. I scan the room hurriedly, the door was over on the other side. The bar appears to derelict and looks like it has not long closed as all the dirty glasses were still on the tables. There's my weapon, now just to get to it. Not yet, it was too risky.

"Jason, you bastard. I fucking knew it," Blake screams down the line, I'd never seen him lose his shit like this before. Now, I'm even more worried. If Blake's that scared, then I'm in even more danger than I first thought.

"You fucking take this up with me, Jase. I swear to god, you touch one hair on her pretty little head, and I will kill you." His threat is filled with promise and gives me hope, but it doesn't seem to bother Jason.

A slow smirk spreads across his face filling me with dread as he calmly replies, "You won't get to us in time, Blake, you're too late. Even your fucking perfect ass can't win them all, kid. Don't worry, you're not gonna miss out; you'll get to watch all the action from right where you're standing. He clicked his fingers again.

"Tie her up, Tiff." She obliges, and although I fight her off as much as I can, two on one is too much, and my arms are soon tied behind my back. I'm forced to sit upright in a chair; all I can do is watch what is unfolding in front of me. A bystander in my own personal horror movie. Except, unfortunately for me, this shit is real life.

He nods to Tiffany, and she withdraws a gun. Fuck.

I try to run, but he kicks me from behind causing me to fall face first into the bar table in front of me. I stumble to my knees trying to get up.

"Blake, please help me." I can see his face in the screen as Jason lets the IPad dangle from one hand and begins undoing his belt with the other.

"Oh, no. Please don't do this," I beg. My eyes darting towards Tiffany trying to make eye contact, and get her attention.

She's gone. Her eyes are dark and her expression distant. It's like she's a million miles away, but she keeps the pistol still pointing directly at my face.

He unzips his pants and grabs hold of my chin, forcing my head around to watch as he pumps his revolting length up and down. The tip is inches away from my face.

"You're going to enjoy this, you filthy slut." I scrunch my eyes shut, and he spits in my face.

"Open your eyes, I've heard you screaming in pleasure for him. Now's your time to scream for me, girl."

Tiffany takes a step forward, and I notice Blake has disappeared, but quickly look away from the IPad, not wanting anyone to realise he is on his way for me. I am confident I'm getting out of here alive, but in what state, I have no idea.

"You enjoying this, bro?" He trailed a finger along my lips making me shudder, and then slowly he traces down towards my bra before ripping through the strap of my dress and bra leaving me exposed and ashamed.

I flinch at his touch, which only appears to piss him off more.

"We're doing this, and like I said, you're going to enjoy it, Candice. I'll show you a better time than that prick ever has."

"Impossible," I croak. Ouch. He grabs my jaw, squeezing it tightly.

"I'm gonna shove my cock so far down your throat, you won't be able to say shit like that again, for a long time. First, I need to get to know you better. Take off her pants, Tiff, I wanna see how wet she is for me."

Tiffany hesitates but steps forward. I squirm in the chair, aware of the gun still pointing directly at me. She manages to wriggle my panties off from under my camisole dress, and I feel my cheeks burn flame red.

I clamp my legs as tight as I can and await the horror of his touch, but he stands back looking amused. His disgusting cock is still in his hand while he slowly pumps up and down.

"Wow, I can't take that from my, so called brother, he's certainly got good taste, that pussy looks fit to fuck." Tiff draws in a breath.

"Please don't do this," I beg. "I won't ever speak about this if you let me go."

"Touch yourself, Candice...and don't be thinking of him, look at my hard cock and imagine me inside you. Go on, get wet for me."

"Never!" I shout in his face the volume surprising all three of us.

"Very well. Tiff, get her wet for me, baby. Go on; touch her like I showed you how to. She falters, his face scowling at her. "Do it." He leans close to my ear and inhales loudly.

"Mmmm, you smell so good. Screw it. I'm tired of waiting. I'll take you dry if I have to, and he bites down on my ear harshly causing me to scream out. He wrestles me to the floor, and I continue to fight him off until my weak body is pinned down underneath him, and his hands are clasped around my throat.

He pulls back about to thrust straight into me, when Tiffany lets out a deafening squeal.

Blake

I'm just finishing up in my office, ready to leave for the day when my phone rings. I don't recognise the number at first, but I know her voice as soon as I answer.

"Blake."

A single word that changes the whole mood of the world around me to black. My chest tightens and joints stiffen as I see the face of my angel, terrified and tied to a chair. It takes a few seconds to register what I'm seeing is real and not straight from some horror movie that my mind's making up. Then I hear his voice. Jason. My first thoughts? I'll. Fucking. Destroy. Him. I desperately try to make out where they are and finally notice an old wall hanging.

There's only one place I've ever seen that piece of art in all of London. I remember buying it from a street art seller in Camden years back. It cost buttons, but somehow the words, 'Just Breathe', were striking against the backdrop of the ocean crashing into the shore.

Ironic, as I can barely breathe now, and I'm feeling choked. I wink at Candice, a silent signal of reassurance before dropping the phone and running faster than my legs can carry me. I'm like a sniffer dog latched onto a scent and nothing can deter me.

My minds racing back through the years, rewinding on speed mode back to where it all began. 'Mokita's'. I turn the corner of Regent Street and onto Piccadilly Circus, almost crashing into someone. A black cab passes, but I don't bother trying to flag it down. I know how grid locked the traffic can get; I'll be with her quicker on my feet. I hold button 1 down, speed dialling Jerry and almost drop the phone I'm running so fast.

"You remember Mokita's?"

"That the old place down by..." I cut him off.

"Get there now, and bring the cops... and a goddam ambulance," I add grimly before hanging up.

Mokita's was the first deal Jase and I had done together. Dad had set everything up when I'd just turned eighteen. Insistent on making me wait until I was adult before letting me enter his world of planning and scheming and landing million pound deals, as easily as Usain Bolt runs a marathon.

We'd built it up from a derelict burnt out shell and put everything we had into making it London's trendiest cocktail bar.

And for three years, it was. We were a good team, and we were turning over a fat profit, but that hadn't been enough for Jason. Always greedy and hungry for more, his shitty decision to push cocaine and any other drug he could get his hands on behind the scenes landed us in a ton of shit.

The cops shut the place down in an early morning lockdown. Luckily, there'd only been Jay and a few of his mates there, but the press were still all over it. Or they would have been, if Dad hadn't paid for their silence in a trade for free interviews with himself and the rest of us at their beckon call for two years. He'd thrown us all into the spotlight, and I pinned every hope of a normal life I had on the army contract I signed just days later.

I never shirked the responsibility for what happened, and we never spoke about it again, but we all knew Jason could have cost Laine Corporations their reputation that night, and we also knew Dad blamed him entirely. He knows I've never touched that shit, while Jase had been shovelling god knows what up his nose since high school. Jesus, had he really harboured and lived with the resentment all these years?

I reach Mokita's, which is exactly as I remember, except the once glossy sign we'd had custom made over the door had turned rusty, and the paint is peeling off the once purple door. I opt for the side entrance knowing it's my best chance of getting to her without being noticed straight away.

I charge up the narrow alleyway that runs alongside the old bar and realise the door is disguised behind a load of old, but full, keg barrels. Probably full of nothing but rainwater now, rather than beers and cider, but that didn't mean they weighed any less.

I heave them out of the way letting them roll down the street and waste no time pissing around with the door.

By recollection, I know the locks aren't great on the old cellar door and use this to my advantage booting the keyhole with everything I have. It falls open straight away, clanging like a swinging garden gate.

I know they'll have heard the bang, and the adrenaline pulsing through my veins, a thick heartbeat full of dread. *I'll fuckin' kill him.*

The odds are in my favour from my army training, but I know this time the ball's in his court. He's got the one thing that matters to me more than anything. Candice is more important to me than my own life, and he goddam knows it. That's what he'll be planning, the scheming little troll, a life for a life. He knows I'll trade places with her in a heartbeat, I think, as I creep along the corridor following the sound of her voice crying...begging.

"Please no."

Her sweet voice filled with terror cuts pulls so fiercely on my heart strings that I'm in physical pain. The horror scene before me, catches me off guard as I see Jason with his dick in his hand and Candy with her legs forcibly spread and her hands tied behind her. Her eyes widen to saucers as she sees me before either of them do.

What the fuck is Tiffany doing here? I have no idea, but the fact that she's staring through me like a deer in headlights with a 44 Magnum Revolver pointed straight at my head does not go unnoticed.

For a moment, everything freezes and no one even flinches, like someone has pressed pause at the peak moment in a Liam

Neeson movie. Tiff lets out a deafening squeal and Jason simply smirks in response.

"Well, well, it looks like we have company. Nice of you to join us Blake."

He signals to Tiffany, "Stand down, Tiff," he watches first. "If he moves, even an inch, then you shoot the bastard's balls off." She nods, but doesn't move a muscle.

He's working her like a puppet on strings. Jason lunges forward to attempt to rape my angel, and I dive towards my girl knowing Tiffany won't shoot me. Despite Jason's best attempts, she's still in love with me.

A loud sound I know all too well as a gunshot, fills the room, and I realise it's not me who's hit. Candice's screams have gone silent. Jason's body is lying motionless on top of my angel. "No. Shit. No. You've killed her, Tiffany. What have you done?"

I am too shell shocked to move. Even all my specialist army training doesn't kick in as it should do. I can't lose her, I just can't.

Tiff doesn't respond, she just stands there in the exact same position. She's eerily still, aside from the tears streaming down her face. I pick Jason up to throw him off my girl, I need to see the bullet hole. I won't believe this is real until I see it with my own eyes. I know it's doubtful, but there may still be time to save her.

Warm blood oozes over my hand as I lift him off Candy, and that's when I realise, my brother is the one who's been shot. I check for a pulse not caring if I find one or not. There's a faint one, but I doubt he'll make it.

I flip him over and off my girl. Underneath his crumpled body, I find Candice completely out of it. I untie her and lay her lifeless body on the ground in emergency position and tear my t-shirt off placing it over her to keep her from going into shock.

The emergency services take over and everything is out of my hands. Everything except, Candice, I'll never let go of her again. Tiffany doesn't even flinch when they arrest her. I watch them pry the gun out of her hands. She doesn't even react and is clearly in a state of shock as they place the cuffs on her.

I hope they throw away the fucking key. Jason is placed on a stretcher and carried out. They seem to take forever to see to Candice, and she's coming around now, her eyes flickering wildly.

The main thing is that she's alive, and I'm going to make sure she is okay. Whatever it takes.

CHAPTER TWENTY-SEVEN

Candice

The last thing I recall is the sound of the gunshot, and now I'm lying in a hospital bed with all my favourite people, and I'm completely freaking out. I can't help comparing it to when I first woke up after the bomb and all those horrible feelings of dread and fear come gushing back over me. It's like I'm caught in a tidal wave of doom, and my body tenses up reactively.

I'm only mildly reassured when everyone around me appears calm and serene, and the reality that I'm okay and have survived that horrific turn of events starts to kick in.

"God, I hate these places when I'm the one whose ill."

Even to me, me voice sounds alien. Dry and croaky, I cough and try to clear my throat. My dad gives me a sympathetic nod in agreement, and Blake looks amused.

"Now you know how I felt cooped up in the centre when you

first found me. Now I get a chance to look after you," he winks playfully.

"Why do I need looking after?" I'm panicking now.

"What's happened to me, Blake? Dad?" Why's everyone grinning when I'm laying here feeling like death warmed up. Before anyone responds, I'm sick over the side of the bed and all over Blake's spanking new Lanvin sneakers. He takes hold of my hand.

"You're okay, angel. You passed out from the trauma. The doctor will be along in a sec to explain better, but there's something else I want you to hear from me first." He smiles. It's another, I-love-you smile and relief washes over me.

"We're having a baby, Candy. Your eight weeks pregnant."

I stare blankly, registering what he just said. He cups my face, planting gentle kisses all over my cheeks and forehead.

"We're having a baby, my angel. That's why you feel so sick." I still don't respond, my hand creeps to my tummy, thoughts of the gunshot run through my mind. He's read my thoughts like always.

"Tiffany fired the shot, baby. She hit Jase. He's been charged too and is going to be locked up for a fucking long time."

"And Tiffany?" I can't help asking.

"She's getting the help she needs to sort her shit out. She's locked up, too, in some psych ward. The woman had major issues long before any of this. Your safe, angel, and I'm not taking my goddam eyes off your sexy ass again. Ever."

Dad purposefully clears his throat. "Sorry, Pops, but it's the truth," Blake clamps a friendly hand on his shoulder, and I watch as Dad covers it with his own.

"I'll hold you to that, son." I let the ocean of tears I've been holding back wash over my face. I'm exhausted and nauseous but relieved to be here with Mum, Dad and, especially, my Blake. I love him so much.

He doesn't leave my side for the next couple of days and caters to my every need. A constant stream of flowers, chocolate and magazines arrive at my bedside, and he even has my mum bring me my own pillow and duvet.

He's spoiling for me and for once, I don't complain. I feel weak, and vulnerable and like I need to be looked after.

After two days resting up in the hospital, I'm sitting on the edge of the hospital bed, my hands resting on my tummy, I jump slightly, when the door knocks and the doctor enters my room. "All set for home, Miss Embers?"

"I'm so ready." I nod.

"I've prescribed you some folic acid, and be sure to book in with your burns consultant to discuss any extra care you might need in the later stages of your pregnancy." He shakes my hand. "And good luck to you, miss, it's not often we have people held at gunpoint walking away completely unharmed. Your one of the lucky ones."

"She's a little firecracker, Doctor, and so is this little flame." Blake places his hand over mine, protectively covering my flat tummy, and offers his handshake with the other.

"Thank you for everything, Doctor." The Doctor looks a little surprised but smiles before turning abruptly and rushing out hurriedly to sort my discharge papers.

"So, if it's okay with everybody, I'd like to take Candy back to my place tonight?" Mum looks a bit disappointed.

"Is that what *you* want, darling?" Oh god, this is uncomfortable, I don't wanna disappoint anyone. Dad smiles.

"Just go, Candice, your mother has enough to do looking after me, I'll keep her busy. I haven't been feeling right for a few days." He winks at me.

"I think I'm coming down with man flu. Get me home, will ya, love, and get the coffee machine, this hospital espresso ain't got nothing on yours."

"You cheeky, sod, I know exactly what you're playing at, and it ain't happening. I'll take you home alright, but *you* can fetch the coffees yourself while I put my feet up and brush up on my crochet skills...I'm gonna need a refresh before the little one arrives."

Dad huffs dramatically making us all laugh. Mum squeezes me tight.

"Love you, Candy. I'll be round tomorrow with some home cooked meals that'll get your strength up now that you're eating for two!"

"There's no need for you to drive all in the way into the city."

"Just you try and keep me away."

"Congratulations to you both," Dad said seeming genuinely happy. "Obviously, Stu for a boy?" Mum swats him away.

"Pack it in, you, you're worse than your mother was." I gave them one last big hug.

"Thanks for everything. I love you both so much."

"We love you, too," Dad replies before passing Mum a hanky to wipe her tears.

I watch them walk down the corridor as far as I can before they disappear, and I'm lost in my own thoughts of how lucky I am to have such great parents, and how much they support me at every hurdle. I hope I can be half the parents they are one day. Blake invades my thoughts again by placing his hand gently on top of my tummy.

"I can't believe we're going to be parents, Candy."

"I know." I smile up at him.

"Thank you so much for choosing me, angel. I don't deserve you, but now that I have you, I promise I'll never let you go, and I'll always protect you and our little flame." He leans down to kiss me, and I wrap my arms around his neck weakly.

"I love you, Blake. Take me home?"

"With fucking pleasure," he growls scooping me up and carrying me out of the ward and all the way outside where Jerry's waiting patiently.

Back at the apartment the moods slightly estranged between us as we disappear into our own heads, both anxious about the unknown. I'd never even considered a baby, until now. These past few months, it feels like my life has been one crazy roller coaster that I've been riding hard. Even though I wasn't prepared to fall for someone and consider having a serious relationship, I wouldn't change a minute of it.

Blake snuggles me up on the sofa, and I flick on the tv, quickly flitting between channels. He takes the remote from my hand and turns it back off so we're sitting in silence.

"We don't need all that shit, baby, let's talk things through." So we do. My mum always told me that men aren't like women.

"They're not wired the same," she says. When a man wants to talk, you should take the time to listen. There's no hidden agenda with a man, so don't second guess them, just take what they say as face value.

"Are you happy, angel? You seem a little off?"

"I'm overjoyed," I answer honestly.

"But I am feeling a little overwhelmed, aren't you? I mean, it's a baby!"

"Our baby," he corrects me, and the words coming from his soft low voice make me smile.

"Our baby," I repeat. "I can't believe it all, it's kind of surreal."

"It sure is a surprise," he agrees. "But it's the best one I ever had."

"Me too," maybe surprises aren't so bad after all."

"I love you, Candice. I'm gonna spend the rest of my life making you happy, and taking care of you and our baby.

Blake

She's looking up at me all wide eyed and beautiful, and tears begin to fall down her sweet cheeks.

"What about Jas..."

"Shhh, baby, don't you even mention his name, he's gone. You're safe now."

"But he was your brother, I know what it's like to lose a brother."

"That bastard stopped being my brother a long time ago, Candy. He's a fucking deadbeat no one, who doesn't give a shit about anyone but himself. He's no one's loss, he made his choices."

Jeez, clearly I said the wrong thing cos' now she's eyeing me like I'm some cold hearted monster. I run my hands through my hair in frustration.

"Fuck, Candice, you think this is the same. You think losing that scumbag is the same as losing your brother?" Even she can see there's no comparison, and she shakes her head and breaks down in tears.

"He's not dead, not that I'd care if he was, he's just banged up. He tried to kill you, angel. I'll never forgive him for that. Plus, if they find the evidence, there's conspiracy to kill my dad, too. He's a sicko, baby."

I can tell she's completely overwhelmed by all this, and I silently scoop her up and let her snuggle into me as I carry her to our bed and lay her down as gently as I can, like she'll break if I touch her too harshly.

To me, her lithe body with my child inside is comparable to a million pound glass ornament, and for the next seven months, I would protect it as such. She weakly lifts her arms, and I follow her signal, peeling the fresh nightie her mum had bought her up over her head and tossing it to the floor.

It's only recently that my woman is okay with undressing around me, and now here she is, in all her naked glory. It's easily the most amazing sight of ever laid eyes on. I'm at a loss and instantly hard, torn between jumping on her and taking every inch of her for my pleasure, and hers, too. Or option two, which I plump for. I quickly undress, hoping she will feel more at ease if I'm naked, too, and hoping my raging hard on doesn't startle her. I don't want her to think I'm expecting anything from her after everything she's been through.

I snuggle in beside her, flipping her softly onto her side so I'm spooning her and almost melt into her. The feeling of her flesh on mine is such a turn on, and I gently run a flat palm over her thigh and up along her side and round to gently cup her breast. She places a hand over mine making me squeeze her tit tighter, and I pull away knowing she's not ready. I wrap my fingers round hers so we're holding hands.

"Don't," she whispers.

"Don't treat me like I'm broken."

"Candice, I..." She takes my finger up to her mouth and presses her lips against it.

"Shhh, Blake, no talking, I need you to make me forget."

Jesus, she's crying again, the sound perforates my ears against the silence. I gently sweep up her hair and kiss the nape of her neck. She lets out a small, anguished moan,

"Please, Blake, take it all away."

Kissing across the top of her shoulder and then deep into her neck, sliding my hand down her side and over her bum, landing gently on her inner thigh. Parting her legs slightly, I waste no time in pressing a fingertip just inside her. The sensation of warm, stickiness confirms she's ready for me and a need to make her feel safe takes over.

I let my cock follow the magnetic force that has me bursting inside her with one steady movement. I lift her leg high into the air, allowing me all the access I need to thrust deeper into her. She cries out, and I'm not sure if it's in pain or pleasure.

"Angel?"

"Don't stop, Blake, I need to feel something that's real." I squeeze her ankle tighter, pushing her leg slightly higher and push myself into her again.

My mind's telling me to be gentle, but my body's natural reaction to Candice is not allowing me to show any mercy. I roll her over onto her stomach, still tightly inside her, and guide her to the edge of the bed, her fingers curling over the edge of it.

"Hold on, like this," I instruct her, my voice low with desire.

"I'm going to make us both forget about anything other than us." I hold myself up on one arm and use my other to lift her hips up towards me, and this time I enter her brutally, pounding her over and over, tilting her hips higher and her fingers turn pale clutching the bed covers.

At first she's crying out every time, and even though, I know I'm not hurting her, I can barely stand the sound of it. Each merciless thrust has her cries growing quieter, and only when they're silent do I let up on her and fall to my elbows and slow our pace to a gentle grinding.

She's attempting to take over now, her hungry pussy missing the hard, fast thrusts, and I watch as her perfect ass circles upwards, riding me from underneath. Her slick walls squeezing around me and pulling me in as tightly as she can, the feeling is almost more than I can bear, but watching it is the biggest turn on of all. I pull back my hand and place a gentle slap on her bum cheek. I pull my hand back and slap her ass cheek.

"Ahhh," she's surprised but carries on circling my cock with that beautiful ass getting higher each time.

I slap her again, a little harder this time drawing my name from her lips.

"Blake," she gasps.

"Take it, I'm all yours." I grab her sweet cheeks and force them to move faster while pushing myself deeper into her. I slap her again, harder this time and the sight of my white handprint against a red circle over her ass is my undoing. I squeeze her cheeks tightly.

"Give it to me, angel, Give it all to me."

"Blake," a peaceful quiet moan from her lips as we both find our release, and I fall to the side of her. I pull her tightly into my arms revelling in the feel of her wet pussy still throbbing around me.

"Love you, Blake," her words given so freely crumple me, and a knot twists in my stomach.

"I love you too. I have loved you since the minute I laid eyes on you, in Bor, you were mesmerising. You're mine, Candice Embers. You always will be." I plant a kiss on her shoulder and she turns around and curls into me. We fall asleep wrapped in each other's arms.

When she wakes I've already made her breakfast. She's eating for two now, and I'm gonna make damn sure she doesn't miss a single meal. I pour out a glass of smooth fresh orange and add it to the tray before climbing the stairs in slow motion trying not to drop anything.

This is the second time I've ever made breakfast for anyone, and I wonder whether I'm becoming one of those soppy melts G and I always take the piss out of when we're on tour. The kind of guys who cry when they get a letter from home, or sleep with it under their pillow.

My concerns fade away on sight of her, and I pause in the doorway taking in the sight of her tangled blonde waves spread over the pillow. She's kicked the duvet off and is wearing my t-shirt from yesterday, which would have been covering her modesty, if she wasn't lying on her side with her ass in the air.

I tiptoe across to place the tray upon the sideboard and decide not to wake her; she probably needs the sleep more than a full English right now. She wakes, and her eyes ping bright as she reaches up, stretching wide.

"Oh my goodness, is that for me?" She eyes the tray beaming.

"It certainly is. Morning, gorgeous."

"Morning, gorgeous, to you." The doorbell rings.

"I'll get it."

"Wait, I'll go. You're not even decent." But she's already running down the stairs. "Easy, baby, it's cool, you can get it. Just slow down."

"Oh my god, Blake, look at these, they're simply beautiful."

"So are you." She takes the huge bunch of blue and lilac roses I had specially dyed for her and smells them before placing them down on the table and running towards me. She jumps up at me, and I catch her, spinning her round and place a kiss on her nose.

"Thank you, that was so sweet of you."

"Now, breakfast?"

"Breakfast."

"You got me a gift, too?" She picks up the brown paper package and unties the rustic string by wrapping around it with her teeth, making me want to take her again, here and now.

"It's to keep you busy while you're resting." I emphasise the 'rest' syllable in the hope she takes note.

"Wow, it's so thoughtful of you; you have to stop spoiling me, though."

"Never," I answer truthfully loving the way her eyes lit up when she saw the paint by numbers set I had made for her. Wait until she completes it, she's going to freak out. I'm so excited, I want to shove the paintbrush in her hand and force her to paint it in right now just to see her reaction, but I know surprising her will be worth the wait.

I shove a piece of toast in her mouth playfully, and we climb back into bed while she eats, and I enjoy the sight of her in my t-shirt.

"So, the fundraiser...You still wanna go ahead with it? No one would bat an eye if you were to cancel, Candy. You've been through a hell of a..." She places her breakfast tray down and hits me over the head with a pillow.

"Course, I want to go ahead, silly, it's took weeks of planning, and I'm not letting all those people down. Plus, the centre could really use the money. It's like, one last thing I can do for them before, you know." Her eyes widen, and she's grinning at me.

"Yes, angel, I know."

"Our fresh start." She smiles.

I press my forehead against hers and whisper, "Us and our baby."

"And that's not all." She's still smiling all excitable, could this be the hormones the doctor mentioned already kicking in?

"It's not?"

"Nope, I've been meaning to tell you since, well I don't know. It all kind of came to me when I was going through, erm, what happened."

"What did, what are you planning in that pretty little head of yours now?"

"I'm going back to school, well technically, college, but

education," she babbles excitedly, "I'm going to study health care and become a proper nurse."

Oh god, she looks so happy, but she can't be serious, can she? My wife, the mother of my child, a college student.

"Baby, you won't need to work or anything. I know you don't like to think about it, but we're rich, as in filthy rich. You don't need to do anything, you will just be here, with me and the baby."

"Excuse me? I most certainly will not." She crosses her arms moodily. "That's not me at all, and you know it. I want to help people, I never had the power as a volunteer, not like Julie. If I train, I'll be a proper nurse. I could really make a difference. Stop making out like we're so different, we're both fighting for the same cause here, Blake. Innocent people are losing their lives, and I can never imagine not trying to save them just the same as you. Don't you see, that buzz you get when you manage to save even one life is the exact same one I do."

"Okay, okay calm down. I'm not saying I won't support you. I'm trying to protect you."

"Well, I don't need protection," she spits out sulkily. "That's something we'll never agree on." She looks completely crestfallen, and her eyes gloss over with a shine of fresh tears about to fall.

"I want to do this, Blake. It's like for the first time, I've really found my purpose, please don't ask me to give it up."

"You know I wouldn't, but it's not just, you now."

I place a flat palm on her slightly swollen abdomen to make the point, and again with this girl, I'm in unchartered territory. Compromising is not a skill I've ever needed before, when your heir to a multimillion pound business you don't have to agree on shit. I'm in the lucky position that anyone and everyone agrees with my point of view, and if they don't to start with, they are easily persuaded at the sniff of a few hundred pound bills flashed in their direction.

Candice is almost the only person to say no to me. Aimee had the exact same annoying habit of being totally unphased by my millions, and it drove me crazy, while endearing me all at once. I soften my voice slightly; I don't want her to think I'm trying to control her life, like she has to change to be with me.

"Will you, at least, consider taking a regular nursing job? You can still save lives here in London, you know, you don't have to be on the frontline to find people who need your help."

A single tear slides down her cheek, and her voice breaks as she replies, "I feel like I'm leaving Marshall behind by staying."

"Baby, he's your brother, he will always be with you." She breaks down.

"I don't wanna fight with you."

"Hey, it's okay, Candy, I've got you." I pull her in close, holding her tight in my arms and stroking her hair in an attempt to calm her. She really is a firecracker at times, there was no point trying to convince her to quit nursing.

I knew from the moment I met her she would never be happy to settle as a housewife, but as long as I have her in my arms every night, I don't care. Nothing else matters more than having her with me every day for the rest of my life. I'm not fully myself without her, so if she wants to complete a nursing course, then I'll support her every inch of the way. Her eyes narrow, and I can almost see her brain ticking over as she pokes a finger in my chest.

"One more thing, Mr. Laine, don't you dare trample this with your flashiness and millions. I fill out my application and get a normal place at a normal college and study the same way any other girl my age would."

I grab her finger and place it into my mouth, dragging it back out slowly between my teeth. I know it drives her crazy.

"There's nothing normal about you, Candy."

"Ugh." She rolls her eyes but smiles as I pull her lips to mine and kiss her fiercely, our tongues colliding with a burning desire for one another that's always there when we touch. A sharp, electric type current that flushes through our entire bodies, flicking an invisible switch whenever we're skin on skin.

CHAPTER TWENTY-EIGHT

Candice

*A*s we pull up outside Jak's, ready for the fundraiser that's taken a small army of us to organise, it's weirdly quiet, and I panic in case no one comes. I need this to be a success, it's, like, closure for me and Marshall. I'm not expecting to make thousands, but a few hundred pounds would make a real difference in keeping the centre going.

Blake gets out of the car quickly moving round the back to open my door, he takes my hand and I'm so excited. As we walk inside, my hand in his, I see all my family and friends clapping and cheering. Blake twirls me around before applauding me himself, and for once, I don't mind being the centre of attention. The atmosphere's unreal, everyone I hoped would turn up is here. The walls are covered in huge photos taken by me and Sally of the children at the Peace Centre, laughing and grinning at the camera.

I spot Sal in the crowd and mouth, "Thank you," to her, I can't believe she made it.

The auction starts promptly with Blake acting as the auctioneer. He's at home with the authority and is a vision in his navy blue suit. I picture myself wearing his white shirt when we eat breakfast tomorrow, and my tummy flutters at the thought.

"First up, we have a make-over day offered by the fabulous Luxe beauty salon. I can see a few tonight who would benefit from this, so don't be shy ladies." I shake my head, scowling at him before everyone shares a laugh. I let him off, only that cheeky smile could get away with a comment like that. He's unbelievable! I start the bidding by shouting,

"Twenty pounds," Rainy immediately counters me.

"Twenty-five," she shouts, and we enter into a bidding war counting up in five's. The competition is on. Rainy is the only person in this room who loves Luxe as much as me.

Then a shriek travels from the back of the room, "A hundred and fifty pounds."

"Oh my god, Mum." I laugh, she hasn't had her hair done in years!

"Soooold to the beautiful lady at the back of the room for one hundred and fifty pounds. Thank you Ma'am. Next up, we have a collection of silver pearl earrings from The Velvet Box."

Myself and Rainy chip in again, but this time more people are joining in. I'm jumping up and down in excitement, handing everyone flutes of champagne, kindly donated by Laine Corporations.

There must have been at least seventy people here, and I can't believe how generous everyone has been. Blake's doing a great job, and I can't wait to thank him in kind when we're on our own later. His next words have my hair standing on end, and my body freezes.

"Next, and for our final auction, I'd like to welcome a guest auctioneer to host this very special collection. Please put your hands together for Mr. Stuart Embers.

Everyone clapping and dad's face is going red and blotchy. He's emotional. What's going on? A curtain I hadn't noticed earlier drops down, unveiling my paintings for everyone to see. I can feel his eyes burning into me, but I can't bring myself to look at him. My mind's racing, how did he know about my paintings?

I can hear the crowd all oohing and wowing, and my dad speaks next, "I would like to thank my daughter, Candice, for putting together this wonderful night that allows us all to share in the success of the Peace Centre in Bor. I know all the money raised tonight will be put to good use, which is why I'm starting the bidding for these spectacular paintings at five hundred pounds. My Candice has done a fantastic job bringing us all together tonight, and I am so very proud of her. Most of you here tonight will know that she is an absolute firecracker, and I wanted to take the chance to thank her for making all of us think about others around the world, who are not so fortunate, and for picking up her paintbrush for the first time..."

He looks directly at me. "...and for showing her mum and I that life goes on, and that in the end, family is all that matters." I let the tears I'm holding back slip down my cheek, and the mood lightens as Aunty Julie shouts,

"Five hundred and twenty five pounds." I'm gobsmacked as I watch the bidding creep up to seven hundred. Blake's wearing a knowing grin, and I forgive him for displaying my paintings, it was a good call after all.

Dad's just about to bring the hammer down when I hear Blake shout, "Five hundred thousand pounds." Everyone's gasping and applause breaks out as Dad slams the hammer down.

"Sold to the only rich guy I know who has a heart bigger than his bank account."

I hurl myself at my man throwing my arms around his neck, and he lifts me higher, wrapping my legs around his waist, not caring who's watching.

A round of applause breaks out, and Dad announces, "The buffet is open, everybody tuck in."

Everyone piles into the side room where Elaine has organised the biggest, fanciest spread possible. The room is filled with laughter, and I'm exhausted by the end of the night. As much as I've loved every minute, I can't wait to get home and put my feet up.

At the back of the room a young girl dressed in smart navy trousers with a white chiffon blouse catches my attention. I recognise her long chestnut locks even when they are neatly tied back in a low ponytail. Something about the way she's walking away tells me I know her, and our eyes meet across the room my heart breaks to see that lonely expression weigh heavy on her pretty face. I dash over to her.

"Evelyn, you made it!"

My brothers wife looked so different, I hardly recognise her.

I'd tried to keep in touch with her over the past year, not wanting her to feel excluded. She'd been like a little sister and was one of my strongest connections to Marshall.

"You came!" I hug her tightly, I didn't see you, or I would have been straight over. You look amazing, girl, the extra weight really suits you.

"Thanks." She smiles, and she almost looks the way she used to when Marshy had made her smile. Her huge brown eyes flashed a brief sparkle.

"Thanks so much for coming, it means the world to me."

"I'm sorry I can't donate any money. Your paintings are really beautiful."

"Thanks, lovely, do you have to go already?" She glances round the room full of people laughing and having a good time, and I get it. She looks completely overwhelmed.

"Don't leave it this long again, missy! Seriously, I missed you bad, and it's so good to see you healthy and happy."

"I won't."

"Promise?" And she holds out her pinkie finger like old times. I watch her walk away for a minute before my mum approaches,

"Who was that, honey?" I shake my head, knowing now's not the time, if they were going to see each other again, it had to be on Evelyn's terms, and I respect that. She's obviously in a good place, and I wasn't about to risk that for anything.

Blake

I bide my time watching from across the room. Mum's sitting next to me chattering on about how amazing Candice has done setting up the night and how surprisingly good her paintings are. I'm zoned out, focusing solely on my girl across the room laughing with Rainy and introducing her to Sally.

Everyone's demanding her attention tonight, and I notice despite the huge smile she's wearing, she looks a little tired around her eyes. I need to get her home and have some alone time. I'm craving it like my own form of therapy. Holding her and kissing her brings calmness to my thoughts, and when it's just the two of us, the world seems to still around us and time has no end.

She works the room, being sure to chat with everyone, before finally she reaches me, she throws her arms straight round my neck like always, and I kiss her like nobody's watching.

"You look tired, angel."

"I am a little."

"C'mon, I'm taking you home."

"I'm not *that* tired," she says with a glimmer in her eyes that sends a rush of heat through my cock.

I pull her closer and growl into her ear, "Good cos' neither am I."

I watch her face as she processes my words and know from her widened eyes that her pussy's already pulsing for me. She glances around the room wanting to say her goodbyes to everyone.

"You've got two minutes."

"You can wait five," she replies.

She's the only person aside from my parents who doesn't do

exactly what I tell her to, and it drives me all kinds of crazy. She takes off and keeps looking over her shoulder at me. I hold two fingers up. She casually throws five back in my direction, not even looking round or giving me chance to respond. My famous negotiation skills go to shit when I'm around her, and I wait the five minutes but when she comes over, I'm on her. I smile at her mum, slipping my arm around Candy.

"I'm gonna get this little wonder woman home, she needs to rest. Goodnight, Joan."

"Night, both of you, take care of each other."

"We will," we say in tandem, and I pull her away before she changes her mind. She's quiet in the taxi, and she lays her head on my shoulder. I notice my hand drifts to her tummy, it's still flat, but I marvel at the thought of our baby growing underneath my touch. Is it weird that it turns me on so much? That I need to fuck her now, and I'm planning on which way would pleasure her most as we sit by side.

As soon as we walk through the elevator doors I am on her, pinning her to the wall as my hands glide round onto her perfect ass and give it a squeeze as I kiss her. She moans loudly into my mouth, since being pregnant she is extra horny, which I am not complaining about. She scratches her nails down my stomach reaching for my cock, kissing me with so much passion and love it makes my head spin.

The elevator dings and the doors slide open. We've barely stopped kissing, other than for a few seconds where I fumble to open the front door with my key card. It eventually flies open, and I take her hand, leading her into the bedroom. I start peeling her dress down her body and find she is completely naked underneath, as usual, not bothering with underwear. I kiss and nibble her neck causing her nipples to harden instantly. I pinch them in between my fingers, knowing she will be soaked already. Walking back so her knees are at the foot of the bed and gently laying her down, I kneel and lick up her inner thighs as she opens her legs for me. I reach her pussy and suck her clit causing her hips to buck off the bed.

"God, Blake, don't stop."

So, I don't. I lick through her slit sucking and flicking her clit just how I know my girl likes it. Her moans grow louder, so I know she is close.

"Come on, angel, come all over my tongue." I continue sliding my tongue in fast hot licks. Over and over again as she comes. Giving her, her full release before I stand and shred my clothes. She pats the bed sheets next to her.

"Come and lay with me," she whispers. I look at her in confusion.

"I want to go on top," she says, simply and with no understanding of the explosion her words cause in my balls.

"Are you sure, baby?"

"Completely." She smiles up at me a sweet unsure smile as I do as she asks and lay down on the bed. She climbs over me stopping at my throbbing cock and licking from the base to the tip. She continues before taking the tip into her mouth and licking it while rolling her tongue around in circles, and I swear I could come in her mouth right now, but I want to feel my angel on top of me. She is kissing her way up my stomach until she reaches my mouth, and her pussy settles at the tip of my cock. She rocks slightly back and forward, kissing me the whole time.

My cock is aching to be inside her. She lifts slightly and lines me up with her entrance before slowly sliding down. Fuck, it feels incredible, better than anything before. She starts slowly and seems unsure, so I guide her with some encouragement.

"Fuck, baby, you feel amazing, keep going." My slight encouragement sets off a switch goes off inside her and a wild animal is unleashed. She's starts riding me with intent and it feels unreal. I reach up, cupping her breasts and kneading them, intermittently pinching her nipples. The way her pussy is clamping down on my cock is a dead giveaway she is close, so I rub her clit in circles as she moans.

"Fuck, Blake...yes. Don't stop." Her hips never miss a beat, and my own release is right there. I grab her hips and thrust with her as we climax together.

"Fuck, angel, that was something else." She giggles, covering her face.

"Are you kiddin'? Don't be shy, you certainly weren't a minute ago!"

"Blake, stop...it's the first time I've ever done that," She slaps my shoulder.

"Well, it didn't seem like your first time, and trust me, sweet girl, it definitely won't be the last."

I hold her in my arms and she soon settles, her breathing evening out, but I can't seem to find the same peace as my mind goes into overdrive. I can't sleep. She knows I'm leaving soon and I've got all the usual adrenalin of a new mission pulsing through me, alongside the force that pulls me to Candy and is telling me not to go. I decide that this will be the last time I ever leave her, and if we finish up quick enough, I'll be back in time for our baby to be born. She's strong. One of the bravest women I know, so I know she will be fine through the pregnancy, she's got her family around her and good friends, too.

I watch her sleep thinking how different my life is now compared to when I met her. I shudder at the thought of the countless fucks with faceless woman I'd snuck out on before they even had chance to wake up. With Candy, I don't want to miss a single moment, this woman captivates me, and all I can do is take in her beautiful features in awe of the fact that out of all the men she could choose, she wants me.

CHAPTER TWENTY-NINE

Candice

I balance the phone between my chin and neck to keep my hands free. "Oh my god, Sally, the college is just amazing, did you love it? Can you believe we'll both be studying at the same place?"

"I know, we're practically on the same campus. It's going to be freakin' awesome."

"Like South Sudan, only with proper toilets and Wi-Fi connection."

"You make me laugh, girl, you can hardly compare Blake's apartment to our pink and orange pop ups in Bor."

"At least I was never lonely there, what am I gonna do here without him for the next few months?"

"Study, eat junk food and watch trash TV?"

"I guess," I reply, trying to dismiss my anxieties and idly

stroking the paintbrush across the watercolours. "Well, mi casa su casa, gorgeous. You're welcome whenever, you know that."

"Candy, you think I don't know that place has a hot tub? I'll drop by next week to test it out."

"It's a date, see ya, Sal."

"Bye, gorgeous." I paint in the final few numbers, finishing another hanging basket full of beautiful pale blue forget me nots and stand back to admire the work of art. It's taken hours, but there's something so relaxing about not having to think about the design and just following the colour number by number.

You don't really think about the finished piece, but it's an absolute beauty. A white cottage with a pale blue front door and a neat row of wild flowers along the front. It's strange how it feels so familiar, almost like a photograph.

Oh. My. God. Realisation dawns on me, and I can barely breathe, goose bumps bubbling up along my arms, and I clench my firsts punching the air, needing an outlet for the surge of excitement that's hit me. What has he done? My beautiful, thoughtful boyfriend. I flip the canvas over re reading the two words scribbled in his messy handwriting.

'It's ours.'

I'd seen the message when I'd taken it out of the box but assumed the artist had put it there, naming his work. I can still hardly believe it, but knowing my man the way I do, knowing how much he loves me. And he did say he liked it at my folks place when he visited.

"Blaaaaake," I scream at the top of my lungs, which must have given him a fright because he's up the stairs and on me in seconds, but I can't speak. The hormones take over again, or perhaps just sheer blissful happiness, but I'm crying. Not the cute few tears in my eye, but the full sobby, snotty mess kind of cry.

"What happened? You're okay, I'm here." He goes to hug me, but I clasp his hands and stand facing him and realise I'm shaking.

"This." I look to the painting.

"All yours, angel. I put in an offer after we visited your mums."

"What!" I gasp, taken aback.

"But we'd only just met."

"When you know, you know," he smirks at me, cupping my face and bringing his face close to mine.

"Even back then?"

"Candice, I've known since the first time I laid eyes on you. I'm crazy about you."

"Me too."

"Well, obviously." He grins, and I kiss him despite his usual cockiness.

"You wanna go and see our new place for real?"

"Well, obviously."

I roll my eyes all diva like and am already heading for the door not even trying to hide my excitement. Blake holds the door to his black BMW, and I realise how easy life's gotten since coming back to England. I used to be so lost here without Marshy, plus my mum and dad constantly on my back was so draining. It's strange how just a few small events can change everything, how just one person can make you feel more like yourself than you even knew you could.

"Bourton on the Water," Blake says to Jerry who tips his hat in response.

"Home," I say the word out loud feeling the warmth of his touch as he squeezes my hand. My thoughts are racing and my tummy's churning with questions.

A rush of nausea washes over me. Oh god, I'm gonna puke. I frantically press the button but panic as the window won't open, "Blake, the window."

"You okay?" *Don't be sick. Do not puke.*

"Jerry, pull over and wind down the windows please, I think Candice needs some air."

Too late, I chuck up all over the leather interior and feel instantly better in one way but dreadful in another.

"Sorry." But to my surprise, Blake just grins at me, and it's a full I'm-crazy-about-you smile that lifts my spirits immediately.

"That's our little one making themselves heard, then. Looks like we've got another little firecracker on the way." I pat my face with tissues and say nothing but notice Jerry's knowing glance in the rear view mirror.

"You wanna turn back?"

"Do I, heck. The man of my dreams just bought me a little piece of paradise. I'm not going to miss going to see it for the world; just, maybe could we relax the window security a little?"

No one speaks, but Jerry adjusts the windows so there's a slight gap, and I feel like I can breathe again. Blake cleans up my sick, which I inwardly cringe at and thank goodness it's mostly water, or I may just have passed out with embarrassment.

"What will you do with the apartment now? We will live in The Cotswolds full time, won't we?" I hadn't even considered that, what if he had bought the place as a gesture, a holiday home or something.

"I guess that depends."

"On what?"

"On whether you like it." I snuggle into his shoulder inhaling his citrus spicy smell, which seems so much stronger today.

"Of course, I like it dumbass, it's stunning."

"Did you seriously just call me a dumbass?"

"She sure did, dumbass." Jerry laughs, raising an eyebrow. It's one of the only times I've heard him speak to Blake or laugh, and it has me in stitches, especially when Blake doesn't hit back and just sits there all sulkily.

"I'll keep the apartment, we'll need a base for when we visit the city, and for when Dad needs me nearby on business." I've switched off, feeling slightly overwhelmed and a little nauseous again. I mostly doze for the rest of the drive and wake only to glance out of the window. The feel of Blake's hand stroking my hair has me in a dream like state, which quickly switches to reality when we pull up outside Snowdrop Cottage. I'm literally speechless. The place is absolutely breath taking. The pale blue door matches the row of meadow flowers that are lined along the front, and there are countless hanging baskets overflowing with tiny forget me nots. It's like a white and blue cloud floating along representing all that is serene and calm.

"Oh, Blake, it's just gorgeous, you must have had a lot of work done. I remember this house from being small, and it was quite run down when I last saw it. I can't believe you've done all this for me... for us."

"It's certainly not run down anymore, check out the inside," he replies casually hurling me a set of keys. I wrestle the heavy lock for a minute before the door flies open, and I'm standing inside my new living room.

"I left it empty, I thought you'd enjoy the project while I'm away," his voice echoes, bouncing off the empty walls.

The rooms surprisingly light with a large bay window at the front. I love that it's all open plan. The kitchen at the back of the room is small but easily big enough for the two of us. Blake must have had it fitted as it's stylish in a classic cream and chrome, country kitchen kind of way.

I picture myself standing in it cooking as Blake watches TV in the living room. I've got a good feeling about the place, there's a real positive vibe here. Oh god, I sound like Elaine now! The double doors in the kitchen open out into a garden that's bursting with flowers of every colour and kind and a neatly mowed lawn, he's thought of everything.

The best things of all is the view of the river, it instantly has me feeling relaxed and at home, and I can't believe our baby is going to grow up playing and riding their bikes along it, just like me and Marshall did. Upstairs there are four bedrooms.

"This will be ours, I couldn't resist the bed." He signals to the huge four poster bed dripping in white voiles and bedding. It looks like something you'd see in an Ibiza beach club.

"I don't know what to say, everything's just perfect." He's beaming. "Can we pop in on Mum, and stay here tonight?"

"You know I have to catch my flight tomorrow, right? Plus, there's nothing here, just empty walls, I was thinking you'd live in the apartment while you do the place up?"

"Nope." I shake my head to make the point. "I'm gonna stay

with Mum and Dad, that way I can keep a close eye on what's happening and move in as soon as possible.

"Okay, baby, it's your call, it does make sense that you stay with your parents. I hated the thought of you all alone."

"So, tonight then?"

"Okay, we'll order take out and christen the bed." His eyes flit wildly between me and our new four poster. He looks primal and so sexy, and I feel his eyes undressing me, working their way down my body savouring every inch.

"Hey you, don't you look at me like that!" He smiles a roguish grin as he walks his way towards me licking his lips and with clear intent on his face.

"Look at you like what?" I go to run around the bed, but he is too quick and soon picks me up by the waist and chucks me playfully on the bed.

"Oh, Candy, I cannot wait to fully christen this bed later, but I cannot resist you right now," he says, while parting my legs and rubbing, stroking and licking his way from my ankle to my thigh before sliding his fingers through my crease. God, it feels amazing. "Candice, you look incredible spread out in front of me," he says on a whisper as he glides his fingers inside me while licking my clit, it's not long before I feel myself ready to explode. I know he knows too as he pays extra attention to my nub, sucking it into his mouth until I can't help it and I orgasm. Fuck, it's so intense, knocking my senses into overdrive until my head is whirling, and I'm feeling dizzy. I lie breathless coming back to earth on my new bed with the love of my life next to me, and finally, after so long, I feel comfortable in my own skin.

Blake gets up quickly.

"Come on, angel, I wanna show you the best part," he says making his way to the other side of the bedroom. He draws back the huge curtains to reveal a set of patio doors, that lead out to a small balcony, overlooking the beautiful river. The view is like something from a postcard, or a stunning oil painting, hung in a gallery.

"Oh my goodness, Blake, this is amazing!" He takes my hand, leading me out onto the balcony. I am mesmerized and cannot believe that I am going to live here.

"Candice, I have loved you since the very first day I laid eyes on you. You're the light in my dull life, you make me whole and you make me want to do better and be a better person."

He reaches behind his back and pulls out a blue velvet box, bending down on one knee, right in front of me. My heart is beating so fast, my hand covers my mouth, and I can feel the tears streaming down my face.

"Angel, will be mine forever? Will you marry me?" I can't speak at the realisation that it's *the* sapphire ring.

"Oh my god. How did you...?" This is all so surreal. My mind flits between his huge green eyes and that day in The Velvet Box jewellery shop. How could he have known?

"Candice, angel, are you ok."

"Yes. Yes a thousand times. I've been yours all along, Blake, I always will be." I can't take my eyes off the exquisite blue jewel shining on my finger. I can't believe he got me the ring of my dreams and by the look on his face, he doesn't even know it.

"You like it baby?"

"It's perfect Blake."

"Like you then."

We kiss for the longest time before standing holding each other. Both speechless for once and both content in the sound of our empty new house. I'm lost in thoughts of my new life, how I'll decorate and learn to cook. Most of all how happy I'll be.

His finger traces gently up and down my side, my torso trembling under his touch. The sensation disappearing then reappearing again intermittently where my burn scars are so deep they block any feeling from reaching me. But I don't need his touch to feel him. He's deep in my heart, locked away for good, spreading heaps of love and passion throughout my soul.

I don't know how I'll say goodbye to him tomorrow, but I feel a million times better knowing I have a little piece of him growing inside me. I rub my hand over my stomach protectively as I feel his heartbeat through his chest and let myself relax and take in my new surroundings.

This is us. I am his, and he will forever be mine.

I almost lost myself, but he caught me. I had almost given up hope of ever sharing myself with a lover again. Hell, I couldn't stand the sight of myself without clothes, let alone consider anyone else seeing me. That was until Blake. He saw through everything, the clothes, my burns, all my insecurities.

His arms provided me with comfort and his arms gave me a safe haven.

He loves me without limits or boundaries and more importantly, he has taught me how to love myself again.

I didn't know I needed saving, but he saved me all the same.

The End.

EPILOGUE

Blake

2 years later...

$\mathcal{L}$ooking around as I watch over the barbecue with a bud in hand, everyone is here to celebrate Easter and luckily for once, it's been a sunny one. My parents are chatting casually with Candice's and Sally is gossiping with Rainy. Stephan's chilling on his own, as usual, and the rest of our friends and neighbours, are all here, too. Along with their wives and children. I let out a deep sigh of contentment, thinking about how amazing the last couple of years have been.

My eyes settle on Candice and the girls sitting around chatting with our handsome boy nestled in his mum's lap, trying to pull off her sunglasses. He's eighteen months old now and me all over, with my dark hair and tanned skin, but our boy has his mother's bright sapphire eyes. Jenson Marshall Laine was born,

1st January at 00:01, weighing in at 7lb 2oz, after sixteen hours of pure hell. Candice was amazing throughout. Me, on the other hand, worried myself sick and paced the floor relentlessly the entire time. But damn, the minute I held my boy, god, I have never felt anything like it. That need to love and protect him with everything I have until the day I die has never faded, and that was it, we were three.

Of course, we're not perfect, the way she's smiling over at me through gritted teeth after our barney over the dreaded potty training fiasco, reminds me of that. The same smile as Jenson's first birthday, after his crazily over the top party that Candice organised. I mean, what one year old needs a petting zoo in his backyard to celebrate his birthday. Yup, that was another argument I'd lost, and yup, it was me that has the pleasure of cleaning up the shit for the weeks after!

I flip the burgers again, and my mind wanders to that night, after the party we'd settled Jensen in his big bed together before my girl had dragged me to the bedroom and told me to wait on the edge of the bed. She'd told me that she had a surprise for me and disappeared into the bathroom. I could hear her rummaging around, so I suspected she would reappear in a sexy little number. She came out holding a gift bag and not much else.

"I have something for you, Mr. Laine."

"Is that so, Mrs. Laine." Her smile growing bigger as she stepped towards me and handed me the bag before settling next to me on the bed.

"Open it," she'd said in a whisper and kissed me on the cheek. I opened the bag to find a small gift wrapped box. I tore off the paper and opened it up and there it was, a pregnancy test with a note, which read a few words I will never forget.

'Pink or blue we're expecting number two.'

I looked at Candice shocked as hell, and she was biting her bottom lip.

"What the hell, we are having another baby?" She giggled and threw herself at me kissing me until we were breathless, and I had a raging hard on.

"Are you happy, Blake. I mean, I am over the moon, but you don't think it's too soon?"

"Angel, I couldn't be happier, you know I have wanted more kids since Jenson was born. If they're anything like him, I want a dozen more."

Candice wanders over and wraps her arms around me bringing me back from one of my favourite memories as I turn around placing my hands on her huge bump.

"How are my girls doing in there?"

"Ughhh, they keep kicking my bladder, and I can't stop peeing." She places her hands over mine on her huge bump. Yes, that's right, she is thirty weeks pregnant with our twin girls, Aimee and Annie.

"Not much longer now, just a few more weeks, you're doing so well," I remind her, placing a kiss on her forehead before shouting, "Food's ready!"

Everyone gathers around the huge tables, Candice has carefully laid out, and Sal pops Jenson into his high chair next to my place. I shoot him a fist bump as I sit down beside him, and he pulls his back laughing cheekily and leaving me hanging.

Everyone is digging in and having noisy conversations

among themselves. Jensen eats for a while, and I see his heavy eyes starting to close then flutter open again. I check my Rolex; yup, it's nap time, and he gets so grumpy if he doesn't have his afternoon nap. I stand and unstrap him out of his high chair and hold his tiny body against me as his head falls onto my shoulder.

"Just going to put him down for his nap," I tell Candy before taking him through the house to his nursery and placing him in his huge cot, switching on the camera monitor and tucking the parent unit into my pocket. Leaning over I sneak a kiss to his chubby red cheek before I turn to leave.

As I am padding down the stairs the alarm beeps, which means someone just came through the gate. I make my way to the front door just as whoever it is knocks loudly. Too loudly for me, since my boy is napping. If there is one thing Jensen hates more than skipping his nap, it's getting woken up from it.

Swinging the door open and about to give whoever it a mouthful, I catch sight of the man before me, and a lump rises in my throat. I can't speak, can't think, and most definitely can't function at this second in time. He looks the same, except his trademark long hair has gone, shaved completely off, and his once bright eyes, looked shady and dark.

"Greyson," I manage to blurt out. It's been six months since I last saw him, and he looked rougher than usual then but had insisted everything was fine. Now he looks downright broken.

"Hey bro, hope you don't mind me turning up unannounced like this," he says to me.

"Of course I don't, man, you know you're welcome anytime, Candice and Jenson will love that you're here. I didn't even know you were due back, how long you here for?" The question seems to make him uncomfortable.

"Well, erm, that's the thing, man, I am out. Done. I ain't going back, and well, I was wondering if it's okay to crash here with you guys while I sort somewhere to live?" Finally, he is out; I have worried about him every time he has been out there without me.

"Fuck, man, yeah, you know that it is, goes without saying."

"Eeeeeek!" Candice squeals from somewhere behind me and waddles over with her bump swaying from side to side.

"Greyson, I can't believe you're here. I am so happy I could pee." He smiles brightly, but I still see the dull in his eyes as he envelopes her in a huge hug, reminding me of the time they arrived in South Sudan together all those years ago. He's the only man I would let put his hands on my wife, well except her Dad and mine.

"What have you done to that gorgeous hair? How long are you back for? Why didn't you tell us you were coming?" She fires questions at him left right and centre. I see her eyes welling up at the sight of him, she loves him like a brother, too. I wrap my arm around her shoulder.

"G is going to stay for a while," Her smile beams.

"That's if you don't mind, sweetheart?" he asks her with a wink.

"Oh, Greyson, of course not. You know you can always come stay with us, Jenson will love having his uncle around. Blake just put him down for his nap, and trust me, if I didn't think he would be a grouch, I would go wake him." She smiles fondly knowing our boy all too well. She links his arm.

"Come out back, everyone is there."

As she pulls him along he appears to relax a little.

"Just goin' to put these bags in the guest room," I call after them. Candy waves her hand in acknowledgment and G shrugs.

I throw his bags down and pop in on Jenson, who's still sleeping, before heading back outside. Noticing Greyson is getting fussed over by my mum and Candice, I walk over to them and attempt to break up the pamper party.

"Come on, let him breath, will ya. You wanna beer, G?" He looks relieved that I saved him from the girls and takes the bud from my hand, we clink them together and each take a long swig.

"You've done well with this place, Blake." He takes in the back yard overlooking the lake that wasn't finished last time he was here.

"Fuck, man. It's good to see you," he says genuinely, but he isn't looking at me when he speaks, his eyes are fixed on Sally.

ACKNOWLEDGMENTS

Firstly, we want to thank our daughters for inspiring us to always aim higher, work harder and love without limits. We hope when the time comes to follow your dreams, you take the chance and believe in yourselves as much as we believe in each and every one of you.

A huge thank you to the men in our lives who are a constant source of strength and support, we couldn't have done it without you and we love you so much!

Lots of love to the beautiful ladies we are lucky enough to call our friends, you know who you are and how much we appreciate you.

To our online book sisters, thank you for sharing this adventure with us. Your endless encouragement has got us through at times, when we have almost given up.

Lastly, Pam Gonzales our book Mum! Without your guidance

and support Saving Her wouldn't exist, and we want to thank you from the bottom of our hearts.

STAY IN TOUCH

Instagram: https://www.instagram.com/autumn_ruby/

Facebook: https://www.facebook.com/autumn.ruby.54

Goodreads: https://www.goodreads.com/author/show/ 17314880.Autumn_Ruby

Blog: www.authorautumnruby.wordpress.com

Twitter: @AutumnRuby3

Before you go
Please consider leaving an honest review xoxo

Printed in Poland
by Amazon Fulfillment
Poland Sp. z o.o., Wrocław